ANCIENT SINS

When a fifty-year-old human skull was discovered in a lorry-load of sugar beet, it came at an inconvenient time. Breckland CID was fully involved in a three-county police operation, with the targets for Operation Longship in their sights. However, the old wartime mystery could not be ignored. DS Judy Kane was assigned to unravel a tangled skein of ancient sins — but a tortuous trail of lost loves and fiery passions would lead her into terrible danger.

ROBERT CHARLES

ANCIENT SINS

Complete and Unabridged

LINFORD
Leicester

First published in Great Britain

First Linford Edition
published 2007

British Library CIP Data

Charles, Robert, *1938* –
  Ancient sins.—Large print ed.—
  Linford mystery library
  1. Detective and mystery stories
  2. Large type books
  I. Title
  823.9'14 [F]

ISBN 978–1–84617–866–5

Published by
F. A. Thorpe (Publishing)
Anstey, Leicestershire

Set by Words & Graphics Ltd.
Anstey, Leicestershire
Printed and bound in Great Britain by
T. J. International Ltd., Padstow, Cornwall

This book is printed on acid-free paper

1

The shock was enough to have given anybody a heart attack. Terry Harrison did, in fact, feel his heart stop still for a moment, his whole body shivered as though an Arctic wind had suddenly cut right through him. Before he began to breathe again he almost fainted.

It had not been a good day to begin with, Monday morning and waking up at five am with a stinking hangover and having to be here to start work at six. It was still dark when he climbed reluctantly into his car, one of those rotten mornings when the thick East Anglian fog filled the beam of his headlights, like driving into a mess of thin grey porridge. He had driven slowly. If he had not known the road like the back of his hand he probably would not have tried it at all. The temptation to go back home and to bed was strong. He had to be careful when he reached the main road, because the bloody sugar beet lorries would already be out in force, crawling in to the giant sugar beet factory on the outskirts of Granchester.

The Campaign had started in September, and would continue until just after Christmas, just as it did every year. Three months to get in the beet harvest from the surrounding fields, then process it into enough sugar to fill the four giant silos that towered into the skyline, enough to keep the adjoining sugar packaging plant going for the next twelve months. Then the cycle would start all over again.

When he arrived the loaded lorries were already queuing up to pass under the bridge of overhead cabins where the samples were taken. Terry was late, no time to stop for a warm-up coffee and a chat with his mates, just straight up into the bloody box and get on with it. The lorries began looming up out of the fog, the overhead arc lights were just about useless and the whole scene was eerie and ghostlike. The lorries, and occasional tractors and trailers, formed three convoys, one passing under Terry's cabin, the others moving below the cabins on either side. Today he could not see much more than the lorries that passed immediately beneath him. Usually most of the drivers would lean out of the cab window and shout up a greeting. Today all the cab windows were closed, keeping in the heat and the muffled sounds of the radio music. Terry was alone in his box in a weird white, cotton-wool world.

As each lorry passed under his cabin a steel cylinder would automatically descend to burrow into its load. Inside the cylinder was a drill shaft that spiralled down and then pulled up a measured portion of the contents. The sample rattled upwards and was swung into the small cabin to be dropped into a thick black plastic bucket. Terry's job was to label the buckets, with the license number of the lorry or tractor that had brought it in, and the farmer supplier from whom it came. The sample would then be sent down a conveyor belt to the Tare House, where it would be washed and topped, weighed at every stage, and finally processed to determine its sugar content. The findings would determine how much the producer was to be paid.

Only half a dozen lorries had passed below him before Terry Harrison received his shock. He still had his hangover headache. A small shower of sugar beet, dirt and stones, crashed and rattled once more into the waiting black bucket. The drill cylinder swung away after dropping its load, and Terry reached for the bucket.

Then he saw the human skull that sat on top of the sample, grinning at him with one empty eye socket and broken teeth. The jaw was twisted, and in the brown hollow of the left eye socket sat an incongruous white pebble, giving the skull a particularly macabre leer.

*   *   *

Judy Kane was not thinking of murder as she drove slowly to work through the November fog. The part of her mind that was not concentrating on the road ahead was still thinking about life, her life in general, and in particular, babies. Her sister Carol had just had her third, and holding her brand new nephew in her arms for the first time had made Judy realize that her own biological clock was ticking away too fast. She would be twenty-nine next birthday, and it was time she and Ben had a baby of their own.

She had said as much when they returned home, after visiting Carol on the Maternity Ward at Granchester General. Ben had laughed at her, 'You're getting broody.' But he had not been dismissive, just teasing. Ben wanted children too. They had decided that first she would move up from Detective Sergeant to Detective Inspector, and that he would jump from Station Officer to Assistant Divisional Officer. They were both doing too well in their respective Police and Fire Service careers to let the opportunities pass them by.

The problem was that parenthood was passing them by. 'Don't wait till you pass thirty,' Carol had said. Too many of her female friends were saying something similar. Thirty was becoming a looming deadline, and now she was not sure she wanted to wait that long. The job was great. Ben loved his job too. But they both wanted children of their own.

She smiled suddenly at the memory of another of their long in-bed conversations. Three nights ago they had been talking about retirement. Fifty-five was the mandatory retirement age in both their services, and hopefully they would still have plenty of active life left. They had both decided that then they would get completely away from this bloody English weather and run a nice little seafront bar in Spain. They had not had their first baby yet and already they were talking retirement. Life was telescoping in too fast.

As she drove into town the street lights battled bravely with the fog. Visibility improved, and by the time she had parked her car she could read the illuminated words Breckland Police HQ above the double glass doors of the large red-brick square building where she worked. She hurried up the steps and passed beneath them, glad to be out of the cold and damp and into the relative warmth.

The feeling did not last. She had barely unbelted her coat, only half way to the policewomen's locker room, when Detective Inspector Ron Harding marched down the corridor to meet her. He was zipping up his own jacket, grinning ruefully from beneath a shock of unruly black hair. His tie, hung loose as always, screaming even louder than usual, a bright orange against a dark blue shirt. He was a few years older, one rank senior, and she still could not stop thinking of him as Flash Ron.

Harding was aggressive Hard Cop, he even had the name for it, and in his own eyes he was forceful and direct, tough as nails. Judy was Soft Cop, she actually liked people, enjoyed talking to them, and she had that invaluable sixth sense of just knowing when people were telling her the truth, when they were hiding something, and when they were just plain lying. They made a good team, which was why the astute Superintendent Grant kept them together, although neither of them would ever have been the other's first choice of partner. Judy thought that it was one of life's ironies that she actually had to spend as much time in the company of

Ron Harding as she did with Ben.

'Don't bother, Jude,' Harding said wryly. 'You're with me, and we've got a nice one to start the day.'

'Another ram raid?' Judy's first thought was of the current top-of-the-heap task that had preoccupied them all for the last few months. Every police force in East Anglia had seen a series of vicious smash and grab robberies, in which the raiders had used stolen vehicles to bulldoze their way violently into small shops and post offices. The raids were always at night, and usually out in the villages. The raiders always relied upon their own speed and violence and the relative isolation of their targets to do the job quickly and get away.

'Not this time,' Harding answered. 'It seems we've got a human skull just showed up in a load of sugar beet. Just the thing for a dark, foggy morning. It scared some poor sod shitless.'

* * *

They took Harding's car. His rank entitled him to let his Sergeant drive, but

Harding preferred to handle his own wheels. He drove fast, and fortunately the fog was beginning to thin. Within minutes they were on the by-pass that circled the town, busy as always with the rush of fog-smeared headlights. On a normal day the giant concrete towers of the sugar silos would loom ahead of them, but today there was only grey cloud. They turned off the main road, passing the roundabout and private slip road where the beet lorries were already winding up toward the Tare House. Harding drove round to the main entrance of the processing plant where a jumble of buildings and tall chimneys formed shrouded glimpses of the offices and processing plant. A large sign showed that they had arrived at BRITISH SUGAR, GRANCHESTER.

Harding ignored the car park on their left and drove straight up to the barrier. They were expected and a tall man wearing a white overall suit and a yellow hard hat waited for them outside the glass fronted gatehouse. Harding stopped the car and pressed the button to slide down his window.

The face that looked in at them was middle-aged, sporting a neat, red-tinged beard, rimless spectacles and ginger eyebrows.

'Jim Collins,' he introduced himself. 'I'm the Operations Manager.'

'DI Harding, Breckland CID.' Harding showed his card. He jerked a thumb at Judy. 'DS Kane.'

'If you give me a lift, I'll take you round there.' Collins was opening the rear door as he spoke. Harding nodded assent and the big man struggled into the car. He was well padded against the cold with a thick jacket underneath his overall. He looked back at the gatehouse and nodded to the guard behind the glass walls. The barrier lifted slowly and Harding drove forward.

'Take a left behind the office block,' Collins said. 'Drive easy because the empty lorries come out this way. We have a speed limit but sometimes the buggers are in a hurry.'

Judy turned in her seat to look at their passenger.

'What have you got to show us?'

'Looks like a human skull. It got picked up from one of the lorry loads as part of the sample. Gave Terry Harrison a right old fright. Can't say I blame him. It's not the sort of thing you expect to see grinning at you first thing in the morning.'

'Where did it come from? Before it came down the sugar beet chute?'

'Well, it came from Sam Arnold's truck. I had him move it to one side to wait for you to arrive. He wasn't too pleased at being held up, but he'll get over it. I think Sam is hauling for Archie Jessup again this year, so the load probably came from Blackberry Farm.' Collins leaned forward and pointed. 'Turn left here, Inspector. Watch the corner.'

Harding turned the wheel as the road swung left behind the main structure of the amalgamated sprawl of the processing plant, and swore as he swerved to avoid an oncoming lorry.

'See what I mean. It's a one way system for the lorries to come in by the slip road

11

and then out through the main gate. Usually there's no other traffic, so they get used to having it all their own way.'

Ahead of them now was a low range of prefabricated buildings on their right, and a bridge of small cabins spanning the road. Two queues of fully laden beet lorries were lined up behind the left and right cabins. There was nothing waiting in the centre line which had been closed off with a pair of red and white traffic cones. One lorry had been isolated and was parked out of the way on their left. Harding pulled up and parked behind it, not too close, so they could still watch the activity under the bridge. On the left hand lane one lorry was pulling away while another inched up behind to take its place. On the right hand lane a lorry stood with its engine running while a steel cylinder pushed down into its cargo.

'What happens here?' Harding asked.

'The lorries get weighed and a sample gets taken from each load. The sample gets weighed and goes down to the Tare house over there. Each sample gets washed to remove the dirt and stones, and then gets weighed again. The tops get sliced off and again everything gets weighed. Then the beet goes into the laboratory where they measure the actual sugar content.' Collins gestured to the laden lorry now moving past them. 'The full load goes through much the same routine. It's tipped on to a hard pad, from there it's fed into a conveyor system, it gets washed, topped, sliced, and then goes into the processing plant.'

Harding's gaze did a full scan of their surroundings. Apart from the lorries there was no movement. The half concealed faces of the drivers inside their cabs and the two men moving inside the left and right overhead bridge cabins were the only sign of life. 'It all seems very quiet for an operation of this size.'

Collins grinned. 'It surprises most people. They all expect a hive of activity when the Campaign is going. Twenty years ago they would have been right, but now most things are computerized. There are about eighty of us working here, half of them are working in the offices, and half of the other half are shut away in the central control room watching their computer screens. This sampling operation is due to be computerized next summer. Then there'll just be one cabin and one operator. Still, Terry Harrison will at least have one highlight to remember his last season.'

'He's the operator who first saw the skull?'

Collins nodded. 'They've got a canteen and locker room in the Tare House block. He's in there nursing a flask of coffee. You want to see him first?'

'Later, first we'll take a look at exhibit A.'

Harding got out of the car and Judy and Collins joined him. Harding gave Judy a grin and asked, 'Had a good breakfast, Jude?'

Judy stared him straight in the eye, 'Bacon and eggs, tomatoes and mushrooms, plenty of fried bread.'

Harding laughed. 'You're a liar. I know you're a healthy fruit and cereal girl.'

They followed Collins up a steel staircase and along the catwalk that led past all three bridge cabins. The Operations Manager stopped at the middle door, opened it, and stood aside to let them pass. There was a conveyor belt passing through the centre of the cabin, still in motion and rattling noisily. It carried a black bucket full of sugar beet from the first cabin past them. There was a table where the sample buckets were filled, and hanging above it the sampling cylinder and its internal drill shaft. There were a few empty buckets, and one full one. The skull sat on top of the full bucket, sitting slightly lopsided on the uneven pile of beet roots, crumpled leaf tops and loose soil. Harding knelt down and stared at it for a moment.

'It's old,' he said at last. 'Brown as an old boot. It's been in the ground for a few years. Even I can tell that.'

'You were hoping for something white and fresh?' Judy managed to hide a smile.

Harding shrugged. 'It would have been more interesting, a possible murder case to get our teeth into. Even if this one is a murder case, the murderer is probably as long dead as old Horatio here.'

Judy stooped for a closer look. 'All the teeth are still there, so he or she was probably not too old, even if it has been in the ground for a long time. The stone in the eye socket is a weird coincidence, somebody's idea of a joke perhaps?'

'Hard to see how,' Harding glanced up at the sample cylinder. 'As I understand it, the thing just dropped like this out of that tube.'

He straightened up and looked at Collins still waiting in the doorway.

'Nothing else, no more bone fragments?'

'Nothing that I've seen, I've just stopped everything as much as I can and left it to you.'

Harding took a pencil from his pocket, squatted again, and tentatively moved a few of the stones and leaves around the skull. He shrugged again, straightened up for the second time and turned his attention to the sampling cylinder that hung over the sample table. After a moment he reached up inside the cylinder and brushed the spiral of the drill. Nothing came down except leaf tops and dirt.

Judy watched through the window as a large white police van drew up behind Harding's car. Three men emerged wearing zip-up one piece suits of white overalls.

'Forensic are here,' she observed, 'Including the Bone Ranger.' It was the general nickname for the police pathologist, a tall thin man named Rawlings who was almost as skeletal as some of his case studies.

'Okay,' Harding said. 'I'll brief them. You can go and get some statements from Terry Harrison and the lorry driver.' He looked at Collins. 'Is there somewhere we can tip up that lorry so the team can sift through the rest of his load?'

'The hard-pad,' Collins said. 'That's where we tip all of them. This time of year it is only half full so there will be an empty corner. We only use the full capacity at Christmas when we build up to a three day supply to cover the holiday break. The deliveries stop, but it takes three full days to charge up the processing plant so we keep the factory running.'

Harding was satisfied and moved out to

meet the three new arrivals. Judy stayed a moment longer, looking down at the skull. She sensed that Harding was losing interest. His instinct was to get back to the three-county ram-raiding investigation which was rapidly coming to a head and promised some possible action and glory. But Judy's intuition was kicking in, and she instinctively knew that this macabre and ancient relic had an equally fascinating story to tell.

2

Judy's interviews were a necessary formality, but also a complete waste of time. The ten minutes she spent with Terry Harrison boiled down to a one line statement: 'It scared the bloody life out of me,' which was all he was capable of repeating. Judy wrote it down in her notebook and left him still shuddering over his tightly gripped cup of coffee.

Sam Arnold, the lorry driver, had a little more to say, but nothing that was useful to their enquiries. He was a burly man with a black baseball cap pulled down over a thick fleshed face that was red-nosed and pinched with cold. His hands were stuffed in the pockets of a black donkey jacket and he was stamping his feet as he watched Harding and Rawlings climbing cautiously on top of his truck.

'How long are they going to be,' he asked peevishly as Judy approached. 'It's bloody freezing standing here, and I've got a living to earn.'

'As long as it takes,' Judy said sweetly, smiling to take the sting out of the words. 'At least we can hurry up my bit if you'll answer a few questions. Then we can all get out of the cold.'

Arnold was only partly mollified but he cooperated, confirming his name, that he was self employed, and that he owned the lorry he was driving.

'This load came from Archie Jessup,' he added unasked. 'Peter Jessup loaded me up last night, ready for first delivery this morning. The beet came from Archie's hard pad at the farm. The first I knew that there was anything wrong with it was when young Terry yelled out. I climbed up into his cabin and had a look with him. The skull just sat there and grinned at us. We called Jim Collins, he told me to pull over and wait here, and that's it.'

And basically, that was it. There was nothing more that Arnold could usefully add. For the rest of the interview he simply grumbled about his bad luck and the delay. Judy wrote down the little that was significant and by then Harding and Rawlings had climbed down from the back of the lorry.

'Okay,' Harding said, 'Take it round to the hard pad and tip it out, but keep it separate from the rest of the heap. We'll sift it there.'

Arnold looked to Collins for a nod of confirmation and then climbed back into his cab. As he drove off the rest of them followed in Harding's car and the SOC van.

The large square of concrete where the beet was tipped was the size of a small car park, but as Collins had promised the small mountain of sugar beet waiting to be processed only filled just more than half of the available space. Arnold's load was tipped in a corner well away from the rest of the heap, and then Rawlings and his team made a careful inspection of the empty truck before Arnold was cleared to go.

The small group stood for a moment, staring at the pile of suspect root crop that remained. So far not one single bone fragment had appeared to suggest that the skull might recently have become detached from a larger skeleton.

'Okay,' Harding said at last to Rawlings. 'I'll leave you and your lads to comb through this lot while we take a trip to Blackberry Farm.'

★　★　★

Judy knew the way. Blackberry farm was out on the East Linden road, only a mile away from the cottage she had shared with Ben for the past three years. The farm buildings were the usual sprawl of black barns and tractor sheds on two sides of the open yard, with the large thatch-roof and cream-painted farmhouse facing on to the yard. The entrance gates stood wide open, and were pushed back against the clumps of brambles and the tilted wooden sign which gave the farm its name.

Harding drove into the yard and up to the house, parking beside an old grey Land Rover that was the typical unwashed farm workhorse. There was a scattering of old farm machinery and two ancient tractors half in and half out of the open-sided farm sheds. Chickens squawked and fluttered as they arrived, and a trio of assorted mongrel dogs dashed out yapping angrily.

The noise saved them the trouble of having to knock on the farmhouse door, which opened as they got out of the car. Harding scowled at the dogs and all three stood off and barked, one slightly closer and braver than the others, while Judy offered soothing words. The old man who had emerged from the house called the dogs by name, shouting and cursing. The two smaller dogs, which seemed to be mostly collie, came sullenly to heel, the large dog, which had a streak of bull mastiff, only backed up a few inches and reduced its savage bark to a sulky growl.

Harding walked past it with a threatening stare. Two kindred spirits, Judy thought, and suppressed a smile as she dutifully followed.

'Morning,' the old man said briefly. He was in his shirtsleeves and old fashioned braces held up his grey work trousers. His hair was white and deep wrinkles lined his temples. He looked to be at least eighty and his legs were slightly bowed, giving him a short stature and making him look as though he probably needed a stick to move any further from his front door. His eyes, below white eyebrows, were a surprisingly sharp blue. 'Don't know you,' he said sourly, and then added, 'You lost?'

Harding grinned and shook his head. He showed his card and made the standard introductions. 'You must be Archie Jessup,' he finished.

The old man nodded warily, saying nothing. Behind him a younger woman appeared. She was fifty something and plain, wearing a worried expression and still wrapped in her dressing gown.

'What's wrong, dad?'

Harding explained. The woman looked puzzled but relieved.

'So it's not Peter then, he's not had an accident.' Then the full meaning of what Harding had said seemed to sink in. Her hand made a nervous twitching move-ment as she raised it to her throat and her face paled. 'A skull you said, like somebody's head, in our sugar beet?'

Harding nodded.

Judy noted that the woman's flustered reaction seemed normal for this sort of situation and she was more interested in the old man. Archie Jessup had stiffened, his grizzled old face locked in its neutral expression, and still he said nothing. Natural shock perhaps, but Judy noticed that the blue eyes were still sharp. Farmers were usually much brighter than they looked and she knew instinctively that this one was no doddering old fool.

'Any ideas Mister Jessup,' she asked politely but directly. 'Has anyone gone missing around here?'

'Well, no,' it was the woman who answered. 'Not as we know of, anyway, is there dad?'

Archie Jessup pursed his thin lips and shook his head. He didn't make eye contact.

'Where exactly did this morning's load of sugar beet come from?' Harding asked.

'Peter is more likely to know that. Peter loaded Sam's lorry last night. Peter is my husband, the woman added. 'I'm Mary.

Dad still runs the farm but Peter does most of the work. He's out now, on the new tractor, taking up more beet.'

'He'll be down by the Old Mill Road,' Archie Jessup nodded in agreement. 'That's where he's lifting this morning. He's already done the Old Bracken and Ten Acre fields. The load that went down to the factory this morning will have come from one of them, I don't know which one.'

'Okay, so we'll talk to Peter later,' Harding decided. 'For now can you show us the hard pad where the beet was loaded.'

'I can do that, it's not far.' The old man pulled on an ancient green canvas coat with baggy pockets which he took from behind the open door. His daughter-in-law helped him to struggle into it and then handed him his walking stick.

'You wait here,' he told her, obviously irritated by the fuss. He snapped at one of the smaller dogs which had started to sniff at Harding's legs, and then led the way across the yard. The dogs trailed silently but watchfully behind them as they walked.

Archie Jessup led them some two hundred yards along the main road before a turn in the hedge revealed another square of concrete hard pad set into the adjoining field. The mound of sugar beet roots waiting there to be moved to the factory was twice as high as Harding's head and he groaned at the sight of it.

Archie Jessup simply shrugged and leaned on his walking stick to watch as Harding prowled gloomily around the edges of the beet mound. If he had hoped for a rib cage or an obvious thigh bone protruding from the dirt streaked harvest he was disappointed. There was nothing and he kicked one or two of the loose beet roots in disgust. Judy glanced sideways at Jessup's lined face and thought she could detect a half smile, perhaps at some secret joke, or perhaps it was just Harding's weary air of resignation that the old man found amusing. Before she could come to any conclusion she saw a new arrival walking briskly toward them along the edge of the field.

'That's Peter,' Archie Jessup said with a note of pride.

Peter Jessup was a big man with a large beer paunch and a round florid face reddened and weathered by long hours of exposure to the sun. He wore a sleeveless grey padded body warmer over a check shirt that even on this cold November morning was open at the neck. His trousers were hard wearing grey corduroy, mud splattered and tucked into the tops of green Wellington boots.

'What's all this then?' He demanded as he came close. 'First Sam Arnold calls me up on my mobile, blowing off steam about being held up at the factory. Then Mary calls up, twittering all in a panic — something about a human skull being found in our sugar beet.'

'That's about the size of it,' Harding agreed. He gave Peter Jessup the official blank-faced look of police appraisal and then asked: 'How can you plough up something like that and not even notice it?'

Peter Jessup scowled back at him. 'The job is all mechanized now — did you think we still pull each one out by hand?'

Archie Jessup chuckled and pointed over to the next field where a large green tractor was parked and hooked up to an elaborate piece of machinery with a short elevator attached. 'Got ourselves a brand new sugar beet harvester,' he told them cheerfully. 'Takes most of the tops off and lifts six rows at a time.'

Peter relaxed and added a grin of his own. 'The beet passes over a set of contra-rotating rollers which allow most of the unwanted dirt and clods to fall through, but I guess your skull must have been too big to get shaken out. The elevator lifts the beet straight into a trailer. I don't always watch it pouring in. Most of the time I just sit on the tractor and steer the whole lot up and down.'

'So you've no idea where the skull came from?'

Peter Jessup was a man of few words. He simply shrugged and spread his hands.

'Okay,' Harding said wearily, 'So where did you take out the load for Sam Arnold's lorry this morning?'

29

Peter pursed his lips, a gesture reminiscent of his father. Judy noticed that he also had the same shrewd blue eyes.

'Over here.' He pointed to where a part of the heap had been scooped away.

Harding took another look. There was an occasional gleam of white in the dirt where part of the crop had been sliced or damaged by the lifting bucket, but still nothing that resembled a fragment of bone.

'We'll let forensic comb this lot over as well,' he decided. Then he looked again at Peter Jessup.

'Do you know which field this lot came from?'

Peter thought for a moment. 'The Old Bracken field, I reckon. That's one of our smaller fields — ' His grin was not quite apologetic, ' — only about fifteen acres.'

★   ★   ★

By the end of the day the Scene of Crime Team had sifted through the load of sugar beet from Sam Arnold's lorry and through half of the great pile remaining on Archie Jessup's hard pad, and it had been a fruitless search. Not even a single knuckle of bone had been unearthed for all their efforts. If there was a grave site and they hoped to find it, then it was beginning to look as though they would have to do a line search over the whole of the Old Bracken field. Harding was bored and fed up with the whole business. It had been a long cold day of mostly standing around in mud and heavy black clay, and Judy was glad to go home.

She found Ben waiting. He had worked the day watch at the fire station and apart from his jacket and cap he was still in uniform. Judy kissed him and loosened his tie, smiling her approval. She liked him in uniform, even enough to tolerate the frequent smell of smoke. When they had first met they had both been in uniform, she had been a policewoman on traffic patrol, and he was the Sub Officer in charge of a crew attending a traffic accident on the by-pass. The uniforms brought back fond memories.

She had soon discovered that off duty

she preferred firemen to policemen. They were all strong, fit young men, serving the public in their own way, but the firemen tended to be much more light-hearted about it. Their work was hot and hard when it flared up, but in between shouts they played a lot more handball and snooker, and they had to listen to less lies and domestics. Generally they were less cynical, and Ben Kane was particularly cheerful. Within a year they were married.

Judy put two ready meals in the microwave and made a side salad to go with them. They ate side by side on the sofa, watching the TV and exchanging their own news of the day. Ben's watch had dealt with two small fires and one false alarm.

'The gypsy camp again,' for a moment he sounded like Harding, as though he were suppressing a yawn. 'The boys there have a sideline in scrap dealing. Every so often they burn the insulation off a pile of old electrical wiring. Some passing motorist spots the smoke and phones in a call. We have to turn out and check it out.'

'It sounds better than freezing all day in muck and sugar beet.'

'But not as mysterious as a human skull. Hasn't anyone come up with any ideas?'

'Archie Jessup did eventually offer up a story. His Old Bracken Field runs alongside the Old Brackendale Airfield. The USAF flew B 17s from there during World War Two. Archie reckons that at least a couple of bombers crashed on landing. Most of the planes got shot down over Germany, some never came home, some only just made it, a few crashed as they came in. Archie's old enough to remember it all. He finally came up with the idea that the skull could be part of a missing airman, someone who was never recovered and assumed incinerated.'

'But you don't think so?' Ben recognized the scepticism in her voice.

'It took him all day to think it up and somehow it didn't have the right ring to it. He admitted that none of those planes actually came down on the Old Bracken Field, most of them crashed on the other side of the runways. He thought that one of the crewmen might have wandered off and then collapsed, but it would have been a bit of a long wander.'

'It could be possible though.' Ben spoke from experience. 'People who are involved in bad accidents can get dazed and disorientated, and then wander away from the scene of the accident before they pass out. It's routine Fire Service procedure to check all around the scene of a road traffic accident. We've had casualties take a knock on the head and then think they are walking home, or go looking for a friend. They get dizzy and confused. They can wander off and then collapse fifty yards or half a mile away. It happens.'

Judy shrugged. 'You could be right, but I still think that crafty old man knows more than he's telling.'

They finished their meal and pushed their plates away on the coffee table. The TV began to report a murder story down in Cornwall and Judy used the remote to switch it off. There was enough police work here in Breckland without worrying about what was happening elsewhere. Ben put his arm around her and pulled her closer.

'Dick rang,' he informed her. 'He called just before you came in. Carol's back home with the baby.' He grinned. 'Big Dick and Little Dick, it suits them.'

'It's Richard and baby Richard,' Judy said severely. But she was glad that Ben had changed the subject. She added casually. 'I've been thinking about that.'

'Oh, oh!' Ben recognized the sign that something was coming and pulled a wry face.

Judy turned to look directly into his eyes. 'Ben, isn't it time we started thinking about having one of our own?'

'We have thought about it,' he protested weakly.

'I know, but I don't think I want to wait anymore. Maybe I should just stop taking the pill, nothing dramatic, no studying the calendar and getting all technical and scientific, I just stop taking the pill and — and let Love decide.'

Ben looked at her thoughtfully, but she knew the long pause was just a tease.

'Well,' he said at last, 'it's mostly your career.'

She punched him hard. 'Oh no, it isn't. I'll go solo for nine months and then it's a joint enterprise again.'

'Okay, okay.' Ben flinched and rubbed his sore arm, but he was grinning. He too had felt the magic of holding their new nephew in his arms.

'I like the sound of it,' he conceded. 'Let Love decide.' He savoured the word as he repeated them and the impish grin that she loved so well grew wider. 'When can we start?'

3

Brentheath was a small Breckland village tucked between the dark Forestry Commission fir plantations and what had once been open heath land. In mediaeval times the heather and bracken covered folds of sandy wilderness had been alive with rabbits which helped to keep the Saxon villagers fat and happy. Now the rabbits were long gone, and the heath land flattened under huge concrete runways, three miles of perimeter fence, and all the high powered might of a modern USAF base.

However, the base was mainly self-maintained, and except for a couple of new housing estates the village was much as it had always been, a picture postcard snapshot of rural tranquillity. The core cottages were ancient, most of them thatched, and there was just one small shop which doubled as the village post office. The new estates had their own small precinct of shops in a neat row, a pocket-sized supermarket, a hairdresser, a bakery, and a newsagent combined with a second small post office.

This last shop in the row was the target.

The time was three am in the morning, the dead hour when most people were deep in sleep. A Range Rover cruised slowly past, showing only dim sidelights. The vehicle had been stolen from a bungalow driveway only a few hours earlier, and would not be missed until dawn. The four men inside were watchful and wary, all of them wearing heavily padded clothes with hoods and gloves.

All around them Brentheath and its two peripheral estates were silent. There was no moon, clouds covered most of the stars, and only a few street lights cast pools of dim yellow. All the upper windows in the shopping precinct were in darkness, the lights in the ground floor shop windows were muted.

The Range Rover drove past the shops and then stopped. The four men inside were satisfied. They quickly donned woollen Balaclava helmets and fitted pairs of heavy duty industrial goggles over their eyes. The driver glanced round and nodded, and the other three men acknowledged in silent agreement. The job was Go. One of the back seat passengers carried a shotgun and the other was armed with a large sledge-hammer. The driver swung the Range Rover into a tight U turn, slammed up through the gears and accelerated back toward the small precinct of shops.

As they reached the precinct the driver again swung the wheel hard over. 'Brace,' he shouted, as the front wheels crashed up on to the pavement. His three passengers were flung up towards the roof but their seat belts held them and jerked them back. Then the bonnet of the Range Rover ploughed into the locked doors of the newsagents with a shattering crash. All four of the men inside yelled out in a triumphal release of tension with the impact.

The entire shop front caved in around them, a thunderous downfall of broken brickwork, splintered timber and exploding plate glass. The windscreen of the Range Rover sagged inward in a sudden craze of star patterns, but somehow held together. The dust settled and there was a moment of frozen silence.

The driver rammed his gloved fist through the windscreen to clear a hole that he could see through as his three passengers scrambled out of the vehicle. One vicious blow from the sledgehammer cleared away the last of the sagging doorframe as they climbed over the fallen rubble into the interior of the shop. The man with the shotgun held it ready, standing where he could cover both the back of the shop and the precinct outside. The third man hauled forward a heavy steel tow chain with a snap hook at either end.

They knew exactly what they wanted. A stand alone cash dispenser stood next to the plate glass corner cubicle that was the Post Office section of the shop. The chain was quickly thrown around it and one hook snapped back onto a link of the chain. The driver of the Range Rover barged it forward, demolishing another corner of the main shop counter but getting close enough for the free end of the chain to be snapped around the front bumper.

The Range Rover was slammed into reverse gear, as it jerked back the bumper bar tore off with a screech, but the cash dispenser was also wrenched off its pedestal, the bolts tearing free from the floor.

The driver jumped out and helped one of his team to manhandle the cash machine over the pile of intervening rubble and debris and load it into the back of their vehicle. The man with the sledgehammer was already attacking the locked post office cubicle and smashing down the glass door. He grabbed the cash till from inside, ripping it away from the counter. In that moment there was a movement from the back of the shop.

The shopkeeper stood there in a beige dressing gown, blinking behind the gleam of his spectacles in the glare of the Range Rover's one unbroken headlight. In his hand he held a stout walking stick, but he was an old man and seeing the odds against him his courage failed and he was too scared to raise it.

'Sod off!' roared the man with the shotgun. He tilted the weapon upwards and fired off one barrel into the suspended ceiling which came down in a white cascade of broken foam plaster. The sound was deafening.

'Bloody hell, Sean,' The man inside the devastated post office cubicle dropped the cash register with the sudden shock.

The effect on the elderly shopkeeper was even more dramatic. He sagged and dropped his stick. He made a gasping, groaning sound as his face drained white, and his hand fumbled toward his chest as though he had actually been shot in the heart. Slowly he seemed to sink down into a shapeless heap inside his dressing gown.

The four raiders stared in a moment of petrified silence as the last dust motes and foam fragments from the ceiling floated slowly down.

'Oh, bloody hell,' the man inside the broken glass cubicle said again.

'Out!' the driver barked the order. 'Leave it now, out quick!'

All four of them hurried back into the Range Rover, panic driving them even faster than the adrenalin that had fired their arrival.

The Range Rover screeched and screamed as its bodywork tore and its gears were crashed. It jerked backward and jolted on to the street, was flung around in another tyre-shredding half turn, and then accelerated away into the night.

★ ★ ★

By the time Judy Kane and Ron Harding climbed out of Harding's car to inspect the damage the whole precinct was alive with lights and movement. Two police patrol cars were already in attendance, plus an ambulance, all with blue lights flashing. The neighbours were all awake, arguing and gesturing over what they had heard and seen. The shopkeeper had been pronounced dead by the paramedics and a tearful widow was being comforted. The cause of death was almost certainly a heart attack, brought on by the violence of the attack and the single gunshot.

All of those who had been rudely awakened assured Judy that there had definitely been a gunshot.

While Judy talked with the various witnesses Harding was fully occupied with his police radio, listening, snapping orders and questions, and gradually becoming more irate. Finally he switched the radio off and climbed over the wreckage to join her where she had paused to stand surveying the mess with two of the patrol car officers.

'We've missed them,' he said in disgust. 'The roadblocks didn't catch them. Either they were too quick, or they've taken another direction we didn't think of.'

This was the fifth ram raid in Breckland so far, and Judy knew that Harding and Grant had spent hours in working out a complex plan on where to deploy their few available patrol cars in the event of any new raid on any post office on their own patch. The net had obviously not been drawn tight enough or quickly enough and they had failed to catch their quarry.

'Bad luck,' she sympathized, 'But we can't win them all.'

Harding snorted, probably choking back some bad language he didn't really want her to hear. 'So what's the picture here?' He finally asked.

'Four men in what sounds like a Range Rover,' Judy summed it up briefly. 'All of them hooded, all masked with goggles. One of them called one of the others Sean.'

Harding looked thoughtful. 'We haven't got a Sean.'

Judy knew he meant that there was no one named Sean in their present list of suspects. She shrugged and said, 'Well, we have now. He was the one who fired off the shotgun. Mrs Kendrick heard one of them shout — ' She paused and checked her notebook. 'Bloody hell, Sean.'

'Mrs Kendrick?'

'The wife of the shopkeeper, I had a brief word, but as you might expect she's almost incoherent. She's with one of the neighbours now. The shopkeeper was

Michael Kendrick, aged sixty. The crash woke them up when the ram raiders hit the shop. They live in the apartment up above. Mister Kendrick had enough nerve to come down with a walking stick for a weapon. He told his wife to stay back. She did, but she was close enough to hear what was said when the shotgun went off. She saw her husband collapse.'

'Was he hit?'

'No the shotgun was a warning, it blasted the ceiling.' Judy pointed upward at the damage, a large, jagged hole with broken shards of polystyrene hanging from the edges. 'But the paramedics say that the old man must have had a weak heart. The shock brought on a massive coronary attack. He died almost instantly.'

'They might as well have shot him instead of the ceiling,' one of the listening patrol officers ventured grimly.

'In my book it's still murder,' Harding said, and there was a note of hard satisfaction in his tone. He now had all the justification he needed for pushing his determination to catch this particular gang of villains to the limit. He finished flatly. 'The way they operate this was always on the cards, so now we'll nail them for it.'

*   *   *

The regular weekly briefings for what had been code-named Operation Longship were scheduled for ten o'clock on Thursday mornings. It was an hour later than the usual daily briefing in the Breckland CID room, but it gave time for the delegated officers representing Cambridgeshire and Norfolk to attend. In overall command was Detective Superintendent Charles Grant, who was also head of the Breckland CID. The Detective Chief Inspector from Cambridgeshire was DCI Dave Pullen, a tall, balding man with a long face that gave him a deceptively melancholic expression. His opposite number from Norfolk was DCI Geoff Geeste, known throughout three forces as Gee Gee, and to some of his own more irreverent lower ranks as 'Horsey.'

Today's briefing had been brought forward by three days and Harding and Judy came straight from the latest ram-raid incident at Brentheath. Despite the short notice call all three of their senior officers were already there.

Harding conferred briefly with Grant before outlining all the known details of the early morning attack. The fact that on this occasion the violent robbery had also resulted in the death of an innocent shopkeeper caused hard faces all round. Judy stood by with her notebook, nodding her head a couple of times when Harding looked to her briefly for confirmation, but his delivery was exact, to the point and complete, and there was nothing she could usefully have added.

'So we have three new leads,' Grant noted as he made the final summing up. He was a handsome and intelligent man who ran a tight ship. His wife, Judy knew, was a lecturer in philosophy at the University of East Anglia, and when they appeared together at social functions it was obvious that they had the easy relationship of contented equals. There was a high-powered, logical brain behind the dashes of silver grey at Grant's temples, and he applied it with precision to all his police work.

He ticked off the three leads on his fingers as he continued: 'One, in their hurry to get away they dropped and left behind their sledgehammer. Two, they also left behind a heavy duty towing chain with snap hooks. Finally we have the name Sean.'

'There's no Sean at Bleak Fen,' Dave Pullen said with conviction. 'We've got a full list of the people there, and we've had no new arrivals in the past few days. Also there was no movement in or out of the camp last night.'

The blunt statement was accepted without question, for the Cambridgeshire side of the investigation was almost complete. Suspicion had fallen early upon the Gypsy travellers camp at Bleak Fen, a small huddle of caravans and motor homes parked in a field between dykes in the middle of the flat, fertile black fenlands. The nearest house was half a mile away, the home of a market gardener who had bought himself a small retirement corner of the seemingly endless furrows of open fields.

What the travelling community did not know was that their nearest neighbour, a man with an unlikely passion for growing Japanese bonsai trees, was in fact a retired police officer. John Padso had once been Dave Pullen's DCI when Pullen was a young detective sergeant. The old bond was still there, and now Padso was happy to keep a discreet but careful watch on Pullen's current quarry. If Pullen said there had been no suspect movement from Bleak Fen during the past twelve hours, then that information came from Padso, and could be taken as gospel.

Geoff Geeste grinned broadly. 'I don't have the godsend of an old boss keeping a round the clock watch on my villains, but I don't think they came from our lot at Dalton Broad. There are only three roads into their camp, and we had all of them blocked within ten minutes of receiving your call, Charles. No vehicle went into that camp, and there is no way they could have covered the distance from Breckland back into our patch before we had our patrol cars in place.'

'We had all the roads into the Brackendale camp covered within minutes, and we passed no traffic on the way from Granchester to Brentheath,' Harding said as a matter of fact. 'So where the hell did they go?'

'Obviously they dumped the Range Rover,' Grant said calmly. 'Sometime in the next few hours it'll turn up somewhere in a forest driveway, or in some quiet lay-by. We know they always have a prearranged pick up point where they can abandon the stolen raid vehicle, and then get a lift home. My guess is that this time they haven't gone straight home. Either they are getting smart, or they are scared now they know that they've caused a death. They'll be laying low until they get a mobile phone call to tell them that our roadblocks are gone and the roads are clear.'

'Or there could be another camp involved,' Judy said quietly. 'This whole crime wave could be more widespread than we think.'

'A good point,' Grant conceded. 'We've worked it out that at least three travellers camps must be involved, and for a while we were kept guessing by the fact that they are all raiding into each other's territories, but we could be missing something.'

'All we are missing is the Mister Big,' Dave Pullen interjected. 'We can be pretty sure that the way this whole operation knits together is too complex for the young hard heads who are stealing cars and ram-raiding shop premises over three counties. Somebody has thought it all out, and that somebody has to be acting as fence and banker for all the proceeds. My bet is that he isn't in any of the three camps that we are watching, and we'll find no loot on any of those sites either. Our man is too smart for that.'

'So we're still left with more police work,' Grant smiled wryly. 'We've got the sledgehammer and the chain. There'll be no prints from last night because the raiders all wore gloves, but they're two old pieces of equipment so there might be old prints that could give us a lead. Or perhaps we can find out whether one or both of those items could have been sold or supplied to one of our suspect sites.'

'What about the road blocks?' Harding asked. 'Ours are still in position.'

'And ours,' Geeste added.

Grant thought for a moment, then looked at Geeste. 'Pull the cars out, Geoff. Keep it low profile and try leaving just one officer behind?'

Geese nodded. 'They'll probably spot him, but it could be worth a try.'

There was a moment of silence as Grant looked around the room for more comments. One of the uniformed constables present coughed, he had been waiting for the senior officers to finish their discussion. Grant gave him an encouraging look.

'Sir,' the constable said, 'I think there is a Sean on the Brackendale camp. I had to sort out an argument a few weeks ago, the usual Saturday night drunks outside one of the Granchester nightclubs. It was the local lads squaring up to some of the travellers, a bit of jostling and shouting but the sight of the uniform calmed it down. The point is, sir, I did hear the name Sean. I'm sure it was one of the gypsy lads reining in his mate.'

'Description,' Harding asked.

'Young, early twenties, thick set, average height, a hard-looking sort, he was the one pushing for trouble.'

'He sounds the type,' Harding nodded.

'We need a complete list of everyone living at that site,' Grant said. 'Get on it, Ron.' He looked at his opposite numbers.

'We've already got one for Bleak Fen,' Pullen said with satisfaction.

'Almost,' Geeste added. 'We're working on identifying everyone at Dalton Broad.'

'When they're complete we need to compare those lists,' Grant decided. 'We need to look for family names, or family connections. If there are gangs on the three sites working together then the links have got to be fairly obvious.'

The discussion went on for another half hour and then began to break up. Pullen and Geeste left to make their respective journeys back to Cambridge and Norwich. Grant shared his final thoughts with Harding as his official 2IC.

Harding acknowledged and then raised the question of the other investigation that had occupied them for most of the previous day.

'What about Blackberry Farm and that damned skull in the sugar beet?'

'Ah, yes,' Grant sighed. 'We could have done without that at this particular moment in time.' He looked to Judy, his glance inviting her to move closer and join them. 'The preliminary forensic examination confirms that the skull is probably around fifty years old,' he continued. 'Doctor Rawlings needs to get it carbon dated to be more exact. It's hardly a priority compared to Longship and now the death of Michael Kendrick, but still we can't ignore it. We'll have to carry on with the enquiry at Blackberry Farm.'

Harding pulled a sour face. 'If we have to start digging up Archie Jessup's Old Bracken field we'll be working beside Old Brackendale Airfield. The Old Brackendale Travellers Camp is on the opposite side of the runways, close enough for them to take notice, and we don't want to scare them into laying low.'

Grant nodded. 'It's a bit unfortunate, but it can't be helped. By lunchtime yesterday the story of that skull was all around the sugar beet factory. Last night you can bet that it did the rounds of every pub in Granchester, and all the surrounding villages. Today it's front page news in the East Anglian Daily Times, and makes the second page in the Eastern Daily Press. It would probably arouse more suspicion now if we didn't continue some level of investigation.'

Harding looked glum. Grant smiled and went on, 'But I need you to head up Operation Longship, we can't afford to slack up on that one now. Judy can look after Blackberry Farm.'

'Yes, sir,' Judy was not sure whether she was pleased or affronted, she was being given her own investigation to run, but it also meant that she was being moved off the main job which everyone considered of paramount importance.

Grant sugared the pill with another

smile. 'Keep it low key and try to get it wrapped up as soon as possible. I do really need both of you back on the main team.'

4

When Judy returned to Blackberry Farm it was mid-morning, and after the previous days heavy fog the weather was a complete contrast. It was one of those crisp, blue sky Autumn days with the red berries gleaming bright on the hawthorn hedgerows, and the leaves turning bronze and gold in the nearby beech wood. Judy recalled the old country saying that a plentiful crop of berries meant that a hard winter was to come. It was nature's way of providing in advance for the birds and squirrels.

The Jessups, father and son, one old and grizzled and the other burly and robust, were both leaning on the sagging gateway and watching the white-suited scene of crime team finishing off their work on the roadside hardpad. They paused in their gossip and turned their heads as her car pulled up behind the small knot of police vehicles that were already in attendance.

Judy climbed out and went to the boot to exchange her black shoes for the pair of Wellington boots she always carried. On a country beat like this one they were standard equipment. Detective Sergeant Jason Roper who headed the SOC team when Rawlings was absent came up to meet her, shrugging his shoulders and with a negative shake of his head. His white overall was streaked with black mud, but even so he was more cheerful than they had all been yesterday. Bright weather brightened moods, she decided.

'No joy?' She asked unnecessarily.

'Nothing,' Roper said. 'We've shifted the whole lot from one side of the hardpad to the other, and sieved it all on the way.'

Judy stared at the small mountain of sugar beet that now stood on the opposite side of the hardpad to where they had started. Moving it this quickly had been hard, dedicated work and she saw Archie and Peter Jessup exchanging grins by the gate. Their irritation from yesterday now seemed to be replaced by an amused satisfaction, or perhaps it was just the improved weather having its brightening effect.

'Your boss now seems to agree that the skull was at least fifty years old, but we still have to keep looking for the rest of it,' she said wearily. 'We'll just have to walk the field where they think it probably came from.'

The SOC DS nodded resigned agreement. Tom Ford, the tall, lean-faced sergeant in charge of the small group of uniformed constables had joined them in time to overhear and exchanged 'Good mornings.'

'We've got as many bodies as we can muster coming up from the station,' Judy told them. 'So we might as well get it organized while the sun shines. Grant and Harding want them all back as soon as possible anyway.'

The two sergeants nodded and went to relay the news to their subordinates. Judy walked over to the two farmers.

'Good morning, Mister Jessup — and Mister Jessup.'

Peter Jessup grinned broadly. 'You'd

best be calling us Peter and Archie. It'll stop us all getting confused.'

Judy smiled in return, noting that he was definitely in a much better mood this morning, and wondering if it was because nothing had yet been found.

'I'm afraid we are going to have to trample all over your field,' she apologized. 'Are you sure that the skull did come from your Old Bracken Field?'

Peter Jessup nodded. He was either unconcerned or resigned to the inevitable. 'Now that I've had time to think about it, it has to be Old Bracken. I know where I've lifted beet, I know where I've dumped it, and I know where I loaded Sam's lorry. Do you still reckon you're going to find anything?'

'We have to look,' Judy said easily, trying to give the impression now that it was all just a routine search. 'Our forensic lab seems to think that we were right in our original guess, and that the skull is fifty years old or more.'

'Goes back to wartime then,' Peter observed, as though that explained it all.

Judy nodded, and looked at his father,

'Any more ideas, Archie, now that you've had time to think?'

Archie Jessup pursed his lips, deliberating before answering. Peter spoke up for him. 'Dad thinks it could be the Nazi.'

'The Nazi,' Judy raised a quizzical eyebrow, it was what Ben called her Roger Moore expression.

Archie Jessup nodded. 'During the war a Nazi fighter plane got shot down. They never did find the pilot.'

'They think he parachuted down somewhere,' Peter nudged his father to continue.

'They found the parachute,' Archie offered. 'There was blood on the harness straps, but the bugger had run off. Some people reckoned he escaped, and some say he must have hid up and died somewhere, but they never did find a body.'

Judy eyed them uncertainly. An enemy airman running away to crawl into a ditch or a hedgerow and die made a plausible theory, but she still wasn't sure. She didn't know whether they were making up stories for her benefit, just trying to be helpful perhaps, or whether they were trying to steer her away from something they didn't want her to find. She wasn't picking up any real clues to help her guess at what they might be thinking.

Tom Ford caught her eye and drew her attention to two more patrol cars full of uniformed constables that had just arrived. She couldn't keep them standing idle and Judy knew that she had to leave things for now and attend to the job at hand.

'The troops have arrived,' she told the Jessups. 'Can you show us the way to your Old Bracken field.'

Peter Jessup nodded. 'It'll be as easy to leave all the cars here. Old Bracken is the next field down.' He glanced at his father. 'I'll show them, you can wait here, dad.'

'I'm coming,' the old man said shortly. 'I've been walking these fields all my life, there's no reason to stop now.'

'Stubborn old bugger,' Peter grinned at Judy and then led off along the edge of the ploughed field. Ford was organizing the new arrivals, so Judy kept pace with the Jessups in order to continue with their conversation.

They were now walking towards the Old Brackendale airfield, one of the many disused WW2 airstrips that were scattered around East Anglia. Much of it was ploughed under, but a huddle of the old hangar buildings remained as small factory units. The old control tower was a ruined square block on the skyline, and somewhere beyond the cracked and grass-grown runways was the gypsy traveller's camp that was one of the three targets of Operation Longship.

'So where did these planes crash?' Judy asked.

Archie Jessup was walking with his stick, although despite his age he didn't seem to really need it. He used it to point to the left of the derelict control tower.

'I can remember one of the bombers came down over there, on one of Charlie's fields. Well, it's not Charlie's field now, young Sarah runs it since Charlie died. It wasn't Charlie's field then, come to think of it, it was before Charlie bought it.'

'Uncle Charlie was dad's brother,' Peter tried to bring some coherence to his father's ramblings. 'He farmed Appledown Farm, next door to us.'

'We were brought up here on Blackberry Farm,' Archie was in a mood to continue his mental wander through the past. 'It was my dad's farm, and his dad before him. Blackberry has been a Jessup farm for five generations. When my dad died I took it over, me being the eldest, me and Charlie ran it together for a few years after the war. Then Appledown came up for sale. I let Charlie have all the money so he could get a mortgage and set up on his own farm. I already had Blackberry.'

'Uncle Charlie died five years back,' Peter finished. 'Cousin Sarah runs it now. She was married but her husband died, caught his arm clearing chaff from an old harvester and bled to death. Sarah runs Appledown now.'

They had reached a corner of the field where a hawthorn hedge acted as a divider, and a cock pheasant flew up shrieking from the grass verge as they pushed through a gap into the next field. Judy jumped in alarm, and Archie laughed, a gleeful cackle.

'This is Old Bracken field,' Peter said. 'The old airfield runs along the other side of that next hedge.'

'So where did this German fighter plane crash?' Judy asked.

Archie pointed with his stick again. 'Over there, other side of the airfield, one night in 1943. It was a winter night, pitch dark, bitter cold. The plane exploded and burned up, a Messerschmitt or something. The parachute was found up at the north end of the runway, so they knew the pilot had bailed out. There was no sign of him though, but I suppose he could have made his way round here.'

Again Judy had to leave it at that. A dozen or more constables were now jostling each other as they filed on to the field behind her, and she had to turn and help Tom Ford get them all into a neatly spaced line. A few of them carried rakes and she spaced them out as evenly as possible with one to comb the undergrowth on each of the hedgerows on either side.

'We're looking for the remains of an old skeleton,' she reminded them as she moved up and down the line. 'So keep your eyes open for anything white or brown that could be a fragment of old bone.'

There was a brief chorus of, 'Dem bones, dem bones, dem dry bones,' which she silenced with a frown. She took her place in the centre of the line and slowly they moved off down the field. With the constables, the SOC team, the Jessups and herself she had less than a score of bodies to cover a width of just over one hundred yards. That meant at least a five yard gap between each pair of eyes, not nearly enough, but it would have to do.

Before switching her concentration to the muddy earth at her feet Judy took a last look round to check that all of them were in place and taking the job seriously. It was then that she saw the small figure watching them, standing on a slight rise of land that had been part of the old airfield. The figure was just visible through a small gap further along the hedgerow. Judy couldn't be sure but her first thought was that it was a woman, the outline might have been a man in a raincoat, but the brief glimpse suggested a woman in a skirt.

The figure moved immediately, disappearing behind the hedgerow, almost as though alarmed by Judy's interest. There had been casual onlookers by the roadside where they had left the cars, but that was normal. Out here in the fields there was no one else to watch them, and no one who had acted as though they might not want to be seen.

For a moment Judy wondered if she might have imagined that quick blur of movement, but she knew she had not.

*   *   *

An hour later they had reached the end of the long field and the slow painstaking search had revealed nothing. The line of constables waited patiently, bored now and ready for a tea break and sandwiches. Judy considered her options briefly. The line was too widely spaced and she didn't have enough bodies. A hands and knees crawl down in the mud hardly seemed warranted by a fifty year old relic and they would still be too far apart. However, she was not going to give up with just one try.

'Everybody step two paces to the right,' she ordered. 'We'll go back up the field, but we'll walk between the lines we walked before.'

There were a few groans and she remembered Ben telling her the first rule of successful fire-fighting: 'Feed the troops.' It applied to policemen as well. She looked at Tom Ford. 'Can we rustle up an urn of tea and a few ham sandwiches from the canteen? A van should be able to get out here and meet us by the time we get back to the far end.'

Ford nodded and patted his radio. 'I'll call them and get it organized.'

The troops were satisfied, they moved themselves as required and started back up the field in the same slow moving line. Harding would have reminded them to keep a sharp eye, but Judy saw that there was no need. Each man had his head down and moving slightly from side to side as they carefully scanned the rutted earth directly in front of them. Even the Jessups seemed totally caught up in the silent spell of concentration.

They were half way down the field again before a welcome shout came from one of the constables walking by the edge of the field on Judy's right, the side that bordered on to the old airfield.

'Over here, ma'am, there's something here.'

Judy walked to him, moving behind the line so that she did not kick over the ground that was still unwalked. Ford and Roper joined her where the constable had stopped to point out a small gleam of brownish white in the clods at his feet.

This was Roper's job. He carried a small hand trowel and a medium sized paintbrush and he knelt to clear the crumbling earth gently away from the dull glint of bone. As he worked he excavated a hollow around what proved to be a human finger bone, pointing upward as though seeking its way out of its grave.

Judy caught her breath and felt a shiver run down from the nape of her neck to the base of her spine, as though that same ghostly hand had stroked her in a sexual caress.

There was silence along the stopped line as they all waited expectantly.

Roper continued to move away soil with his trowel, brushing gently and patiently with his paintbrush, slowly exposing the skeletal hand. As each knuckle was cleared he nodded with satisfaction.

'It is human,' he confirmed, with all the guarded reservation of the forensic team who rarely offered more than the obvious in the first instance.

Judy knelt for a closer look, and became aware that the Jessups had also come up to see what was happening. With an effort she tore her gaze away from the slowly materializing dead hand to study their faces.

Peter Jessup was leaning forward to get a closer look over Roper's shoulder. His ruddy face showed no expression other than curiosity, and perhaps faint surprise.

Archie Jessup stayed further back, drawn to the scene, but hesitant, as though reluctant to take that final step. The old man's face was masked with a day's growth of dark stubble, and she wasn't sure if he was pale underneath. His lips were tightened to a thin line, and she sensed more than saw the faint flash of fear in his eyes. They met her gaze for an instant and then flickered away.

'It looks as though that is it.' Roper had cleared the earth away from the hand and wrist bones, but there was no attached arm. He dug away carefully, widening the search area, but after ten more minutes of digging the rest of the skeleton was still missing.

Judy straightened her back, which was beginning to ache, and looked all around the field. The search line was still in place, calmly awaiting her next instructions. She looked toward the old airfield where she had briefly seen the mysterious figure, and then she froze. The lone watcher was back, standing in the same place as before, but Judy was closer now, almost opposite the gap in the hedge, and this time she could definitely see that it was a woman, stooped with age and wearing an old grey coat.

She tapped Peter Jessup on the shoulder. 'Who is that?' she asked quietly. She refrained from pointing but the farmer turned his head to follow the direction of her gaze.

'That's Crazy Alice,' he said simply, as though he was not surprised and her presence was unimportant.

However, Archie Jessup's reaction was startling. The old man looked round at the sound of his son's voice, his whole body jerked and stiffened and his eyes flashed with anger.

'Peter, you don't talk about your aunt like that.'

The big farmer blushed, looking remarkably shame-faced and sheepish for a man of his age and bulk.

'Sorry, dad, I forgot, that's what everybody else calls her.'

'She's family,' the old man snapped. 'Crazy or not.'

He turned abruptly and began to walk back up the field.

'Come away, Peter. They've found what they wanted. They don't need us anymore, and we've got real work to do.'

Peter Jessup hesitated. He was still curious, but then he slumped his broad shoulders and obediently followed his father.

Judy watched them go, one marching briskly, the other trailing reluctantly, but neither of them casting a backward glance, and she wondered at the old man's reaction. She had a dozen questions to ask but this was not the moment to chase after them. There would be a better time, she decided, preferably if she could catch Peter Jessup alone.

She looked through the gap in the hedge, but the solitary figure of Crazy Alice had again vanished, slipping out of her line of vision like a phantom in a dream.

She had to return her attention to the skeleton hand, which lay palm up in the small hole of cleared earth. Ford and Roper were waiting for her to speak first.

In Harding's absence it was her call, she had to make the decisions. She looked up and down the length of the field, her eyes following the lines of the plough furrows.

'Well, they obviously harvested lengthways, so that's the way we'll run our trenches. My best guess is that if there is a whole body then the beet harvester probably dragged the skull and the hand away from the rest of the skeleton. If we work up and down the plough lines from here we should find it.'

Roper nodded, 'A small trench, just a foot wide and a foot deep should do to start.'

Judy looked to Ford. 'Tom, if we can keep a couple of your lads to help SOC here, then I think we can release the rest and send them back to the station.' Beyond a far hedgerow she saw the top of a white police van approaching and added diplomatically. 'That's after they've had their tea and sandwiches.'

Ford grinned. 'It's what keeps coppers happy.' He turned to go but on impulse Judy caught his arm.

'Tom, you've worked in Granchester

for several years, do you know anything about Crazy Alice?

They both looked back to the empty space where the old lady had briefly been standing. The tall uniformed sergeant stroked his lean jaw thoughtfully.

'Crazy Alice, I believe she's Alice Jessup, so that would make her Archie Jessup's sister. She's got a cottage on the lane that runs past the end of the old airfield, Wheatsheaf Cottage I think it's called, a yellow washed place, thatched roof. She lives there alone.'

'Why do they call her Crazy Alice?'

Ford shrugged. 'She's just a bit odd, I suppose. She's an old spinster, never married, although she is supposed to have had an American boy friend during the war. Before my time of course, she must have been a teenager then.' He paused, and his tone became wry but sympathetic. 'They say she's often seen walking alone around the old airfield, especially at night. They say she often stops and looks up at the sky. Her boyfriend flew out on a mission and never came back, so now she's always looking eastward, as though she's waiting for a plane to come home.'

★　★　★

While the police search line gratefully broke ranks and converged around their tea van, a diesel engine pulled a single coach train into Granchester railway station. The train was the 12.45 from London, via Ipswich, and there were only a few passengers. Only one of them was getting off at Granchester.

He was a well-dressed man of about fifty years of age, and he watched the familiar twin Victorian towers of the station building's as they slowly drew closer, until finally the train stopped in their shadows.

Those who attended the stage productions in provincial theatres might have vaguely recognized him. He had a fine-boned face and a wave of thick, dark grey hair. He was not famous, but he trod the boards regularly enough to make a living, which was more than most actors could manage. His name was Rupert

Drake, and it had appeared often on theatre programmes, usually about half way down the cast list of various comedy and mystery plays.

As the train stopped he stood up from his seat, buttoned up his fawn overcoat and lifted his small overnight case from the luggage rack. He was home, he thought, without much emotion. He had lived away from home, usually on the move from town to town, for far too long.

Almost as an afterthought he picked up the paper he had been reading on the journey. It was one of the national dailies, but the story of the human skull in the sugar beet chute had enough novelty value to make the fourth page. The paper was folded so that the picture leered up at him.

Rupert Drake shivered before he folded the paper again and stuffed it into his overcoat pocket. Then he dismounted from the train. The skull story and the picture had brought him back here. There was something he had to know, an old mystery that might at last be cleared up.

5

The November days were short and by late afternoon the light was failing. The sun was low in a dark red haze over the old airfield and the shadows of the beech woods and hedgerows had lengthened out into huge dark patches over the fields. Roper and his team had excavated a series of narrow trenches north and south from the spot where the skeleton hand had been unearthed, but so far they had found no trace of the main grave.

If there had been any real urgency, a fresh murder or any current mystery to be solved, then they might have brought up arc lights and a generator to enable them to carry on working. However, even if there was any more to be found it had all been buried there for fifty years or more, and so Judy decided that all night overtime was hardly warranted. Roper agreed and they called off the search until the next day.

The site was far enough from the main road to remain undisturbed, and in any case there was nothing yet to guard. Roper bagged up the skeleton hand and took it away to join the skull for further forensic analysis. Judy arranged for the police cars that would be on patrol duty throughout the night to pass by on their rounds and give the field a passing glance, and they all departed.

For Judy there were still a couple of hours of her working day left. She had to call in at the police station and type up a report, but first she made a small detour.

She had driven past the small lane that ran past the north end of the old airfield many times, but tonight she slowed her car and turned off the main road to enter it. She saw a sign saying Bracken Lane half buried in long grass and blackberry bushes heavy with unpicked fruit. Then there were hawthorn hedgerows passing on either side. When an opening came on her left she saw the gable end of a small thatched cottage. The walls gleamed pale yellow in her headlights and the early moonlight, and she could see why it was called Wheatsheaf Cottage.

The lane wound round to the front of the cottage, and here there was just enough room for Judy to stop and still leave enough room for another vehicle to pass. There were lights showing in the windows of the lower half of the cottage, leaking out from behind the drawn curtains.

Judy sat thinking for a moment, and then switched off her lights and engine and got out of the car. There was a white-painted wooden gate, again gleaming softly in the pale moonlight, and as she walked up the short path she could see that two or three of the last roses of summer still clung defiantly to the trellis arch around the front door. It looked an idyllic little place, but then she was biased, she and Ben had chosen something very similar for their own home. She knocked on the door and waited.

There was no response. After a minute Judy knocked again, a little louder this time in case the old lady was partially deaf, another minute ticked by, and then she heard a reluctant shuffling behind the closed door. The catch clicked and a security chain rattled, the door opened a few inches, and light flooded out through the crack.

'Who is it?' The voice was old, quavering and frightened.

'My name is Judy Kane,' Judy said calmly. 'I'm a police officer. I know it's late and it is nothing serious, but I would like to talk to you.' She passed her card into the crack in the doorway. 'This is my identification. I'm happy to wait if you want to telephone the police station to check.'

There was a pause, and then the card was taken out from her fingertips. Another pause, and then:

'Detective Sergeant?'

'Yes, that's why I'm not in uniform. May I come in and talk, please.'

She put a gentle emphasis on the please, making it a polite request and not an official demand. She knew that she would learn nothing unless she could win the old woman over and gain her confidence.

There was another short wait and Judy

could imagine the old lady pondering slowly and deliberately over what to do next. Then the door closed, Judy wondered if she had wasted her time, but then she heard the chain rattle as it was unhooked, and the door opened wide. Alice Jessup stood in the doorway. She was small, frail and slightly stooped, barely coming up to the height of Judy's shoulder. She wore a brown woollen skirt and a thick brown wool cardigan, clearly dressed for warmth although the cottage seemed cosy. Her hair was grey, almost white, and Judy was reminded briefly of a small, white-headed, brown sparrow. There was no such bird, of course, tree sparrows had a chestnut crown, and house sparrows a grey crown and black bib, but the thought persisted and would not go away. The eyes behind the plain rimmed spectacles and beneath wrinkled brows were bright and beady, nervous, just like a sparrow.

Judy rubbed her hands lightly together and smiled as she affected a small shiver. 'Brrr, it's cold out here. Do you mind if I come in?'

Another silent hesitation, and then the old lady inched back and stood to one side. Judy stepped into the small hallway and the door was closed behind her.

'Thank you,' Judy kept her smile and tone as friendly as possible. 'Oh, it is nice and warm in here, just what I need.'

'I was making a cup of tea,' Alice Jessup said slowly.

It wasn't exactly an offer, but Judy was grateful. 'I'd love a cup of tea, thank you.'

Alice led the way into a small sitting room that looked like a 1950s time warp. There was an old settee with a rose flowered cover and a highbacked chair with a matching pattern. There was an old fashioned fireplace, although now the fire in it was an electric one with a burning log fire effect. There were china figurines on the mantelpiece and a colourful cuckoo clock on the wall. The few pictures were all old paintings in heavy gold paint frames, a rose garden, and autumn woodland, and even a Scottish stag in the glen.

The table was laid with a white lace cloth, and a teapot, milk jug and sugar bowl sat on a small silver tray with just one cup on a saucer. A single plate contained two brown bread sandwiches and a slice of fruit cake, the old lady's tea.

Alice waved Judy toward one of the two chairs at the table and then found a second cup and saucer from a long sideboard, predictably the cups and saucers had a pattern of small red roses.

'It's Mrs Jessup, isn't it?' Judy said as her host poured two cups of tea.

'Miss Jessup,' Alice Jessup corrected her.

'I'm sorry, Miss Jessup,' Judy smiled brightly. She accepted her cup, sipped appreciatively, and politely declined the offer of a sandwich. 'Just the tea is fine. It's been so cold out there, on your brother's field. The sun has been bright, but the wind has a bite to it.'

'A lazy wind,' the old lady agreed. 'It won't go round you, cuts right through you.'

Judy nodded. 'You felt it too, but then, you were watching us. I saw you twice, I think.'

Alice Jessup pursed her lips, a gesture

reminiscent of her brother Archie. She seemed about to say something, but then changed her mind and asked a question instead.

'Are you married?'

Judy knew she was being sidetracked. She smiled and said simply, 'Yes.'

'Does he mind — your man — about you being a policeman?'

Judy suppressed a chuckle. 'Sometimes it's a problem,' she admitted. 'But my Ben is a fireman. So he has a job that sometimes proves awkward too, like being called out at weekends or in the middle of the night. We both love our jobs and each other, so we've learned to put up with it.'

The old lady nodded approvingly, a small sigh escaped her lips, and for a moment her mind seemed far away.

'And you,' Judy said softly. 'You never married?'

'No,' Alice Jessup left it at that. She obviously did not want to be drawn any further.

Judy sipped her tea. 'Do you know why we were digging up your brother's field?'

Alice Jessup met her eyes, but her face

gave nothing away. 'It's all around Brackendale village,' she said. 'They found a head in Archie's sugar beet.'

Judy nodded. 'It was an old skull, perhaps it goes back to the war days. Archie thinks it might be a missing airman. He says there was a bomber that crashed on landing. He doesn't think they found all the bodies.'

'Could be,' Alice admitted cautiously. Her head bowed and she looked down at her cup. 'Could be,' she repeated unhelpfully.

'Do you remember it?' Judy asked.

Again Alice sipped at her tea, stalling for time. Then she made a brief, reluctant nod of her head.

'How old were you then?'

'Sixteen — seventeen,' Alice spoke slowly. Her thoughts were far away, she was remembering more than she was saying.

'Seventeen,' Judy kept her voice soft, as unintrusive as possible. 'You were a young girl, just becoming a woman. It must have been an exciting time, the war, the American Air Force coming here, the big bombers flying missions over Germany, all those brave young men.'

Alice Jessup nodded again, but she refused to look up from her teacup.

Judy sipped some more tea and changed tack. 'This is a lovely little cottage, have you always lived here?'

For a moment she thought that she was going to be ignored again, but then Alice began slowly. 'In a way, I suppose, not always in this cottage, but here in Brackendale. My mum and dad had Blackberry Farm, I was brought up there. When Dad died Archie took over the farm, but half of it was Charlie's, he was my other brother. Then Appledown Farm came up for sale, almost next door. They mortgaged Blackberry Farm to get the deposit to put down on Appledown for Charlie.'

Her voice trailed off. Judy waited for a minute and then asked, 'What about you?'

'I went to London for a few years. I didn't want to stay with Archie.' Alice continued to speak without looking up. 'I worked in a few hotels, as a chambermaid, jobs like that. But the big city was not for me. I suppose I'm a country girl. I came back here, rented a room in Granchester, worked mostly in shops. I liked shop work, it was better than cleaning hotel rooms. Both of the farms were doing well and eventually both Archie and Charlie had paid off their mortgages. They helped me to buy this place, feeling guilty, I expect.'

The last words held a note of anger, slipping out almost involuntarily. Judy's police antennae prickled up and she wondered what Archie and Charlie might have done to feel guilty about. She wanted to ask, but knew that this was not the moment, it would be too soon.

'So you wanted to stay close to Archie and Charlie?' She knew that was not the reason, but it was another probe and a safer question.

'Not exactly,' the old woman shrugged, and then finished, 'Charlie's gone now, the stomach cancer killed him off about five years ago. Young Sarah manages Appledown now, she's Charlie's daughter, a good girl, Sarah.' Her tone implied that the rest of her family were perhaps not so good.

'Archie and Charlie were your older brothers?' Judy ventured.

Alice nodded. 'Charlie was about three years older than me, Archie two years older than him.'

'So when you were seventeen, Charlie would have been about twenty and Archie about twenty two,' Judy reflected aloud. She had the picture now: Wartime East Anglia with Royal Air Force spitfires flying overhead, and then the Americans arriving with their fleets of heavy B 17 bombers, the old Flying Fortresses, and a young farmer's daughter, just flowering into womanhood amid all that glamour, danger and excitement, with two, possibly jealous older brothers. She wondered how many fascinating scenarios could be concocted out of that heady cocktail, but again she knew it would be fatal to ask too soon. Alice Jessup was again concentrating tightly on her teacup, as though she knew that she was already in danger of revealing too much.

Judy eased off the pressure and again

changed the subject slightly. 'Archie said that there was also a German fighter plane that crashed near here. He said that the pilot baled out but was never found.'

Alice nodded too quickly. 'Yes, there was him too, him, or one of those poor bomber crews that blew up when they landed.' She was grateful to be back on more solid ground, with a ready-made explanation for the skull in the beet field.

Judy had to control and conceal her frustration, but now she was sure that there were answers here, even though as yet she wasn't getting any. She felt like a fisherman with a large juicy fish on a line that she knew was too weak. If she pulled too hard the line would snap and all would be lost. She made one last try, still keeping her voice soft and friendly.

'Alice, why were you watching us today?'

Alice looked up from her cup and met her eyes. She smiled brightly in return.

'Just something different to watch, I suppose. Nothing much ever happens in this part of the world. It made a change from watching the beet grow.'

Judy continued to smile and finished her tea. She knew it was time to go, before the old lady bottled up completely. If she kept it low key then perhaps the next time she could tempt out a little more.

'Thank you for the tea,' she said. 'It was lovely. The trouble is, now I need the loo, would you mind?'

Alice Jessup hesitated, distrust and uncertainty flickering behind her eyes. Finally she nodded her grey sparrow head.

'It's upstairs,' she said, 'The door opposite at the top of the landing.'

'Thank you,' Judy went out into the hallway and glanced briefly into the small, meticulously tidy kitchen before starting up the narrow stairway. The stair carpet was dark green, the stairway papered in green and silver vertical stripes. It was all still 1950s décor. The stairway made a dog leg to the right, taking her out of sight of the landing, which was better than she had hoped for.

She stood for a moment on the small landing, there were three doors and the one on her right was partially open. She gently pushed it back and found herself looking into what was obviously the main bedroom. The single bed was neatly made, but with a pink and white knitted patchwork quilt instead of a modern duvet. The wallpaper was roses again, small yellow and pink flowers, and the carpet was pink. It was a little girl's bedroom from fifty years ago.

There was a dressing table with the usual female things, hair brushes and hand mirror, all neatly arranged, and a single photograph in a silver frame. It was, she realized thoughtfully, the only framed photograph she had yet seen in this house.

Judy took a step into the room, close enough to study the picture. It showed a young man, with a lean but handsome smiling face and high cheekbones. His skin was slightly dark, his hair sleek and black and combed straight back. He wore denim jeans, a check shirt, and a belt with wide, silver cowboy buckle, oval shaped and with what looked like a buffalo head and horns as its emblem.

The picture was old, fading to a brownish yellow behind the edges, although the glass and frame were clean and polished. Judy stared at it for a moment, and then silently she backed away and returned to the landing.

A few minutes later she went back down the stairs, the sound of the toilet cistern flushing behind her.

★   ★   ★

'I'm sure that old lady knows something she is not telling,' Judy said to Ben as he joined her in the sitting room of their own cottage later that evening. She had changed into a comfortable pair of old jeans and a sweater, and because they had both worked late there were again two quick ready meals in the microwave. Ben had just descended from the bathroom wearing clean trousers and a shirt and was still pummelling his thick blonde hair with a towel.

'What makes you so certain?' He asked, sitting down beside her, 'The old female intuition again?'

'She didn't gossip,' Judy said simply. 'Old ladies usually love to gossip, even when they've got nothing to say they can't stop chattering.'

'That's women generally,' Ben nodded agreement and she gently cuffed him.

'Shut up, I'm serious, and don't forget to take that towel back to the bathroom when you've finished. Now where was I?'

'Old ladies love to gossip.'

'Yes, and Alice Jessup was just too restrained. She didn't even ask me any questions, and yet she was obviously very interested in what we were doing in her brother's field.'

'Perhaps she's just a rare one who doesn't get much chance to gossip, so she's out of practise. She sounds an odd bird, and you said that even her own family call her Crazy Alice.'

'There was something else,' Judy said, 'I realized as I was leaving. There were no other photographs in that house, no family photographs. Okay, so she never married, but she had two brothers, she's got a nephew and a niece and they will probably have children. So there should have been something, even for a spinster aunt, instead just hints of hostility.'

'So, just the one picture of an old lover,' Ben commented. Judy had told him about the lone photograph on the dressing table.

'We can only assume he was a wartime lover, he wasn't in uniform but I'm guessing a US serviceman. He looked, well, he wasn't white and he wasn't Negro, Hispanic or something, perhaps a Red Indian.'

'Nothing else. You must have had a good look round.'

'A Bible,' Judy remembered. 'And a picture of Jesus on the wall, The Good Shepherd. That was it, all quite bare for a bedroom.'

'So what do your bosses think?'

Judy shrugged. 'I haven't had a chance to talk to them yet. Ron was out somewhere, and Grant was tied up with a long telephone call, probably to Norwich or Cambridge. They are both totally immersed in Operation Longship. It's been a long day, so I didn't hang around.'

'Uh, huh,' Ben finished towelling his

hair and threw the towel on to the nearest chair. He turned to face her, grinning, 'Better now?'

Judy smiled. He had come in late after spending several hours at a fire in the paint shop of one of the small factory units on one of the industrial estates, and his hair and clothes had reeked of smoke. This time it was too much and she had ordered him straight up to the bathroom.

'At least you smell a little sweeter,' she said, and gave him a delayed kiss.

Ben snuggled closer but she heard the click of the microwave door as it opened in the kitchen.

'Time to eat,' she said and pushed him away. 'And you can pick up that towel and take it back where it belongs, and comb your hair. You look like a demented golden golliwog.'

⋆ ⋆ ⋆

Much later, as they lay in bed together, drifting into sleep, she heard the sudden but familiar bleeping of a pocket alerter. She groaned into half wakefulness, her

97

mind picturing another midnight ram raid, but then realized that the bleeps were too sharp and too close together. This call was for Ben.

She settled back and heard him sit up and speak to his control room. Then she felt his parting kiss on her cheek.

'I have to go, a house fire in Barford. Their Sub Officer is off sick and the pump has booked out with a Leading Fireman in charge. It's Persons Reported, so they need an officer.'

Judy sighed and wriggled deeper under the duvet. She heard the front door bang, and then she fell back into sleep.

6

After Judy had left Alice Jessup sat for a long time simply staring into her cup of tea. It was cold when she finally drank the last few sips. She ate her ham and cucumber sandwich and her single slice of fruit cake without any sensation of taste. Her movements were slow and mechanical as she took her plate and the cups and saucers into the kitchen to be washed.

She always spent her evenings watching television. The news bored her, there was always too much foolishness and violence but if she was late switching on then she might miss Emmerdale. She loved the soaps and watched all of them, but tonight the gossip and storylines of her favourite characters passed almost unnoticed on the small colour screen in the corner of the room. Tonight even Eastenders failed to raise a snort of derision or a chuckle of approval. She kept thinking instead of the visit from the young policewoman, about the old skull that had been found in Archie's sugar beet, and about the disturbing bustle of digging in Archie's Old Brackendale field.

At last it was time for bed and she went upstairs to the landing. She stood for a moment looking at her half open bedroom door. Then she stepped carefully into the doorway.

The floorboard beneath the carpet was part of the original flooring, worn from years of use, mostly by occupants now long gone. It creaked very faintly under her weight, just as it always did. A stranger might never notice, but Alice Jessup had perfect hearing that was tuned to every squeak of her own environment. She had heard that soft squeak when the young policewoman had gone up to the bathroom, and so she knew that the policewoman had stepped into her bedroom doorway, she had come this far if not further.

Alice wondered what the policewoman had been thinking, what had she been looking for, what she had seen.

There was only one thing that might have been a clue to the mystery the policewoman was trying to solve. Alice moved to her dressing table and picked up the photograph of Joe Crowfoot.

Navajo Joe, her Joe, it was all so long ago. Without the photograph she might have forgotten his face, the memories might have faded. The old eyes that had been vacant all evening slowly misted over as a single tear trickled down the brown parchment skin of her ancient cheek.

She remembered meeting him at a dance held in one of the large aircraft hangars. It was a vast steel barn of a place and it had been crowded, everyone packed shoulder to shoulder. All the local girls were there, and there were hundreds of young American airmen, all in their smart brown uniforms and their close cropped haircuts. She had gone with Grace and Mavis. 'Safety in numbers,' they had giggled, but the yanks had soon split them up. Glen Miller had played, or perhaps it was a band that modelled itself upon Glen Miller. She could still hear the music in her head: 'In The Mood,' 'Little Brown Jug,' 'Pennsylvania 25000.'

She held her arms around a memory and swayed to the silent music. She could almost feel his strong arms around her, lean muscular arms that had held her as though she was as light as a feather. They were safe arms. She had always felt safe in Joe's arms. With all the other boys she had always been tense, slightly nervous, wondering about what they might be thinking, how far they might be hoping she would go, but in Joe's arms it didn't matter, she always felt safe. Joe was always the gentleman. His kisses were never too hungry. And with Joe, even if things had got more passionate, she would have welcomed it. Another tear trickled down her cheek as she remembered.

On that first night she had been wearing a new blue gown, a tight bodice with bare shoulders and a wide flared skirt that twirled as she danced. And blue gloves, in those days it had been so fashionable to have bared shoulders and matching silk gloves.

He had called her 'Alice Blue Gown,' because of the song, and her name and the dress.

And he was Navajo Joe, her Joe, the tail gunner of a B 17 Flying Fortress bomber crew, a hero from a different culture, and a romantic land across the sea.

They had gone to the pictures several times, some of them Cowboy and Indian pictures, but she had always cheered the Indians when she was with Navajo Joe. That was in between the kissing and cuddling, of course, on the later dates they had always tried to get in the back row.

Joe had told her stories about his homeland, and about the Navajo way of life, stories so vivid that she could still see in her mind the vast red rock mountains and the stony Arizona deserts, all changing in fantastic patterns of colours in the sunrise and sunsets. He had told her of the Bear Dances and Buffalo hunts, of the sweat lodges and other rituals, and of the enigmatic ruins of the old Hopi culture that had preceded his own. He had been a fluent storyteller, with a gift for making everything sound exciting and alive.

Alice reluctantly stopped dreaming, opened her eyes and put the picture down gently in its place on the dressing table. Her face became bleak and her mood darkened. It was such a shame that Archie and Charlie had never been able to like Joe. In fact, both of her brothers had hated him, and had done everything in their power to try and stop her from seeing him.

'Her Red Nigger,' Archie and Charlie had called Joe, and she had hated Archie and Charlie for that. The old wounds cut deep and she had hardly spoken to Archie and Charlie over the next fifty years. It had been a hard thing just to give Archie a sister's peck kiss on his cheek at Charlie's funeral, but she felt no remorse. They had deserved fifty years of silence. Helping her to buy this house had not paid her for what she believed they might have done.

After five glorious months Joe Crowfoot had vanished from Alice Jessup's life just as suddenly as he had appeared. His

B 17 had flown out one dark night, never to come back. It had been shot down, Archie said, somewhere over Germany.

She knew how it must have been, for Joe had described it to her many times, the long, cramped flight through cloud and darkness, or the even greater terror of a bright full moon that would have illuminated every plane in the sky to make them easy targets. Then the screaming, exploding nightmare as they flew through a barrage of artillery fire. The horror of seeing another aircraft, another crew of close buddies just like your own, being blown to hell in fire and debris and scattered all over the sky. And this time it had been them, Joe's plane, the Kentucky Belle, blasted into oblivion, or sent on that last howling death plunge to the unyielding earth. No one had survived. The entire crew had perished.

So Archie said, but she had never been able to get any real confirmation. She had asked, of course, all around the village and at the airfield gates. However, the Americans were trying to play down their losses and keep morale up, so the bad news only leaked, so nobody really knew what was happening. Some local people counted the planes flying out, and counted those that came back home, and said that the numbers on the second count were always less. Sometime a plane would crash land and then everybody knew. Sometimes an airman, or a group of air crew, who had become well known locally would just disappear.

After the war it all came out, much, much later. The USAF had lost more than six thousand aircraft and twenty six thousand servicemen had been killed during the wartime operations from East Anglia. Alice had studied the long columns of commemorated names at the US war cemetery near Cambridge, but she had never been able to find the name of Joe Crowfoot.

Alice moved over to her bedroom window where the curtains were half parted, the view there looked out at the eastern sky. Rain threatened and a few stars glinted bravely between the dark patches of slowly moving clouds. There were no other lights, no descending aircraft dropping down towards the Old Brackendale Airfield, no sound of returning engines, the night was deathly still and quiet.

It always was.

It always had been for the last fifty years.

The Americans were still in East Anglia, mainly at Brentheath and the other bases on the other side of the Breckland forests, but the modern fighters flew so high that they were rarely seen or heard above Granchester. Old Brackenfield was dead, like so many other old wartime airfields it was obsolete and almost forgotten.

She still walked around the bracken-choked perimeter, or along the crumbling, grass and weed-grown runways, but not so often now that the rheumatism was getting into her left hip. She knew the villagers all called her 'Crazy Alice,' and most of them knew why she occasionally stopped to search the eastern sky.

Sometimes, in the early years, she had climbed up on to the old control tower, out on to the sagging balcony where the senior officers had once watched with their binoculars, watching and waiting for their planes and their crews to come home. Alice had stood there in their place, long after it was all finished and all the Americans had gone, watching as they had watched, waiting and hoping. It had all been in vain, and now the old watch tower was too dangerous, the balcony had shifted once beneath her feet, dropping a few inches, and making her heart pound with the sudden fright. It was all crumbling away and she had not dared to climb up there again.

'Joe,' she thought, repeating his name in her mind as though it might call him back: 'Joe, Joe, Joe . . . '

She thought about the other one then, The Wild One. She didn't think of him so much, but sometimes when she had been thinking a lot about Joe the other one would also creep into her mind. It was strange that they had both come into her life at the same time, and then that they had both disappeared, almost simultaneously.

Her heart had always been for Joe, but

The Wild One had fascinated her and excited her. There had been many similarities between them, he too was from another country and another culture, and she had been only seventeen at the time. Having two fantastic men chasing after her had been thrilling and daring, putting her head in a whirl and making her feel breathless and giddy.

Joe was her true love, she knew that now, but when The Wild One had burst into her life she had been briefly undecided, blissfully, painfully, ecstatically torn between the two. Now she sometimes smiled and asked herself, what woman would not have played them both for a while?

Her mood darkened. Archie and Charlie hadn't liked The Wild One either, but at least he wasn't a 'Red Nigger.' Perhaps that was what had pushed her more quickly and firmly into the arms of Navajo Joe.

Alice Jessup sighed. It was all so long ago. Joe was gone. The Wild One was gone. Teasing, flirting little Alice Blue Gown was also long gone. Now she was just a silly old woman getting moody with her memories. She sniffed back a tear and turned away from the window.

She thought again of the human skull that had been found, and all those policemen digging in Archie's sugar beet field. People were saying that the skull could be fifty years old, and for fifty years she had been wondering what might have happened to her two missing lovers. She had always been fearful of what Archie and Charlie might have done. Now it seemed that she might at last find out, but now she was no longer so sure that she really wanted to know.

For a moment her loneliness weighed down heavily upon her bowed shoulders, the empty house, silent now that she had turned off the TV, and outside the empty, silent airfield, where the grass and bracken grew tall and no planes ever flew. She was a strong person, and most of the time she could cope with being alone, but there were times, like tonight, when she felt that she needed someone to talk to.

As if in answer to an unspoken prayer a knock sounded on her front door, and then she heard a key click in the yale lock. Alice suddenly remembered that after the policewoman had left she had failed to put the safety chain back in place, but whoever it was had a key. That could only mean one person. She went back down the stairs to where they turned and she could see the front door as it opened.

'Oh, it's you,' she said calmly.

7

As Ben reached the open road he switched on the flashing blue light on the top of his car and shifted up swiftly through the gears. Within minutes he was doing 100mph along the by-pass, but soon he had to turn off the straight dual carriageway and take the smaller B road that dipped and wound through the dark Breckland forests to Barford.

The actual report had been for a 'House Fire, Persons Reported Trapped,' which meant that there were one or more people believed to be still inside the burning building. The rest of the message had been brief for his information: 'Pumps made three, Breckland-three-five responding with Leading Fireman Slade in charge of a crew of six.'

Technically it wasn't Ben's shout, he was the operations commander for the full time day watches at Granchester, but Station Officer Reg Watson, whose patch included Barford and three other out stations, was currently on holiday and sunning himself in the Seychelles. Ben was providing extra cover in Watson's absence.

Ben had covered Watson's area in the past, but he wasn't familiar with all the men now under Watson's command. He knew the Sub-Officer in charge at Barford, a reliable man with thirty years of fire-fighting experience, and it was bad luck that he should be off sick at the same time that Watson was on holiday. Ben was only vaguely familiar with John Slade, the young Leading Fireman who was now in charge of the Barford crew, but he knew that Barford had recently taken a big shake-up in personnel. Several of the old hands had reached retirement age, new young replacements had come in, and the average length of crew experience had gone way down.

Ben knew from his own days as a Sub-Officer that sometimes he had been able to look round the five faces of the crew around him and count up to eighty or ninety years of collective fire-fighting experience. That gave a good feeling of support. At other times the crew could be all fresh young faces, plenty of eager young blood, but no wise old heads, and then the job would need careful watching.

Such a crew with a new Leading Fireman could get into trouble. That was why control was sending three pumps instead of the usual two for a house fire, and why Ben felt that it was imperative that he should get there as quickly as possible.

The 'Persons Reported' part of the message always pumped up the adrenalin and screwed up the tension. On all three of the pumps now speeding on their way to the Barford incident there would be two crewmen struggling into their breathing apparatus sets, strapping air cylinders on to their backs and checking their breathing masks and pressure gauges.

The actual rescue job would be Barford's, their pump would be the first to arrive. The back up pumps and their BA crews would be fifteen to twenty minutes behind them. One of them would be Granchester's full time pump, almost certainly on the road now, following on somewhere behind Ben. The other would be the retained pump from East Lynden, almost as far away. Ben put his foot down to the floor and drove as hard as he could.

The road dipped up and down over a series of low hills, occasionally making twists to the left or right as it plunged through the black plantations of fir trees. Usually at this time of night it was a quiet road. The biggest dangers were the herds of fallow deer which sometimes emerged from the forest depths to graze after dark on the sweet grass at the edge of the road. Normally they would freeze if caught in a car's headlights, just standing there as the vehicle swept past with large, unblinking eyes reflecting back the gleam. On rare occasions they had been known to bolt into the road, killing themselves and doing a few hundred pounds worth of bodywork damage to the oncoming vehicle.

Tonight Ben was taking a chance on the deer, taking the hilltops and the bends with less than his usual caution.

It was the combination of a hilltop and a bend that caught him by surprise. At that crucial point a dazzling glare of headlights that had been hidden by the forest and the valley beyond suddenly flashed full in his eyes and leaped toward him. Ben realized too late that there was an oncoming car in the middle of the road. He stamped on the brake and swung his steering wheel hard to the left, but there was no road to spare. The speeding car hit him broadside and he felt the explosion of agony as the right hand side of his car was caved inward and his right leg was shattered. The sound of the impact was a blast of pure, screeching, crashing pain in his eardrums and he lost consciousness.

He didn't feel the two cars being flung apart by their own momentum, spinning away on either side where they smashed into opposite tree lines, spraying broken glass and flying fragments of metal all over the road and the roadside verges.

There was a flicker of red where torn wiring sparked and the petrol dripped from the ruptured tank of the second car,

116

then a roar of ascending flame.

Fortunately the Granchester fire engine that had been following Ben to the Barford house fire came powering up the hill a few minutes later.

★　★　★

Judy was awoken by a polite but persistent knocking on the cottage door. She sat up in bed, startled, curious, and then alarmed. The white glow of the alarm clock on the bedside table showed 3.05 in soft green numerals and the space beside her was empty. She remembered Ben going out on a shout. He never forgot his key. A dread premonition rushed into her heart.

She threw aside the bedclothes and grabbed for a night robe that hung behind the bedroom door. She put on the landing light as she passed and almost ran down the stairs, only just remembering to close the night robe and knot the belt as she reached the front door.

She opened the door and her worst fears were realized. She felt as though her heart had collapsed inside her chest.

The tall man on her doorstep wore full Fire Service uniform and the silver impellers inside the silver laurel wreathes on his shoulders, together with the loop of red braid across his shoulder, showed his rank of Divisional Officer. His long face under the silver braided peak of his cap was familiar but strained. He stood stiff and uncomfortable.

'Ben?' Judy said in a strangled voice that did not even sound remotely like her own.

'His car crashed,' Colin Bradshaw, the officer commanding the Breckland Fire Brigade spoke awkwardly. He moved to steady her, both hands clasping her shoulders, and added quickly: 'He's alive, Judy. They've taken him to the Accident and Emergency Unit at Granchester General Hospital. Our Ben is a tough customer underneath all that bonhomie. I'm sure he's going to pull through.'

'What happened?' Judy asked.

'He was on his way to the call at Barford. Our first pump was about half a mile behind him. They saw Ben's blue

118

light spin off the road at the top of the hill. Another car had hit him almost head on.'

'Oh, no,' Judy said weakly, her heart was now hammering uncontrollably.

'The second car caught fire. Fortunately Ben's car did not. He ended up in the trees on the opposite side of the road. Our crew dealt with the fire, then cut Ben out and the driver of the second car.' Bradshaw paused, the brief factual report over and now unsure of how to go on.

'Ben?' Judy insisted, staring into his eyes.

'He was unconscious when they got him out. The ambulance crew think perhaps a broken leg. By the time we get to the hospital they should know more. I'll take you there.'

Judy saw the white fire service car parked behind him. She had heard it arrive, she now realized, but her half-sleeping mind had assumed it to be Ben.

'I'll get dressed,' she said.

Bradshaw nodded. He came in and waited in the hall while she ran back up to the bedroom. Two minutes later she was down again, wearing a hastily donned pair of jeans and a thick white woollen sweater. Like Ben she always had a set of warm clothes ready to hand for an urgent night call. In some ways the demands of their police and fire service careers were very similar.

Bradshaw drove fast but carefully to the hospital, where a receptionist in Accident and Emergency informed them that Ben was still unconscious and undergoing examinations and X-rays. A break in his right leg was already confirmed. After that there was nothing to do except to sit and wait through the long anguished night. Bradshaw sat with her, making some attempts at small talk, and periodically getting up to fetch coffee.

It was dawn before a nurse came to tell them that Ben was in the operating theatre where the surgical team were setting his broken leg. Two more hours passed, and finally a young doctor came to tell them that the leg was set and that Ben was now sleeping comfortably in the recovery room.

'We won't know for certain till he

wakes up and speaks to us, but the leg breaks appear to be the most serious damage. The impact fractured his thigh bone in two places.' The doctor spread his hands in an apologetic gesture. 'That is as much as I can tell you for now.'

Judy thanked him and he went away.

Bradshaw said slowly. 'I could take you home if you want. It could be hours before Ben wakes. I'll make sure the hospital calls me and then fetch you again as soon as there's some news.'

'I'll stay,' Judy said. The thought of waiting alone in the empty cottage was worse than waiting here. She smiled faintly, 'But you don't have to stay, Colin. I'm grateful for all that you've done, but I'll be alright.'

'I'll stay until you have some other company,' Bradshaw said firmly. He looked at his watch. 'Nearly nine o'clock, the day watch will be coming on. We can spare one of Ben's colleagues, one of the Fire Prevention officers, Dave West or Chris Tyler.'

Judy smiled. She knew that any one of Ben's fellow officers would gladly come out and sit with her. 'I have to make some family calls,' she said, 'Ben's Mum and Dad, my Mum, and my sister Carol, she'll probably come here and sit with me.'

Bradshaw nodded. 'Whatever you want, Judy, the Fire Service is here for you for as much as you need us. Ben was one of ours. You are one of ours. We try to look after our wives too.'

'I know,' Judy said. She suddenly felt warm and choked. Bradshaw patted her arm, and then gave her a brief fatherly hug.

When she broke away Judy fumbled for her mobile phone. She pulled herself together and called Carol. Her older sister answered and she heard the baby gurgling in the background, it was a contented feeding sound. She and Ben had talked of having their own baby and suddenly a wave of pure anguish swept over her. Her eyes flooded and when Carol spoke she found that for a moment she couldn't answer.

Finally she blurted out the news. Carol was shocked, and then suddenly business-like. She would tell their mother, she would phone Ben's parents then she would leave Little Richard with his father and come straight over to the hospital. Judy felt suddenly helpless, feeling that she was being taken over and yet grateful as it was all arranged.

'I'll wait until she gets here,' Bradshaw promised.

It was all beginning to get a bit too much and Judy's emotions again threatened to overflow. Then she received another surprise as Ron Harding suddenly appeared.

Harding sat down beside her and put his arm around her shoulders, her second unexpected hug of the day.

'Bad news, Jude, I heard as soon as I got into the station this morning. Tom Ford had the report from the patrol car that attended Ben's accident last night. I guessed that you would be here. How is he?'

Judy told him, struggling to keep her voice level.

Harding nodded soberly. 'Ben's fit and tough.' His assurance echoed Bradshaw.

'He'll make it, better than the other guy.'

Judy stared at him, 'The other driver?'

Harding flinched and looked apologetically at Bradshaw. 'You haven't told her — me and my big foot.'

'I thought it best to leave it.' Bradshaw also looked apologetic.

Judy looked from one to the other, and then back at Harding again.

Harding sighed and explained. 'There were three teenagers in the other car, two boys and a girl. Two of them crawled out okay. They were given breath tests at the scene and both of them were well over the alcohol limits. The other boy died at the wheel, but we are pretty sure that his blood will prove alcohol positive too. All the measurements, tyre marks and the usual accident reconstruction factors show that they hit Ben the driver side of Ben's car on his side of the road, so Ben was not at fault. He was just unlucky.'

'One boy dead,' Judy said faintly, 'Oh, no.'

They were all silent for a minute.

'Grant sends his sympathy,' Harding said at last. 'You're officially on leave,

Jude. The crimes and the villains can all wait. Grant said to take off as many days as you need.'

'Thanks,' Judy said quietly.

There was another uncomfortable silence which neither of the two men seemed able to fill, and then Carol arrived. Judy's sister was a slightly older version of Judy herself, her figure a little bit fuller, her eyes the same pastel blue, her blonde hair a little longer and worn loose instead of being tied back in the short pony tail that Judy favoured when she was working. Judy rose to meet her and to receive her third hug of the day, this time with more unashamed feeling and a big kiss on the cheek.

By the time the two women parted and the greetings and the explanations were over, Bradshaw and Harding were both ready to leave.

'I should have been in Norfolk half an hour ago,' Harding excused himself, 'Another meeting with Geoff Geeste. If there's anything I can do, just call.'

'Likewise,' Bradshaw said. 'I think I can leave you with Carol now, but if there's anything that you need — ?'

Judy thanked them both and they left together. Judy sat down again with Carol and began another long period of waiting.

★   ★   ★

It was two hours before a nurse came to tell them that Ben was awake, and yet another hour before the doctors had finished their post op checks and examinations and they were allowed a brief visit to his bedside.

'He is still very weak and sleepy,' they were told, 'But he's been moved from the recovery room to the main ward and you can see him for a few minutes. He's got a few cuts and bruises and a badly sprained left wrist, but except for the leg no more broken bones.' This doctor was a young woman about the same age as Judy with weary eyes but a warm smile, she finished gently, 'He'll be with us for a while, but he's going to be OK.'

It was a warning to prepare them, for Ben looked pale and battered. His left eye was almost closed by a great yellow and purple bruise, and there were long red scratches down his cheek. His right leg was encased in plaster and suspended in traction and his left wrist was bandaged. He wore hospital pyjamas and there was more lurid bruising to his neck and chest where he had been slammed against the steering wheel. He smiled faintly when he saw her, 'Hi, Sweetheart.'

'Hello, Hero,' she kissed him with tears in her eyes.

'This time the hero didn't get there,' he said ruefully. 'The cavalry fell at the first fence.'

'It doesn't matter, you're still my hero.' She sat down and held his good hand. For a moment they could only look at each other with all their emotions threatening to surface and overwhelm them.

After a few minutes a watchful nurse gently reminded them that Ben needed to rest. His eyelids were drooping, and so Judy gently kissed him again and allowed Carol to draw her away.

'You had best come home with me,' Carol decided as they walked away from the ward. 'We know he's OK and he's going to sleep for most of the day anyway. We'll telephone this afternoon and come back when he's awake.'

Judy was too tired to argue. The sleepless night had suddenly caught up with her and relief was taking over from anxiety. She was glad that her older sister was here to take charge and organize things.

Carol drove her back to the cottage to collect a few clothes and toiletries, and to pack a smaller bag to take to Ben later. Then they drove to Carol's home, a large, detached four bedroom house on the modern Seymore Estate on the northern edge of Granchester.

Carol's husband Richard was waiting for them with the baby in his arms. He was a large, athletic man, with, like Ben, an easy grin. He and Carol were into keeping fit together, with regular visits to the Granchester Sports Centre where they swam, played squash and weight lifted. Now he was serious and considerate and when Carol had relieved him of the baby Judy was again duly hugged and kissed.

Carol bustled around getting lunch, a chicken sandwich and salad which she insisted the reluctant Judy must eat. Richard joined them, but then had to leave for the office where he worked. As the office manager he had simply phoned in to say that he was taking an unscheduled morning off, but, he explained apologetically, his paperwork would be piling up.

Judy helped Carol to wash up and then they went to check on the baby who now lay wide-eyed in his cot. Little Richard had big blue eyes that regarded them gravely from a solemn but curious little face.

Judy felt her eyes water again. 'He's lovely,' she said, and then she blurted out in a rush, 'Ben and I had only just decided that we want a baby of our own. We didn't want to wait anymore.'

Carol picked up Little Richard and placed him in Judy's arms.

'I'm sure you will have one of your own soon enough,' she said, and then risked a teasing giggle. 'After all, it's only his leg that's broken, isn't it?'

Judy realized that her big sister was trying to cheer her up, and suddenly she was laughing and crying at the same time. The last of the tension broke and she knew that what they were all saying was true. Ben was a tough customer. He was going to be OK.

★   ★   ★

Judy stayed with Carol and Richard for the next two days, visiting Ben as often as possible and in between times glad of their company. The baby was soon demanding attention from its aunt as much as from its parents, and the gurgling delights of her new nephew provided Judy with the best possible diversion from her own worries. She was soon adept at changing nappies and administering a feeding bottle.

After the first day Ben was more wide awake and receiving a constant stream of visitors, including family and friends and a constant parade of fire service colleagues checking up on his progress. Judy also found herself fielding endless telephone calls, she had never realized just how many people they knew, and decided, with pangs of guilt, that she really must extend their Christmas card list.

Ben had soon learned that the Barford House fire he had been trying to reach had been a malicious false alarm. The Barford fire engine had arrived at the given address to find the occupants fast asleep and no sign of smoke or fire. The call had been some idiot's idea of a joke, or perhaps some late-night drunk who just liked to see fire engines go flashing by.

Ben had cursed bitterly at the news, and he had also been bitter to learn that the car which had crashed into him had been driven by three drunken teenagers on a joyride. However, it was difficult to dampen Ben's mood, he had a philosophical nature which could rise above most things, and with so many friends rallying round he did not stay depressed for long. Teenagers were always getting drunk and driving cars, and malicious false alarms accounted for a regular percentage of turnouts. These were things the Fire Service normally took in their stride.

For Judy it was a busy time with too many other things to think about, and she spared barely a thought for her job and the cases in which she had been involved.

On the second night after Ben's accident Carol was cooking a meal in the kitchen and Richard was upstairs in the bathroom and singing loudly in the shower. It was a song about 'Cowboys and Horses,' and Richard had a fair baritone voice that only occasionally slipped out of tune. The baby was quiet in his cot, and his school age siblings were busy with their homework. With a few unfilled moments Judy picked up the local paper that Richard had brought home with him and dropped on the settee on his way through the living room.

On an inside picture she suddenly found herself staring at the small picture of a face she instantly recognized. The few brief lines of post mortem announced that seventy-six year old Alice Jessup had died in her sleep. The old lady had been found dead in her bed at her home in Wheatsheaf Cottage.

8

The following morning Carol drove Judy back to Hawthorn Cottage to collect a change of clothes and her own car. The past two days had again been grey and foggy, a typical English November, but today with the fickle vagrancy that was equally typical of an English Autumn the morning was once more bright and sunny, with a charming pattern of white fleece clouds strewn over blue skies. As they passed Old Bracken Lane Judy noticed an old Land Rover parked in front of Wheatsheaf Cottage. Someone was there before her.

'Phone it in,' Carol had said, half a dozen times at least. 'Your boss did say you could take off as much time as you liked.'

Judy had tried to explain. There was something the old lady had known, something Alice Jessup had been holding back. Judy was sure of it. If she had only been able to talk to her again, perhaps a couple of times, then she was sure that she could have eventually won Alice's confidence. Whatever it was, Alice would never tell her now, and perhaps that was why Alice was dead.

'You think the old lady was murdered?' Carol was horrified.

'I don't know,' Judy was frustrated. 'But she was holding something back, and now she is dead. It could be my fault. She may have been killed because of what she might have been able to tell me.'

'Phone it in,' Carol had insisted again. 'Leave it to your Inspector Harding and Superintendent Grant.'

But Judy knew that Harding and Grant were almost totally involved with Operation Longship. The ram raids were their current top priority, and rightly so. If anyone was going to check whether Alice Jessup had really died in her sleep, then it had to be her.

'What about Ben?' had not worked either, it was an argument that Carol had used almost as often as her urging to, 'Phone it in.' It was now three days since

Ben's accident and Ben didn't need her sitting at his bedside for every minute of the day. The hospital wouldn't allow it anyway, Ben was out of danger now and there were long gaps between the set visiting hours. It had been nice playing with the baby in between times, but he was Carol's baby and she couldn't just sit around playing Auntie Judy for ever. She was grateful to Carol and Richard for all that they had done for her, but it was time to go back to work.

'Come and eat with us tonight anyway,' Carol insisted as Judy got out of the car. Judy promised that she would, and with a sigh Carol finally gave up, waved a hand and drove away.

Judy let herself into the cottage and went upstairs to change quickly into one of her working outfits, a tan leather jacket and blue jeans. Then she got into her own car, and drove back to Old Brackendale Lane. It was almost a relief to be behind the wheel and in control of her life again.

She had intended to report first to the police station, but the sight of that parked

Land Rover had necessitated a quick change in her plans. The Land Rover was still there, a mud splattered vehicle that looked as though it had spent more time driving across fields than on the main road. Judy parked behind it and then walked through the open gate, up to the trellis porch doorway and knocked on the door.

The middle aged woman who eventually opened the door was short and sturdy, dressed in a sensible black skirt and a dark green jumper that had been chosen for warmth and comfort rather than fashion. Her black hair showed just the first hints of grey. The pale blue eyes had that alert brightness that allowed Judy to immediately guess that here was another Jessup.

Judy introduced herself and showed her card.

'Ah, the policewoman,' There was a purse-lipped nod of understanding, another Jessup family characteristic. 'Aunt Alice was cross about you — you went poking about in her bedroom.'

'I didn't poke about,' Judy protested.

But it was a fair cop, she thought ruefully, and admitted, 'But I did look inside, just for a second, how did she know?'

'Aunt Alice wasn't as crazy as some people like to think. She heard that old floorboard creak just inside the bedroom door. That old floorboard always creaked, ever since Wheatsheaf Cottage was built, I reckon. Not so a stranger would notice, but Aunt Alice always knew.'

Judy smiled. 'I knew she wasn't crazy. She struck me as a very sharp old lady, mentally, I mean, she definitely had all her wits about her. I very much wanted to talk to her again.' She paused, 'If you are her niece, then you must be Sarah Jessup?'

'Sarah Kent, actually, but since my poor Fred passed away everyone still calls me Sarah Jessup. I don't mind. The Jessups have farmed around here for five generations, first at Blackberry Farm, and then my dad, Charlie, he had Appledown for the last forty years. Jessup is a good local name around here. My Fred was okay, but the Kents didn't count for so much.'

'I was sorry to hear about your aunt,' Judy said. 'Who found her?'

'I did, and it was quite a shock, I can tell you. She seemed as right as anything just the day before.' Sarah Jessup sighed and looked down at her hands for a moment, twisting them nervously. Then she looked back into Judy's face. 'I suppose you had best come in.'

They went inside and into the small sitting room where Judy had talked with Alice Jessup just four days ago, sitting facing each other over the same small table. Sarah Jessup rested her elbows on the table, again twisting her fingers nervously together. Judy wondered if the agitated mannerism meant anything. However, the woman in front of her had suddenly lost her aunt and was now confronted with an inquisitive police officer. That in itself was enough to make most people nervous. She didn't have to have any feelings of guilt.

'What happened to Aunt Alice?' Judy asked.

'I found her dead in her bed,' Sarah said simply. 'I thought she was asleep at first, although it would be unusual for her to sleep in that late, she goes to bed early so she's usually up with the lark. But when I tried to wake her she didn't wake up.' Her face crumpled and her blue eyes were suddenly wet. 'I shook her shoulder but she wouldn't wake up. Her poor old face was white and she was so cold. She wouldn't wake up.'

Judy reached out and held the other woman's twitching hands in her own. 'I'm sorry,' she said, knowing that as always in these circumstances the words were so inadequate.

There was a pause while Sarah Jessup bit her lip, looking down at the white lace tablecloth, then Judy asked softly, 'When was this?'

'Wednesday morning, middle of the morning, I'd brought her round a few bits, a cabbage, a few carrots, some beetroot — Aunt Alice always liked a bit of fresh beetroot.' She looked up again. 'I grow my own vegetables, there's plenty of room on the farm, and I usually bring Aunt Alice a few bits round once or twice a week.'

Judy nodded understanding. 'What happened then?'

'I called the doctor and then I came down here and waited. There wasn't anything else I could do. The Doctor said she was dead, that she must have passed away in her sleep. He arranged for the funeral people to come and take her away.'

'Which doctor?'

'Doctor Brownlow, the Lark Valley Surgery — he's her GP.'

'And where is the — ' Judy stopped herself and began again, 'Where is Aunt Alice now?'

'Jenkin's Funeral Parlour, in Granchester. She's in their Chapel of Rest, the funeral is next week.'

It will have to be cancelled, Judy thought, we need an autopsy and I want to know exactly how that old lady died. Aloud she said, 'When did you last see her — alive?'

'Tuesday night, the same as you, I came round after you had gone, getting late it was, she was getting ready to go to bed. Aunt Alice was upset about you going

141

into her bedroom.

Judy grimaced, feeling uncomfortable. 'Did she talk about anything else?'

'We talked about all that digging your lot were doing in Archie's field. She was upset about that, too. As a matter of fact, that was why I came round. It was the talk of the village — that skull being found at the Sugar Beet Factory, and then all of you digging in Archie's field. I knew Aunt Alice would have heard, and I just wondered if she knew anything about what was going on.'

'And did she?' Judy hardly dared to hope.

Sarah shrugged. 'I don't think so. She asked me as many questions as I was asking her. She did seem worried though, she wanted to know who it was buried in Archie's beet field. That was before they found the rest of the body, but of course, she was dead herself by then.'

'The rest of the body,' Judy was caught by surprise.

'The skeleton,' Sarah looked at Judy uncertainly, 'After Aunt Alice died, your lot found the grave.'

'I'm sorry,' Judy said. 'My husband had a car accident and I've been off duty for a few days. I seem to have missed a few things.'

'Oh, well, they've found a grave now, but they still don't seem to know who was in it.'

'Did Aunt Alice have any ideas?'

'She might have,' Sarah shrugged again. 'But she wasn't saying. Like I said, it was all questions and no answers.'

Judy was silent for a moment. The cuckoo clock ticked quietly on the wall. Then Judy said, 'You visited Aunt Alice a lot, kept an eye on her, she must have talked to you.'

'She talked about most things, yes, more than anyone else in the family, but not about that.'

'About what?'

Sarah frowned, then again twitched her shoulders. 'Aunt Alice was a private person. I always respected that. But I guess it doesn't matter now. Older folk know why they called her Crazy Alice, so someone will tell you sooner or later anyway. Archie won't, my dad's dead, but someone will tell you.'

'Tell me what?' Judy persisted.

'Aunt Alice had a lover, when she was a girl, back in the war days. He was an American, one of the crew on one of the B 17 bombers that were stationed here, the old Flying Fortress, they used to call them. The Kentucky Belle, I think his plane was called. It got shot down over Germany in 1944. Her man was missing in action, all the crew were lost. Folk say that's why she went crazy — why she was always walking around the old airfield, waiting for him to come home.'

Judy thought about it, then said carefully, 'A wartime romance, a nice story, but not that unusual surely. Lots of local girls must have fallen in love with American servicemen in those days. Some of them got married and went off to live in America.'

'Yes, that was Aunt Alice's dream, no doubt about that. But it didn't happen that way.'

'So, a lot of girls must have got left behind, when the Americans went home — or when their planes failed to come back. What was different about Alice?'

Sarah pursed her lips then said reluctantly. 'I don't think Alice's boy friend was a white American. Some people say he was a black man. A lot of Negroes came over with the American forces. But he wasn't black. He was a red man, a full blooded American Indian from one of those tribes, a Navajo, or something. That's why Uncle Archie and my dad Charlie hated him so much. Aunt Alice never forgave them for that.'

Judy remembered the old photograph on Alice Jessup's dressing table, and now the puzzle pieces were fitting together. The young Alice had taken a Native American for her lover, or at least as her boy friend, and her two older brothers had been furious.

She had to pick her words carefully, not wanting to turn Sarah hostile and defensive of her remaining family. She smiled softly and ventured, 'I can imagine your Uncle Archie being unhappy about that. He is a bit of a patriarch, isn't he?'

'If you mean he's the head of the family, yes, he's always been that, even when my old Granddad was alive. He was a soft one, my old Granddad. Archie was always the top dog, just as soon as he was old enough. Granddad wasn't a well man, he had to retire early, but Archie was running Blackberry Farm long before that.' Her voice became bitter, 'And he's thick-headed, thick-headed and stubborn. My dad was too, God rest his soul, but Archie was the oldest. Charlie always followed Archie's lead.' She shook her head sadly, 'Poor old Aunt Alice.'

'Aunt Alice rebelled,' Judy murmured softly. She didn't want to break the flow, but it needed a gentle prompt to keep it going.

Sarah Jessup sighed, 'Aye, she was a stubborn one too, in her own way. She wasn't going to be bossed about, and she wanted her red man no matter what Archie and Charlie had to say. It's caused a rift in the family ever since, all three of them too stiff and bloody-minded to ever forgive or forget. Now Dad has gone and Aunt Alice has gone I guess it doesn't matter any more.' She sniffed back a tear, 'What a waste of fifty years.'

Judy waited, but there was no more. Sarah Jessup was silently brooding, looking down at her hands which were now still on the crumpled tablecloth.

'The Red Indian,' Judy said at last. 'Do you know his name?'

'Joe Something — I think it was Joe Crowfoot.' Sarah didn't look up, her hands didn't move.

'You said his plane crashed on a mission over Germany during the war.' Judy paused before continuing quietly, 'So why was Aunt Alice so concerned about all the police digging in Archie's beet field?'

'I don't know. She didn't say.' Sarah straightened up and looked her directly in the eyes. 'It was just an old story, to help you understand Aunt Alice, but I don't think it means anything. I think I've told you all I can.'

'Thank you,' Judy knew how to push gently and when to stop pushing. She leaned back and looked up at the ceiling, a pattern of square white polystyrene tiles that were never used now in modern buildings. Everything here was old

147

fashioned and out of date and she wondered what other secrets Wheatsheaf Cottage might hold.

'This time I'll ask,' she said wryly, looking back at Sarah Jessup, 'Can I take another look at your Aunt's bedroom?'

Sarah hesitated. 'I can't see as how it can do any harm now,' she conceded, and got up to lead the way.

On the landing she stood aside to allow Judy to step first through the open bedroom doorway. At first glance it seemed that nothing had changed. The bed where Alice Jessup had been found dead was again neatly made up, Sarah's handiwork obviously, and nothing seemed to have been disturbed. Judy felt herself shiver a little and then turned her gaze to the neatly dusted dressing table. The Bible was still there, the hair brushes and the few small trinkets and ornaments, but the photograph of Joe Crowfoot was missing.

9

When Judy finally returned to Breckland Police HQ she found Grant and Harding together in Grant's office. As Superintendent and Head of CID Grant was dressed as always in a neat grey suit with a freshly pressed white shirt and a pale blue tie with a perfectly shaped knot. His Inspector, as always, wore a casual jacket with his tie hanging loose from an open collar. They were a clash of fashion styles but worked surprisingly well together. Grant ran a tight ship in most things, but didn't impose his own dress sense.

Grant welcomed Judy warmly and asked immediately after Ben.

'He's doing well sir, as well as anyone can do with a broken leg. He's going to be in hospital for a few weeks yet, but he'll mend.'

'Good,' Grant smiled as though he meant it, 'And it's good to have you back on the team. Things have been getting hectic around here. Ron, bring her up to date.'

Harding grinned. 'The main thing, Jude, is that we now have our own round the clock watch on the travellers at Old Brackendale Airfield. It's as good, if not better, than Dave Pullen having his old boss spying on the buggers at Bleak Fen.'

'How?' Judy was intrigued, even though she was eager to tell her own story.

Harding's grin widened. 'The old observation tower, it's a broken down old ruin, cold and draughty as a wet night in a shop doorway, but it's still the ideal place.'

Judy had a mental picture of the old square, concrete block building that was virtually collapsed at the north end of what had once been the main runway. All of the windows were smashed, with just jagged pieces of broken panes hanging from the rotting frames, most of the old outer balcony had fallen away, and the top of the tower looked like a decapitated square grey eggshell. She could see that it would still make a good look-out point over the relatively flat airfield, except for one thing; it was too close to the gypsy camp, fully exposed and isolated from any kind of cover. There were no bushes, no bracken and no trees, just bare, sandy heath-land all around.

She said doubtfully, 'I still don't see how.'

'It was John's idea,' Harding said modestly. Detective Sergeant John Kershaw was one of Harding's favourite aides, almost a Harding clone. He was also a local boy, born and bred in Granchester. 'John remembers playing out there on the old airfield as a boy. There's an old ditch that runs along the northern edge of the airfield. It takes you right up to about twenty yards from the back of the old tower. The local kids used it to play commando games, sneaking up on the tower and such like.'

'Those last twenty yards were a bit of a problem,' Grant took over. 'But John crawled up the ditch with a tripod and a pair of heavy duty binoculars two nights ago after dark. Now we change the shifts just before daylight and after sunset. The days are short at this time of year, and so far we've been lucky, there's been very little moonlight.'

Judy began to share some of their cheerful satisfaction. 'So what have we learned so far?'

'We've seen Sean Ross return,' Harding said. 'He's one of a gang of four who drove in bold as brass just a few hours after you went off duty. They all fit the general descriptions of the four men who hit the Brentheath Post Office. Right now we're trying to fix names to the other three faces and waiting for them to make another move. The Range Rover they used for the ram raid wound up burned out in a field twenty miles away, just as the Guv predicted, but we'll get them eventually.

'So Operation Longship is all coming to a head,' Grant said confidently. 'We know that three separate traveller's camps are involved. Dave Pullen has enough to raid Bleak Fen now, and the next time our lot pull another ram raid we may well be in a position to nail them in the act. It's the Norfolk end that we still need to tie up and Ron has been working on that with Geoff Geeste.'

'We've identified family links with all three sites,' Harding said. There's a family named Farrel at River Farm, Irish background with a history of petty thieving and general law-bending that goes back for two or three known generations. In the old days they were horse traders, probably horse stealers. They have cousins at Bleak Fen, and we believe we've got a couple of Farrels at Old Brackendale, they're part of the group that includes Sean Ross.'

'The head of the family is the Grandfather,' Grant took over again. 'They all call him Gaffer Jim, or sometimes Tinker Jim. He's got quite a plush, ornamental caravan at River Farm, which is the site by Dalton Broad. Norfolk is where the first ram raids took place and afterwards the young Farrels from River Farm were noticed flashing a lot of money around the pubs in King's Lynn.

'Then they suddenly went low profile and the post offices and off licences started getting hit in Cambridgeshire and

153

Breckland. We think that's probably when Tinker Jim stepped in and took control. He probably reined the River Farm boys in because they were making themselves too obvious, but spread the idea and the operation through the rest of the clan.'

Harding nodded, 'Geoff reckons that Tinker Jim, or Gaffer Jim, whichever you like to call him, has to be our prime suspect for Mister Big. The old man almost certainly cut his teeth horse stealing when he was still a kid, and he's been a rogue and a fence ever since. He would know how and where to get rid of all the loot. He's got to be the master mind and banker.'

'So we've put together the picture and all we have to do now is prove it,' Grant spread his hands wryly. 'We could probably raid all three sites now and unearth enough evidence to prove a case against the boys who have been doing the actual ram raiding, but we really need to have everything nailed down in advance so that we can also prove the case against Tinker Jim. When we go it will be a coordinated operation in Norfolk, Cambridgeshire, and here. They've been acting like Viking pirates, looting all over our three counties. Operation Longship will hit them in turn, with all three police forces acting at the same time.'

It was a good plan and had been coming to fruition over six months of hard, painstaking work. Judy had been part of it and she was as pleased as her male colleagues, but Alice Jessup had been niggling at the back of her mind. She had been waiting for her opportunity, and now that they were finished she reminded them of the case that had almost been overlooked.

Briefly she outlined her talk with Alice, and then her more recent visit to Wheatsheaf Cottage and her meeting with Sarah. She finished seriously, 'There's something there, sir. I'm not sure what it is, but Alice Jessup had her own fears or suspicions about that skull in the beet field, and she wasn't crazy. Her death may look like natural causes, but she seemed fine when I spoke to her, and her death immediately afterwards strikes me as too much of a coincidence.'

'Damn it,' Harding swore softly. 'I think I did hear some mention that the old girl had died in her sleep, but I didn't know that you had any interest in her. I didn't make any connection.'

'It was my fault,' Judy apologized. 'I never got round to making a full report. Ben's accident took it all right out of my head.'

'Unfortunate circumstances,' Grant said slowly. 'Ron, you've spent more time in Norfolk than you have here in Granchester over the past few days. If anyone should have spotted a link it was me.' He looked back at Judy and continued firmly, 'But you are right, we have to look more closely into this. You'll need to interview Doctor Brownlow, find out exactly what he's put on the death certificate and why. And call Doctor Rawlings, we need a full pathologist's report ASAP. We need to know exactly how that old lady died. And we need to get a SOC team into Wheatsheaf Cottage, to give it a thorough examination.'

'We may be a little late,' Judy said

ruefully. 'Sarah Jessup has already been tidying up. I have asked her to leave it now and not touch anything else. She wasn't too pleased, especially when she realized that our enquiries might mean a delay to the funeral arrangements, but she said that she would cooperate.'

'Good,' Grant thought for a moment then made a decision. 'Judy, I want you to run this investigation. I need Ron and the rest of the team to concentrate on Operation Longship. I know you've still got the worry of Ben being in hospital, but can you handle it?'

Judy was pleased. 'I can manage, sir. Ben seems to have a constant stream of off-duty firemen filing through his ward in the afternoons, so as long as I can see him in the evenings I can still do the day job.'

'Then the Alice Jessup case and the skull in the beet field is yours,' Grant affirmed, 'One of us needs to give it our full attention.'

'I've missed three days,' Judy reminded him. 'Sarah Jessup told me that we have now found a grave and a skeleton.'

Harding brought her up to date. 'Roper and his team found it the morning after Ben's accident. They extended the line of trenches you proposed and cut into the grave after another ten yards of digging down the field. The whole skeleton was there except for the skull and the hand which had already been discovered. I went out later and had another chat with Archie and Peter Jessup. They claimed total ignorance again. Archie said that there was a lot of rain last winter, which may have washed away some of the topsoil and brought the bones nearer to the surface, or the new sugar beet harvester they've bought this year could be digging deeper. Either of those factors could explain why the grave has now come to light after all these years, and either way they are still insisting that the bones are as old as the ark.'

'They are nearly right,' Grant agreed. 'We have Rawlings's report now so it's official that the bones are at least fifty years old, which is what we've been guessing all along from their general condition and discolouration. They belonged to a young male of about twenty years old. The way the skull plates have knitted together is a good indication of the age. The length of the major bones shows that he was a medium size man, about five feet and eight inches.'

'I seem to remember that Red Indians have high cheekbones,' Judy said slowly. She looked at Harding, 'Would you say that our skull in the beet chute had high cheekbones?'

'I'm not sure,' Harding looked curious.

Grant raised his eyebrows.

Judy told them about Alice Jessup's Red Indian lover.

'We'll have to ask Doctor Rawlings for his professional opinion,' Grant decided. He opened the drawer of his desk and withdrew a flat, clear plastic evidence bag which he passed across the desk to Judy. 'Here's something else you ought to see. It was found in the grave with the skeleton.'

Judy held the bag up to the light. Inside was a heavy oval belt buckle. It was the type of large, elaborate silver buckle that a cowboy might have worn, or an Indian.

The silver was badly tarnished and blackened, but the horned buffalo design was unmistakeable. It was identical to the belt buckle worn by the man in the photograph which had disappeared from Alice Jessup's dressing table.

★ ★ ★

Judy spent the rest of the day trying to catch up, first a long telephone call to the Bone Ranger, next an interview with Alice Jessup's GP, and then supervising the SOC team as they made their detailed examination of Wheatsheaf Cottage. Finally she knocked off, drove home for a quick shower and a change of clothes, and then kept her promise to eat with Carol and Richard. Then at last she was free again to visit Ben.

She found him depressed and gloomy with an unusually long face, when she leaned over to kiss him his smile was only a faint flicker. He had seen two doctors earlier in the day and the news was not good.

'They reckon that when I get out of

here I'm going to spend at least six months hobbling around on sticks,' He told her despondently. 'I can handle that, but I asked them how long it might be before I'll be fit enough to resume active fire-fighting. They didn't want to commit themselves to any answer to that.' He looked up at her miserably. 'Jude, I think my Fire Service career is over.'

'Don't say that,' She took his hand and squeezed it. 'You'll be up and running eventually, it's just going to take some time, that's all.'

'Maybe, but for the Fire Service I need to be A One fit. The fireground is no place for slow movers and half cripples. I'll be no use for fast running and ladder work if I'm dragging a limp.'

Judy was silent for a moment, then she said quietly, 'Well, that must be the worst scenario, but even then there must be other work you can do, fire prevention or the control room. All firemen don't spend all their time fighting fires.'

'Fighting fires is what I want to do,' Ben said stubbornly. 'It's what I'm good at. I'm a fire-ground officer, not a desk

161

Johnny or a sweet talker. I wouldn't be any good at visiting schools and telling kids not to play with matches. And I couldn't sit in the control room all day long just listening to the action elsewhere, it's not me.'

'It may not come to that,' Judy said positively. 'Whatever the future does bring, we'll face it together when it comes.'

Ben was silent for a minute, and then he looked into her eyes, 'Of course we will, I'm sorry, Jude, I guess I'm just feeling bloody sorry for myself.'

'You've got every right,' she answered softly, and kissed him again. This time he responded by pulling her closer and when they came apart he was smiling a little, showing a shadow of his old self.

'Enough about me,' he said firmly. 'Don't let me get self-centred. Let's talk about you. I'm guessing you're back at work, so tell me about your day.'

'You're never self-centred,' Judy said. 'You're just down a bit, and with good reason.' She felt both guilty and relieved at being able to change the subject, but decided that perhaps for now it was best. She settled down and told him all about Alice Jessup.

'We won't get a full pathology report on Alice Jessup until tomorrow.' She finished. 'I've talked to her GP and he's put the cause of death down as a heart attack. He seems a competent doctor so I'm assuming that he's probably right. The question is what caused the heart attack, was it natural or was it somehow induced. She seemed fit enough when I saw her, so that makes me suspicious.'

She paused, considering for a moment. 'Some sort of fright or shock could have brought on that heart attack, something had to have happened. Maybe somebody held a pillow over her face, I don't know. Sarah Jessup has washed all the bedding and tidied everything up, which could be because she's just a fusspot, or because she had something to hide. SOC searched and dusted the whole cottage but so far they've only come up with a couple of unknown fingerprints. They didn't belong to Alice or Sarah Jessup, and they were not mine, so it seems that Alice may have had at least one other recent visitor.'

'They could be her brother or her nephew.'

Ben was taking an interest, and anything which took his mind away from brooding over his broken leg was good. He often listened to her more difficult cases, treating them like shared jigsaw puzzles they could tease out together. Sometimes he brought a fresh approach that could be more helpful than anyone down at the nick.

'They could belong to Archie or Peter,' she admitted. 'But I'm told the old man never visited his sister, and it seems that Peter is pretty much under his dad's thumb. We'll take their prints to eliminate them for certain, but my feeling is that they won't match.'

'Were there any signs of a forced entry?'

'None, but I got the feeling she was a trusting old lay. I showed her my card, but she hadn't asked for it, and she didn't do anything to check it. She had a chain on her door, but when I left I didn't hear her hook it back into place. She seemed sharp in some ways, but naïve in others.'

'So you think someone could have talked his or her way in.'

'Maybe, or it could have been someone she knew. This all goes back to that grave in the beet field. I think Alice was afraid that the skeleton we found could have been her lost wartime lover.'

'The Red Indian, but didn't you say that his plane was shot down over Germany?'

'According to Archie Jessup, so far I haven't got any official confirmation. And even if the Kentucky Lady was shot down in flames, it doesn't necessarily follow that Joe Crowfoot was on board for that last mission.'

'You've picked a twisted one to unravel this time,' Ben said wryly. 'And it all happened so long ago. I suppose in practical terms the answers hardly matter much now.'

'They matter to me,' Judy said grimly, 'Especially if poor old Crazy Alice was killed to cover them up.'

'I can see that,' Ben frowned. 'So what's the next step?'

Judy shrugged, 'Go back over the same old ground, I suppose, talk again to Archie and Peter Jessup. The standard police routine, keep chipping away until something cracks open.'

'They probably won't tell you any more than you know already.' Ben was thoughtful for a moment, and then said, 'You mentioned that the old girl had a Bible on her dressing table.'

'Yes, what of it?'

'So she was probably religious,' Ben offered patiently. 'Religious people go to church, church congregations are made up mainly of old ladies. Go along to Brackendale village church and you may well find a few more old ladies of Alice Jessup's generation. They could be your best bet for some informed gossip.'

Judy smiled, 'Thank you, Ben. I've always said that one day you might come up with a bright idea, this could be it.'

'Well how about this for number two,' Ben said modestly. 'Think about that old pub in Brackendale, the Coach and Horses. We've had a meal and a drink in there a few times. Remember all those

166

model airplanes behind the bar, and all those old photographs of the old bomber crews and the B 17s around the walls. The Coach and Horses was the nearest pub to the old airfield, and old Tommy Gallagher who runs it now collected all the memorabilia himself. Go and talk to him, he'll know as much as anyone about the planes that flew in and out of Brackendale during the war.'

10

When Judy arrived at her desk the next morning there was a report waiting from the Bone Ranger. The cheekbones on the human skull that had appeared at the sugar beet factory were slightly higher than the average norm for a white Caucasian, but it was not enough for Rawlings to positively determine any other racial origin. It meant that perhaps the skull was that of Joe Crowfoot, and perhaps it was not, which was not much help.

The skull almost certainly belonged to the skeleton they had found later in the Old Brackendale field, the report continued, and with the skull and the detached hand the skeleton was intact. Most of it was undamaged except for the right wrist bones and the neck vertebra. These had been ripped apart when the tines of the sugar beet harvester had clawed the head and hand away from the rest of the body.

Most of the damage was recent, but some of the neck vertebra damage could have occurred at the time of death, which meant that death could have been caused by an act of violence. Again Rawlings could not be certain.

Again Judy felt frustration. The skeleton might be Joe Crowfoot, or it might not. Whoever he was he might have died violently or he might not. She still had only questions and possibilities, with no firm answers.

A second message from Rawlings caused her to grimace even more. He had scheduled his post mortem examination of Alice Jessup for 9 am in the mortuary at Granchester General. If Judy would meet him there at ten he could convey his conclusions without her having to wait for his written report. Judy hated morgue visits, it was the one part of the job she definitely did not enjoy, but being designated officer in charge of the case had its downside, she had to go.

By now Judy was familiar with the hospital and its grounds and she knew that her only hope of finding a parking space at this hour of the morning was at the far end of the overspill car park. It meant a long walk back through the rows of parked cars, and then down the long hospital corridors. The corridor walls were all painted in bright buttercup yellow and decorated with pictures and artwork by local schoolchildren. An elevator finally took her down to basement level and the more clinical white tiled world where Rawlings was waiting for her.

The Bone Ranger was dressed in a green surgeon's gown and he pulled his face mask down below his chin as he turned to face her. His face had its usual deep-hollowed, mournful expression and his eyes blinked behind his spectacles. Judy thought that he looked like an actor born for his particular role.

The body of Alice Jessup had been retrieved from the funeral parlour and lay on the steel table behind him. He had finished his work and the body was covered in a rubber sheet, leaving the face and shoulders bare.

'Good morning, sergeant,' he was

polite and formal. 'Your timing is perfect, I've only just washed up.'

Judy returned the greeting, forcing herself to look briefly at the shrivelled death mask of Alice Jessup's face. 'What can you tell me?'

'Well, in her stomach there were traces of an undigested digestive biscuit, and a cup of ovaltine. That suggests that she had already had her supper and was ready for bed. The cause of death was definitely a heart attack, which occurred soon after she had taken her last bite and the drink. However, there is something here you should see.'

He moved closer to the body and reluctantly Judy joined him. Rawlings touched a gloved finger to each of the skinny shoulders in turn. 'Here you can clearly see some hard bruising, I'd say those are probably thumb prints, and there are more bruises on the back of her shoulders. My guess is that someone gripped her shoulders hard, facing her as he or she did so, and possibly shaking her hard. That could have brought on the heart attack that killed her.'

Judy stared at the incriminating purple marks and then said slowly. 'How could Doctor Brownlow have missed them?'

'I spoke to the people at the funeral parlour,' Rawlings said. 'She was delivered to them wearing an old fashioned nightdress, which buttoned up at the neck and had elbow length sleeves. Brownlow would have opened the neck of the nightdress to put a stethoscope to her chest, but he obviously missed the bruising. Her shoulders would have been covered and he had no reason to look too close or to suspect anything other than old age and inevitable decline.'

'So this could be murder?'

'If you can catch whoever is responsible a good lawyer would get them off with manslaughter, but someone did grip her shoulders and shake her, the sort of thing that might happen in the course of an argument and that could have been the cause of her heart attack.'

'Did she have any coronary history?'

'No, but her arteries were narrowed, and there is no doubt about the actual cause of death. I'm afraid it's an occupational hazard that goes with old age.'

Judy thanked him and left as soon as she decently could. She was glad that she hadn't had to watch poor old Alice being cut open. Rawlings had spared her by doing that part of the job before she arrived. Now she had plenty to think about as she walked back through the car park. The sun was shining and it was a relief to be out in the open. The fresh air tasted particularly good.

She sat in her car for a moment, tempted to take some time off and visit Ben, but it was too early for the designated visiting hours. Reluctantly she started the engine and began to exit the hospital grounds. Rawlings's written report would not reach the police station until much later in the afternoon and she knew that Grant and Harding would be preoccupied with Operation Longship. This was her case and she had been given a free hand to run it. She decided to take Ben's tip and visit the Coach and Horses, after that she would go to church.

Brackendale was a close knit little

Breckland village, almost self contained with its own pub, post office, general stores and a fish and chip shop. They were all clustered around a small, triangular village green, overlooked by the square flint tower of the church and shaded by two magnificent old sweet chestnut trees. The core buildings were all white plaster and golden thatch, with a couple of grey timbered Tudor structures thrown in for good measure. The chestnuts were in their autumn glory, their fallen leaves making a mottled red and yellow carpet on the green. Judy thought of it as one of the prettiest of the Breckland villages.

It was interesting, she thought, that its tiny post office had never yet been ram raided. Perhaps it was too close to the traveller's site on the old airfield. There was an old local saying that even the dirtiest dog didn't mess on its own doorstep.

She drove into the car park of the Coach and Horses and got out of her car. The well-named pub was a rambling old 16th century building that looked as though it had probably been a coaching inn. It had ancient stables that were now converted into a stylish restaurant. The meals there were excellent and for Judy and Ben it had become one of their favourite haunts. The memories evoked went back to their courting days.

She went into the main bar, where the original ceiling beams were low and twisted and the wartime memorabilia adorned the smoke-dulled walls. Every alcove had its painted portraits of bombers in flight, or the faded brown photographs of the smiling young aircrews posing in front of their ancient B 17s. From 1943 to 1945 this had been the nearest watering hole for the thousands of young American servicemen stationed at the Old Brackendale airfield. They had made it their own, and five decades later the memories still lingered.

Tommy Gallagher was at his usual place behind the bar, serving a handful of local farmhands and villagers with their lunchtime pints and sandwiches. Gallagher was a large, pot-bellied Irishman, at least seventy years old, with blue eyes under bushy white eyebrows, a thick wave of snow white hair, and a full white beard.

'Me mammy was frightened by a Yeti in the Himalayas,' was his usual chat-up line to any new young female who happened to stray into his domain. Gallagher was a bachelor and was well known as a character. He loved young women and he loved life, and his life was his pub. He rarely took a day off and claimed that he had no intention to retire. Once he had suggested that when he shuffled off his mortal coil then his customers might like to just pickle him in one of the barrels in the cellar.

He recognized Judy as she came in and smiled a huge, white bush welcome. He finished the punch line of the dirty story he was telling and left his other customers laughing as he came to serve her.

'Well, if it isn't the Police Force, but without the Fire Brigade,' he said cheerfully. 'Are you working, or will you be drinking?'

Judy sat at the bar stool she had chosen away from the other customers. 'A bit of both,' she answered. 'For a start I'll have a half of shandy and a roast beef baguette.'

Gallagher called the food order through to the back of the bar and served her the drink. 'So what will you have to finish,' he asked as he set the glass in front of her.

'Just a chat,' Judy smiled at him. 'You know we've found a skeleton in Archie Jessup's beet field.'

Gallagher shrugged. 'Everybody knows that, it's all they've been talking about in here just lately.'

'So what are they saying, Tommy, what do most people think, are there any interesting opinions.'

Gallagher leaned his elbows on the bar, bringing his shaggy head forward and cupping his chin in his hand, a sure sign that he was ready to gossip.

'There are almost as many opinions as I have customers. Most of them dating back to war time, because the skeleton was found next to the old airfield, I suppose. A few of the old bombers crashed on landing, the body could have come from one of those. There were all sorts of things going on in those days, the Yanks coming and going, all sorts of strangers appearing and disappearing, talk of spies and traitors and black market jiggery-pokery. Take your pick.'

'You pick for me, Tommy.'

'Well, the oddest tale I've heard so far is one man who thought it could be one of the old mediaeval pilgrims on his way to Norfolk and Walsingham. There were a lot of them wandering about and heading that way in the Dark Ages, some of them half starved and mad enough to do it in the middle winter when the weather was freezing.'

Judy shook her head. 'These bones were too tall and too recent for a mediaeval pilgrim.' She looked at him severely. 'Come back to the war years, Tommy, tell me about Alice Jessup and her war time lover.'

'Ah, so you are chasing that one are you, well, I have to say that it is the favourite.'

'Tell me about it.'

'Well, some people say that he was a black man, but I happen to know that he was a Red Indian, a real Navajo Indian from a reservation somewhere in Arizona, that's the place with all those lovely red rock hills. Anyway, young Alice really did go crazy for him. The talk was that he was going to take her back to America with him, another Breckland war bride. Of course, her brothers hated his guts, they thought she should only look at the nice local ploughboys like themselves. A real Romeo and Juliet story it was, even better than Shakespeare could have written it. I remember it created quite a buzz in the village at the time.'

'You actually remember it?'

'Oh yes, although I was only a nipper, ten years old I was when they sent me up here as an evacuee. Us London kids got sent out all over the place when old Hitler started the Blitz, but I was old enough to understand what was going on when I heard it.'

Judy was intrigued, even if she had not been working on solving a crime she still had a woman's fascination for a good love story. 'So what exactly did you hear?'

'Well, the man's name was Joe Crowfoot, a full blooded Arizona Indian, and for the duration of the war he was a tail gunner on a B17.' Gallagher straightened up and lifted the flap in the counter beside them. He came through into the bar and said simply, 'Follow me.'

Judy did as she was asked, her curiosity now fully aroused, and he led her to one of the side alcoves where the courting couples usually sat. Gallagher pointed out two framed and hung portraits, both browning with age behind the clear glass. One showed a B17 bomber in the foreground of a whole row of similar aircraft. The other showed the same airplane with its crew of eight lined up all in sheepskin flying jackets just in front of the wing and under the cockpit, all with their arms around each others shoulders.

'The Kentucky Lady,' Gallagher said, 'And there's Joe Crowfoot.'

The pictures were similar to a score of others that hung all around the walls of the bar, but Judy could clearly read the name painted with a flourish under the cockpit window above the closely grouped crew, and she could also count the twenty two small black bomb stencils that represented the number of missions the aircraft had already flown over hostile Europe before the picture was taken. Many of the crew pictures around the bar had been personally signed by the men they portrayed, but this one simply had the list of eight names printed in brown-yellow letters of faded ink.

The fifth name down was that of Sergeant Joe Crowfoot, tail gunner. Judy looked more closely at the fifth man in the line. He was black haired and smiling, and like the others he wore a zipped up brown leather jacket with a high sheepskin collar. The bottom edge of the closed jacket hid his belt buckle, but Judy could see that this was the same man as the one in the missing photograph from Alice's dressing table.

The faded brown lettering continued below the list of crew names and was now only just readable:

THE KENTUCKY LADY FLEW HER 24th AND LAST MISSION ON JULY 14th 1944. SHE WAS SHOT DOWN SOMEWHERE OVER GERMANY. NONE OF HER CREW SURVIVED.

Judy stared at the two old photographs.

In her mind she had started to believe that the body in the beet field had to be that of Joe Crowfoot, but now she was not so sure.

'How official is this?' She tapped the final words on the photograph with her finger.

Gallagher shrugged. 'Who knows, most of these pictures were here when I bought the pub, probably left behind by the aircrews themselves. I've added others that I've bought or had given to me, but I think these two were originals.'

They went back to the bar and resumed their places. Judy's beef baguette had arrived and she took a disconsolate bite. Gallagher hovered, looking round to check that no one needed serving then he leaned on the bar again.

'There is another story you might want to think about.'

Judy looked at him over her sandwich, 'Okay, I can eat and listen.'

'Well, like I said, I was a nipper in wartime, and I first came to this part of the world as an evacuee. My family were Londoners, but my mum had a sister up here, so when it looked certain that it was going to get hot in London I was packed off up here to live with my Auntie Joan. I liked it here, and after the war, while Aunt Joan was still alive I made lots of return visits. I spent forty years in the Merchant Navy, ship's cook and then chef on a P and O passenger liner. In between trips this place was as much home to me as the East End of London, all green and rural, a nice contrast if you like. Aunt Joan managed to live a bit longer than my mum and dad, so eventually it was just this place that I came back to. When I left the sea I just had to come and buy a pub down here.'

'Tommy, you're rambling,' Judy said between bites at her sandwich.

'So I am,' Gallagher agreed cheerfully, 'So back to my story, the evacuees. You know that during the war most of London's children were shipped out to the countryside where it was hoped we would escape the worst of the bombing. Most of them were sent west to Wales or Cornwall to get them as far out of danger as possible, but there were a lot of us so

183

we were pretty widely scattered. Some of us came this way because at least it was out of London and there were relatives or friends to take us in.'

Gallagher paused, looking down into his beard, remembering those far off days. Judy waited for him to continue.

'So I came here, to Auntie Joan, and there were half a dozen others in and around Brackendale. Most of us arrived before the Americans, when it was thought to be relatively safe. There were two other lads who became good pals of mine, because they came from the East End the same as me. I don't remember their surname, but they were Freddie and Herbert. Freddie was a right little tearaway. He was ten, the same age as me. Herbert was Freddie's little brother, he was about seven, he just tagged along with us. They were billeted with the local vicar.'

Two young building workers had just come in and Gallagher went to serve them, leaving Judy wondering exactly what he was leading up to. For a moment she thought that he was going to be distracted by other conversations as all those with empty glasses took the opportunity to get them refilled, but eventually he came back to her.

'Now where was I?' he asked, fingering his beard as he settled his folded arms comfortably back on the bar.

'You were telling me about Freddie and Herbert,' Judy said. 'And the vicar.'

'Ah yes, they were taken in by the vicar and his wife, and they hated it. A right old Bible-basher Freddie called him, always preaching at them and forcing them to go to church on Sundays, Freddie wasn't used to that. And always making them take their clothes off and have a bath, touching them too, Freddie said. Freddie hinted a lot and Herbert cried a lot. They were not happy. Freddie said that if the old vicar made him take his trousers off one more time he'd do for him.'

Gallagher paused again, and Judy prompted him.

'So what happened?'

Gallagher shrugged. 'I don't know, they just vanished, one day Freddie and Herbert just disappeared, and the vicar,

George Wilkes, he disappeared too.'

He grinned at her wryly through the white bush of his beard. 'So it's not just Joe Crowfoot's old bones that you might have dug up. There's more than one candidate for that old grave in Archie Jessup's beet field.'

11

When Judy left the Coach and Horses the sun was still shining and the idyllic village of Brackendale still seemed the ideal rural retreat. There was no one else in sight and momentarily not even the sound of a passing car. The ancient shops seemed to sleep around the leaf strewn green in the benevolent shade of the solid church tower. It was hard to believe that there were dark secrets to be uncovered in this drowsy setting, but she was still thinking over Tommy Gallagher's story, and there was definitely a fifty year old skeleton that still had to be identified.

She paused by her car, looking towards the church, and then decided that the church was so close that she might as well leave the car here in the pub car park while she made her next call.

She walked across the green with the red and gold leaves from the two chestnut trees crunching under her feet. As far as she could remember the vicarage was behind the church, which meant that her quickest route was to walk through the churchyard with its mixture of old, lichen covered unreadable grave stones and the new marble stones with their crisp black letters and pots of bright flowers. However, as she walked the gravel path between the headstones she saw that the church door inside the porch was open.

The porch was constructed of thin red bricks with a black timber roof and red tiles, a Tudor addition to a hotch potch of architectural styles. She went inside and saw that one of the double oak doors set in the old Norman archway of the main building was also open. She heard voices inside the church and stepped into the cool of the aisle.

A dark hammer-beam roof, complete with carved wooden angels, soared high above her, and light streamed in large beams through the tall arched windows. A group of three elderly ladies, all in bright flowered dresses, clustered down by the chancel, engaged in chattering, dusting, polishing and arranging flowers. A short, tubby man wearing a grey jacket and trousers had his back to her as he tidied a variety of books, leaflets and postcards on the trestle table behind the font. When he turned at the sound of her approach she saw the white dog collar at his throat.

'Do come in,' he smiled a welcome. 'Please don't mind us if you want to have a look around.' He came towards her, offering one of his folded leaflets. 'We have this little guide if you're interested. It tells you the history of our church and there's a floor plan to show you what's what. Our roof has twenty-four angels looking down on us, and the font is 14th century, which is the same age as the tower.'

'Actually,' Judy said, 'I'm looking for the vicar. I just want to talk.'

'Well, I am the vicar,' His smile was guarded now, pitched mid-way between cheerful and sympathetic, not sure whether her need might be for either a wedding or a funeral. He said calmly, 'My name is Brian Davies.'

Judy showed him her card and his smile faltered. Now he was at a loss.

189

'Oh dear,' He fidgeted with his glasses and then pushed them back up his nose. 'I do hope we're not in any trouble.'

'I shouldn't think so,' Judy reassured him. 'I'm just making some routine enquiries, about a lady who may have been one of your congregation — Miss Alice Jessup.'

'Oh, poor Alice, yes, yes I see. Alice was a regular, she came every Sunday. She seemed fine at our last morning service. Her loss was such a sad and sudden shock.' The implications of Judy's card and her visit suddenly struck home and his tone sharpened a little, 'I've been told that I may have to delay the funeral.'

'We hope that won't be necessary,' Judy kept her smile in place. 'Could we talk about Alice?'

'Of course,' he looked at her shrewdly, 'But I've only been with this parish for a few years, so it would probably be more helpful for you to talk with Grace and Joyce. They've known Alice since they were all schoolgirls together.'

He led her toward the altar where his trio of helpers were still pretending to be

190

absorbed in their dusting, although their chatter had ceased and they were obviously straining hard to listen.

'Ladies,' Davies said as though he were presenting her on stage, 'this young woman is a police sergeant, she wants to talk about Alice.'

They gathered round promptly in a bright, flowery flock, all grey haired and lined faces, but bright eyed behind spectacles. They were all well past their three score years and ten. The vicar introduced them.

'This is Joyce Bennet, and Grace Wilkes, and Muriel Abbot. They are the most senior members of our little congregation and I must say the hardest working. They volunteer for everything that needs to be done and I don't know how I would run this church without them. We have a rota of course, for the church cleaning and all the other little tasks, but they virtually are the rota. They — '

Judy had stopped listening. She was looking at Grace Wilkes. For a moment the prime reason for her visit was suddenly forgotten.

'I've heard your name before,' she said, hardly daring to hope. 'Wasn't there a vicar here named Wilkes during the war?'

'Oh yes,' Grace Wilkes seemed pleased at the unexpected attention she was getting. She looked to be the eldest of the three, and the smallest. Her dress was of blue and yellow irises under a blue cardigan. To Judy all these old ladies seemed alert and bird-like, Alice had been a grey sparrow and she could see Grace Wilkes as a perky blue starling.

Grace said cheerfully, 'My George was the vicar here for four years, from 1939 to 1944. He was the youngest vicar this church has ever had. We were only just married, and he was only just ordained.' Her voice became wistful, 'They were short years, but good years, before George was called home.'

'What happened?' Judy asked softly.

'It was wartime, dear, he died in the Blitz.'

'The Blitz,' Judy was confused, she wasn't aware that the Luftwaffe had ever bombed Brackendale.

'The Blitz in London,' Grace explained. 'George went up there, you see, looking for the two lost boys.'

Judy realized that her perplexed look was serving her best and so she simply repeated the last words, 'The two lost boys?'

'Yes, dear, you see we had two little evacuee boys billeted with us during the war, Freddie and Herbert Burroughs. They were sent down from London to escape the bombing. They were two sweet little boys, but they were a bit difficult. They didn't want to leave their mum and dad, you see, and they couldn't really see why it was necessary. They were sent down late in the war and it was always other streets that had been bombed, never their street. They thought it couldn't happen to them, and so they were not happy with us.'

'A lot of them thought that, they all wanted to go home.' Muriel Abbot nodded her head in jerky agreement, and Judy thought of an old grey thrush banging a snail on a stone.

'The poor things,' Grace carried on.

'We tried to teach them about Jesus, but they had never been to church before, so that didn't go down too well. It was impossible to teach them God's love when there was so much evil in the world. They were quite difficult, and so dirty. I mean they hated having to wash themselves and they always seemed to be playing in the mud somewhere. Getting them to take a bath was quite a battle.'

'Very difficult,' Judy agreed, and waited.

'They loved climbing trees. I don't suppose there were any trees in London, so that was something new they did like. But they always seemed to be falling out of the trees, or falling over somehow and getting all dusty and dirty. And they were always in and out of the hedgerows, robbing bird's nests and collecting eggs. I think the local boys must have taught them that. It was another thing we tried to stop them doing, robbing the birds and killing their unborn babies. Oh, it was all battles with Freddie and Herbert, I can tell you.'

'What happened?' Judy tried to channel the flow of words, 'You said George went up to London, after the two boys.'

'Yes, dear, they ran away you see, such naughty boys, but I suppose they just wanted to go home. George had to go up to London on business, so he said he would call in on Burton Street, that's where they lived, just to make sure that they had arrived home safely. We were responsible for them, you see.'

'So George followed the two boys back to London?'

'Yes,' Grace Wilkes nodded, and looked down sadly at her feet. She paused for a moment and the gossipy momentum of her story was gone. 'I never saw him again,' she said at last, her voice subdued and pathetic. 'Nor those two poor little boys. It was on the radio the next day that Burton Street had been bombed, fifty two people died, and I don't remember how many were hurt. Some of the dead were never found, they were blown to bits, I suppose.'

There was another long, respectful moment of silence.

'You're sure the two boys went back to London?' Judy asked softly.

Grace Wilkes opened her eyes wide behind her spectacles. 'Why, yes dear, where else could they have gone?'

'And George went after them?'

'Yes, dear.' Her eyes were misty and the flow of words had now dried completely. The Reverend Davies put a comforting hand on her shoulder and patted gently, his manner was reassuring and defensive.

'But you were asking after Alice,' he reminded Judy.

'Yes,' Judy wasn't sure that she was ready to be dragged back to the real purpose of her visit, but she had to agree. 'I was looking for anyone who might have known Alice when she was young.'

'Oh, we all knew Alice,' Joyce Bennet said. She was the one with red roses on a white dress, together with a short brown woollen jacket. Judy thought of a cheeky chaffinch. 'We were all girls together.'

Muriel, who wore a jacket and skirt with green leaves and yellow lilies nodded brightly. Judy was already mentally distinguishing them by their bird mannerisms and the flower patterns they wore.

'Tell me about Alice,' she prompted.

'When she was young.'

'Oh, she was beautiful,' Joyce said. 'The prettiest one of us all. We were all jealous of her then. She turned all the young men's heads, always had them all flocking round her at the dances.'

'Like bees to the honey,' Muriel nodded. 'Especially at the dances.'

'Especially when the Americans came,' It was Joyce who was in full flow now. 'They held lovely big dances, not like the ones in our poky little village hall. They used to clear one of the big aircraft hangars on the airfield, moved all the big bombers and all the other stuff out on to the runways. We all went there. They had much bigger bands, much better. Glen Miller came once. We all danced until our feet dropped off, or at least it felt as though our feet were going to drop off. We were all young then.'

'And Alice was popular?'

'Oh yes, even us girls liked Alice, even though we were jealous of her. And the American boys were all over our Alice, until she met Joe. Then it was love at first sight, as they say, Alice fell for Joe like a ton of bricks, and Joe fell just as hard for her.'

'They made a perfect couple,' Muriel said. 'Our Alice in her Alice-blue-gown, and Navajo Joe, he was a real Red Indian, very handsome, all sleek black hair and large brown eyes, you could just picture him in one of them big feather head-dresses.'

'But her brothers didn't like him?'

Joyce snorted derisively. 'Archie and Charlie hated anyone who had an eye for their Alice. They thought they owned her because she was their little sister. They scared off most of the local boys, Archie even punched poor Billy Ruddles on the nose, and he'd only kissed her once. The Americans they hated even worse, and Joe being, well, not white, that really fired them up. Archie even threatened to kill him.'

'That night in the Coach and Horses,' Muriel said in a hushed whisper.

'Oh yes, I was with Archie that night. I only went out with him once or twice, mind, he was a bit too black tempered for me. And you were there with Little Lenny — what was his name?'

'Lenny Smithers,' Muriel said. 'I only went with him a few times, he was not really my type, but he made me laugh a lot. He used to pull those funny rabbit faces — '

'Joe and Alice,' Judy steered them back on track.

'Oh yes,' Joyce continued. 'They came in to the pub together, arm in arm, all happy and smiling. Archie and Charlie were there, Archie with me and Charlie with blonde Dolly, the one he eventually married, only just in time as I remember. Anyway, we were all drinking. When Alice and Joe came in Archie saw red — ' She giggled. 'Literally red, you might say, Red Indian, see. Archie wanted to fight Joe there and then. He swore he was going to kill him.'

'But Joe didn't want to fight,' Muriel remembered. 'He was a nice, quiet man. He had no real business being in the American Air Force. He didn't want to fight anyone, but his government had called him up. They were all drafted in those days. They had to join the war and fight.'

'No, Joe didn't want to fight Archie,' Joyce agreed. 'But Archie and Charlie wanted to fight Joe.'

'But Joe had friends there, some more of his crew from the Kentucky Lady. They all came over and stood by Joe. They thought Archie and Charlie and some more of the Brackendale boys were all going to gang up on to Joe, and they wouldn't allow that.'

'Archie was still going to fight Joe, he wanted One to One. I had a hold of Archie by his arm, trying to pull him back. Dolly, Charlie's girl, she tried to help me, but Archie was strong, he just about threw us both off. Then Bald John who kept the pub shouted at them to stop. He had a piece of broom handle he kept under the bar, remember? When Bald John smacked that old broom handle down on the bar, most people decided to stop causing trouble and behave themselves.'

'Oh, and he did smack it down hard that night, made all of the glasses jump and rattle, and made all the boys shut up. Then the American boys said they would leave, and Joe and Alice went with them.'

'And Archie still wanted to follow, he was furious that Alice went with them and he kept shouting for her to come back. She ignored him, and me and Dolly kept hanging on to his arm. Then Charlie saw some sense and he pulled back on Archie's other arm. Charlie was mad too, but he could see that they would be only two against six if they went outside so he helped to hold Archie back. He kept saying that there would be a better time, they'd catch the 'Red Nigger' without his mates and sort him out then. Oh, that was a night that was.'

'Yes,' Muriel agreed with Joyce, 'that was a night.' They looked at each other and chuckled at the memory.'

'Did they catch up with Joe?' Judy asked. 'Did they sort him out?'

Muriel frowned, 'I don't know, I don't think so.'

'It was soon after that that Joe's crew were lost,' Joyce explained. 'The Kentucky Lady flew out to drop some more bombs over Germany, and they never came back.'

'Poor Alice,' Muriel sighed. 'She never got over it.'

Joyce nodded, 'And there was the other one, too, the Wild One, she called him. He disappeared at the same time.'

'The Wild One?' Judy was intrigued, and confused.

'Oh yes, like we said, Alice was very popular, a bit of a flirt sometimes, she had more than one admirer.'

'He was a Gypsy boy,' Muriel said. 'One of the travelling Irish, Danny something.'

'Danny Farrel,' Joyce filled in the gap. 'Gypsy Danny, but Alice always called him her Wild One. Because Joe was so quiet, I suppose, and young Danny was full of fire and life. Joe was her Gentleman Joe, and Danny was the Wild One.'

'How did she meet him?' Judy kept her prompts short, half afraid to interrupt, but desperate to keep the flow coming.

'In those days the Irish came over every year to help work the sugar campaign,'

Muriel explained. 'The travelling people always moved and worked with the seasons. In spring they would be apple picking, and then it would be pea picking, strawberry picking and the wheat harvest. Then they would be hop picking down in Kent, and in winter back here for the Sugar Beet campaign. They moved where the work was. Before everything got mechanized and they had computers, the farmers and the sugar factory always relied on the travelling people for the seasonal work.'

'So Alice had another love affair,' Judy tried to get it straight. 'At the same time as Joe?'

'That's right,' Muriel and Joyce spoke together, and then Joyce continued, 'Archie and Charlie didn't like Danny either, and Danny didn't like Joe. Danny didn't want a rival, see. Oh, it was a right old mix-up, our Alice had them all in a whirl.'

'And then Danny disappeared at the same time as Joe,' Muriel finished the story. 'They say some money was stolen from the sugar beet factory and Danny ran off with it, but nobody knows if that was really true. Danny just vanished. Poor old Alice never saw him again either.'

By this time Judy's head was reeling. She had started the day with one possible candidate for the skeleton in the beet field, and now she had three.

* * *

She told the whole story to Ben when she visited him in hospital later that evening. Ben was pain free now and in a much better humour, he lay back on his pillows with his hands cradled behind his head and laughed at her frustration.

'Perhaps you should dig up the rest of Archie Jessup's beet field,' he suggested. 'You might find it full of skeletons.'

'One is enough,' Judy assured him. 'If I can just identify this one, and find out who killed Alice, that will be enough to satisfy me.'

'Well, it could still be Navajo Joe. He's got to be your best bet. Just because his plane was lost over Germany doesn't necessarily mean that Joe was on board. If he was already dead and buried in the beet field, then the plane going missing could have proved very convenient for Archie and Charlie Jessup.'

'Joe is still my favourite,' she agreed.' 'But it is not all so clear cut now, these other disappearances are clouding the issue.'

'So what about the missing vicar, let's suppose that he was abusing those evacuee boys, that sort of thing did happen. The vast majority of evacuee children were well cared for by those who took them in, but there was the occasional horror story. Is it possible that these boys could have turned on their tormentor and killed him before they disappeared?'

'They were ten and seven years old,' Judy protested. 'It's not really feasible.'

'Perhaps there was a paedophile ring, more abusers, and more children being abused. Perhaps a gang of kids got together and killed the ringleader. Remember Lord Of The Flies? Kids can easily slip back into being little savages.'

'Now you are going on flights of fancy.

This is Brackendale we're talking about, not Stephen King territory. Besides, if something like that did happen, a bunch of ten year olds wouldn't be smart enough to cover it all up.'

'Maybe, but if there was a paedophile ring, then maybe the rest of the ring would have quietly buried the vicar to protect themselves. The abusers would have as much motivation as the abused to keep the whole thing quiet.'

'I don't believe it,' Judy decided. 'I think Grace Wilkes was genuine, and all we have here is a culture clash between a couple of grubby free spirits and a Holier than Thou couple who probably thought that cleanliness was next to godliness.'

She paused. 'The story that her George went up to London to look for them and died in the blitz did ring true, but I do wonder why Tommy Gallagher told me all the rest but left that bit out.'

Ben shrugged, 'You know Tommy, always one for a wind-up. He probably just wanted to get you going.'

'Yes,' Judy said thoughtfully, although she was not sure. She knew that Tommy did like to play games within all his talk, but this time she couldn't work out exactly what game he might have been playing.

However, Ben was moving on.

'I'll lay seven to three on Navajo Joe,' he said firmly. 'Fifty-fifty on the vicar. What odds do we give to the Gypsy boy?'

'I'm a detective, not a bookmaker,' Judy pulled a face at him. Then she became serious again, 'But the Irish boy does interest me, he's another link to Alice, another wartime lover, hostile to Joe and at odds again with her brothers.'

'So there is no link between Alice and the vicar?'

'There's none that I can see, but it seems that there was the old three corner triangle between Joe and Alice and Alice and Danny. Somewhere there has to be a link between the skeleton, Alice, and whoever shook her hard enough to scare her to death.'

'You think that's what happened?'

'Something like that, it seems the most likely scenario.'

Ben was silent for a moment, considering, 'So what do we know about this Wild One?' he said at last.

'He was Irish, a seasonal worker who worked at the sugar beet factory during the winter campaigns, and he may have disappeared with some money.' Judy ticked the facts off on her fingers. She looked around and lowered her voice, although the beds on either side of them were empty. The occupant of the bed behind her had been taken down to the operating theatre earlier in the afternoon and was still in the recovery room. Ben's neighbour on the other side had wandered down to the far end of the ward to talk to another patient.

'His name was Danny Farrel,' she said quietly. 'Now there's a family of that name still living on the old airfield travellers site, but Grant and Harding have got them in their sights for this spate of ram raids. So, I can hardly barge in there asking any questions about Alice. It could jeopardize all the time and work they've put into Operation Longship.'

'Tricky,' Ben agreed. 'What are your

guvnors saying about this?'

Judy made a rueful face. 'I haven't had a chance to speak to either of them. They're like a couple of blinkered racehorses on the finishing straight, totally focussed on their own task. Plus I've had a busy day and I didn't want to hang about. I wanted to come and see you.'

Ben smiled and squeezed her hand.

After a few more minutes the bell sounded to signal the end of visiting hours. Judy kissed him goodnight and reluctantly left.

12

When Judy walked into the large CID room the next morning the lower ranks were already busy at their telephones and computer screens, but there was no sign of either Grant or Harding. Tony Marsh, the lanky young DC with the irreverent grin who was sometimes her partner when she was not paired with Harding noted her questing look. He replaced his telephone and leaned back in his chair to greet her.

'Morning, Jude, if you're looking for the guvnors they're in another meeting, top brass only this morning, just our two and the two guys from Cambridge and Norfolk. They're in Grant's office. The rest of us were not invited, or at least not yet. My hunch is that Longship is getting close to go, so the timing and the final details are on a need to know only.'

Judy felt mildly annoyed at being shut out. She had spent a long time working on the Longship team, and she realized that she didn't want to miss the climax. Then, with a mental shrug, she accepted that she did have her own enquiry to run, and life rarely allowed you to have everything.

'Thanks, Tony, I'll try and catch up with them later.' She decided against the dull routine of typing up the report on what she already had in favour of hopefully learning some more, and added: 'If anyone is interested I'm going out to Appledown Farm to talk to Sarah Jessup.'

'They managed to find some old prints on the sledgehammer,' Marsh called after her. 'And there were smoke smuts grimed into the handle which probably came from burned insulation rubber. That suggests scrap dealing so the chances look good that we can tie it to the traveller's site when we do go in there.'

'Good,' Judy smiled back at him. 'I'm glad it's all coming together.'

She went out and returned to her car. She was glad that the Longship investigation was paying dividends, but suddenly she realized that she was more interested now in finding out what had happened to Crazy Alice. Longship was almost a foregone conclusion, but the story of Alice and her lovers was still a mystery. She was trying to untangle an elusive skein of ancient sins, and possibly a related murder, and she had almost a free hand to pursue her own investigations.

Suddenly she didn't care so much about Longship. She put her foot down and drove out almost happily to Appledown Farm.

The two Jessup farms were side by side, the farmhouses almost in sight of each other and separated only by a few fields. Even the layouts were the same, the farmhouse facing on to the central yard with barns and storage sheds on either side. The Appledown farmhouse looked slightly smaller and smarter than the one at Blackberry Farm, it had been recently painted, the masonry fresh cream and the door and window frames still sparkling white. The rest of the outbuildings were just as dilapidated and as Judy got out of her car she was aware of the strong smell of cow manure. The farmhouse was silent and appeared deserted. A cockerel strolled out from between two hay bales and fixed her with one beady and disdainful eye. Nothing else moved. Judy felt uncomfortable.

She walked up to the farmhouse door and knocked. The echoes faded slowly away with no answer. Judy frowned and looked around the farmyard again. The cockerel had vanished. She was alone and somehow the silence didn't seem right, she had always thought of farms as busy and noisy places. There should have been more chickens, yapping dogs and lazing cats.

She moved along the front of the house to the nearest window and looked inside. She saw an empty living room, comfortable armchairs facing a large open fireplace. A large television set now filled the space where once a log fire might have burned. The heating, she could see, now came from modern streamline radiators along the wall.

She moved back past the closed door to the window on the other side. This one looked into a large kitchen, old-fashioned red tiles on the floor, but all the fittings were up to date, all the appliances the latest models. She stood with her hands on the window sill, wondering why the place was so quiet.

And then it wasn't. A low, throaty growl sounded from close behind her.

Judy spun round, her heart skipping a beat. A large black mastiff dog glowered at her, for a second she thought that it was Archie Jessup's dog, but this one was older, more grizzled and grey bristled around its half open jaws. There was white slaver dripping from its teeth. Judy froze. The dog looked dangerous and its hot stare seemed to bore into her.

'Snooping again,' Sarah Jessup's voice broke the silence.

Judy looked past the dog. Sarah had appeared from between two of the sheds on her left. She wore a black raincoat, Wellington boots and a black, waterproof hat. In her hand she carried a stout stick. She looked almost as menacing as the dog.

'Good morning,' Judy said steadily. 'I

was looking for you.'

At the sound of her voice the dog hunched back and growled again.

'Easy Jess,' Sarah came forward, holding the stick firmly in her right fist. The dog cocked its head to one side, its left ear pricked up, but its hot eyes stayed on Judy. It growled again.

Judy could feel her muscles tense, although she tried not to let it show. Suddenly it occurred to her that Sarah Jessup was a strong and competent woman who would have been physically quite capable of strangling her frail old aunt.

'Why do you need the stick?' She asked as calmly as she could.

Sarah looked down at the stick in her hand, suddenly she grinned. With her left hand she took a grip on the dog's collar before she answered.

'I use it for driving the cows. I usually herd them down to the pasture after the morning milking.' She gave the stick a little flourish. 'I suppose it could come in handy for clouting trespassers and intruders, but so far all I've ever done is tap the odd Friesian on the rump or the shoulder.'

The dog looked up at its mistress and seemed satisfied with the tone of her voice. It settled its hindquarters and sat down, its front legs still stiff and erect. Its tail wagged briefly in the dust of the farmyard and a large tongue lolled out to lick the slaver from its lips.

'Old Jess has been running a bit,' Sarah explained fondly as she stroked the dog's head. 'That's why she's slavering and panting. Her wind is not as good as it used to be.'

'She reminds me of Archie's dog,' Judy said.

'She would do, Toby is one of Jess's pups. Don't know who his father was though.' She leaned the stick against the wall. 'So what can I do for you?'

'A few more questions,' Judy said. 'Some new thoughts, some things I forgot to ask.'

Sarah shrugged, and dug into her raincoat pocket to produce a door key. 'You'd better come in then. I'm going to make a cup of tea.'

She unlocked the door and led the way through to the kitchen. Judy followed and tried to ignore the dog which trailed silently behind them. Sarah filled an electric kettle and switched it on. Then turned and leaned her back on the kitchen worktop.

'So what do you want to know?'

'Anything you can tell me about Danny Farrel might help.'

'Ah, the Wild One, you've been listening to that gossip. Well, I don't suppose I can tell you more than any of the other gossipers. Aunt Alice never talked about him, so what I know came much the same way as what you know already, just the village gossip.'

'Didn't you ever ask her?'

'I suppose I might have done, but Aunt Alice had a habit of just tapping her nose and shaking her head. It was her way of telling you to mind your own business. It was the same with Navajo Joe, all the village knew, Aunt Alice couldn't hide it, but after it was all over she didn't want to talk about it much. I suppose some old aunties might tell their favourite nieces all about their love lives, but Aunt Alice wasn't that sort. She went a bit prim and proper, lived with her memories, but got so she didn't really want to share them with anyone.'

'So what do you know?'

'He was Irish, came here with the travellers. They came every year to do the winter work at the sugar beet factory. Aunt Alice had her fling. He talked about taking her home to the Emerald Isle where they would take to the road and live in a gypsy caravan. I think Aunt Alice loved the blarney, but it didn't quite match up to the idea of going to America and living on a Red Indian Reservation. Joe Crowfoot had the edge, but then she lost them both.'

'How did she lose Danny?'

'He turned out to be a thief as well as a rogue, stole some money and vanished into the moonlight.'

'Where did he steal the money?'

'From the sugar beet factory, he stole the wages. In those days they paid the men in cash every week, all the money in coins and notes in little pay packets. At least, that's the story — you've heard the gossip.'

'The village gossip,' Judy agreed. 'What about the family gossip?'

'The Jessup family don't gossip.' Sarah's grin was becoming more irritating, making her plump face almost jovial. 'I asked my Dad once, when I was a little girl and first heard the stories. He just told me not to listen to the village gossip. I think Peter got the same sort of answer from Uncle Archie, although in his case a clip round the ear came with it.'

The kettle boiled and Sarah made two mugs of tea. She offered one to Judy and added milk and sugar. The dog thumped its tail on the red-tiled floor and she tossed it a biscuit from an open box by the window.

Judy had been thinking. 'On the last night that you saw Aunt Alice, did she speak about Danny?'

Sarah sipped the hot tea, flinched and put the mug down. 'Now you mention it, I think she did. Just hints, nothing I can quite remember, but she seemed to have them both on her mind. And she was definitely worried about what you found in Archie's beet field. She didn't say it, but I got the impression she might have thought that it could have been one of them.'

Judy nodded. 'Okay, we'll leave that. How long were you with her that evening?'

'Oh, about half an hour, I didn't usually stay long, just sort of looked in regular to see that she was okay.'

'What time did you leave?'

'Got there about half eight, left her about nine o'clock, I suppose.'

'And then came home here?'

'No, I went to the pub.' Sarah grinned. 'Ladies aren't supposed to go alone into the pub, but I'm no lady. I'm a working farmer, and a damned hard working farmer. It's not easy running this place since I've been left alone. So I go into the pub for a drink. I usually meet Peter there. He likes a pint after a hard day's work. Mind you, I don't drink pints. I'm just lady enough to drink a small light ale.'

This was news to Judy, something she

should have asked before. Her interest sharpened, 'Did you meet Peter that night?'

Sarah nodded.

'What did you talk about?'

'Aunt Alice, the skeleton in the beet field. That's what everybody else was talking about. Anyway, we are family, cousins and all that.'

'Close cousins?'

Sarah grinned again. 'Not kissing cousins, but we run neighbouring farms, and we played together as kids. Uncle Archie and my Dad Charlie were always close.'

'What time did you leave the pub?'

'About ten o'clock, got there at nine, had one drink, so there about an hour I suppose. We never make a night of it. Farmers have to start work fairly early in the mornings.'

'Which pub did you go to?' Judy asked, although she knew there was only one public house in Brackendale.

'The Coach and Horses,' Sarah answered. She threw the dog another biscuit and resumed drinking her tea.

* * *

Judy's next stop was Blackberry Farm. There was no point in passing it and it was time to talk again to Archie and Peter Jessup, and now she particularly wanted to talk to Peter.

Her timing was fortunate. The morning tea break was a regular Jessup habit and at Blackberry Farm she found them all in the kitchen. The farm dogs loudly announced her arrival and Mary Jessup opened the door to her, looking immediately anxious. Peter and Archie sprawled on hard backed chairs with the kitchen table between them, each with a large tea mug in one hand and a cheese and onion sandwich in the other. Mary shooed Judy inside and the dogs out and then closed the door. They all looked at each other and exchanged good mornings, Judy's tone was bright and cheerful, the male Jessups both guarded.

Mary found another chair and Judy sat down. They all waited for her to speak first.

'I've just come from Appledown,' Judy

explained. 'Sarah has told me that you were both in the Coach and Horses on the night that your Aunt Alice died.'

Peter Jessup frowned and looked uncomfortable. 'That's right,' he admitted. 'What of it?'

'Do you meet her often?'

'Two or three times a week, just for a drink.' The big man looked puzzled.

'There's nothing in it.' Mary Jessup spoke up sharply. 'Sometimes I go with him, sometimes I don't. They're cousins, that's all, when Sarah's Fred was alive we all went to the Horses together.'

It was the first time she had volunteered anything and Judy noted the quick reaction. She nodded as though she understood, filing her thoughts away for later as she returned her attention to Peter.

'What did you talk about that night?'

'Oh, general stuff, I suppose.' Peter was trying to avoid his father's glare. 'Lifting up the beet, how much barley we're going to plant next year, farming talk.'

'You talked about the skeleton in the beet field,' Judy reminded him. 'You talked about Aunt Alice and her wartime lovers.'

'Well yes, the whole pub was talking about that.'

'What were you and Sarah saying about her?'

Peter put down his mug and grimaced as he tried to remember. 'Sarah said most of it, about how Aunt Alice seemed worried and upset. That old skull and the skeleton turning up like that, it made her all fretful.'

'Aunt Alice thought that it might have been Navajo Joe, or the gypsy boy.'

Peter shuffled his feet and stared up at the ceiling. 'Well, I don't know about that. I don't think Aunt Alice said as much, Sarah sort of thought that was what she was worrying about. Nothing there for you to worry about, though, Aunt Alice always had some odd ideas. That's why they called her Crazy Alice.'

'Peter,' Archie Jessup almost snarled.

Reluctantly Peter looked at his father. 'It's got to be said, I suppose, Dad. She's hearing all about it in the village anyway. And she's from the police, she's a

Detective Sergeant. I can't not talk to her when she asks me.'

Archie snorted, 'Well I don't have to talk, and I don't have to listen. I'm going upstairs.' He slammed his half eaten sandwich back onto the plate, pushed himself up from the chair and deliberately turned his back on them. He stamped out and slammed the door behind him. They heard his boots clumping loudly as he went up the stairs.

Too loudly, Judy thought. The slammed door had bounced slightly open again and noise echoed in the high hallway of the rambling old house. She felt certain that Archie Jessup could still hear, and was probably still listening.

Mary Jessup was biting her lip, looking flushed and embarrassed. Peter fidgeted in his chair but finally looked back at Judy.

'Sorry about, Dad. He's always been a bit touchy about Aunt Alice. They had a row a long time ago and never seemed to be able to make it up. What you found in our beet field, that's upset him too, and you coming here and asking questions and all that. And now Aunt Alice has died, and that's upset him. She may have been crazy and obstinate, but she was his sister. He's an old man. It's all being a bit too much for him.'

'What did they row about?' Judy said softly.

'Old stuff, when they were all young. Dad and Uncle Charlie didn't approve of Aunt Alice courting strangers. They thought she could do better with someone local.' Peter shrugged. 'You've heard it all, you know.'

Judy knew. She was listening for a reaction from the upstairs bedroom but there was silence. She wished that she could see Archie Jessup's face.

'What about the body in the beet field? Your Dad seemed to think he must be from a crashed aircraft, so why should he be worried about it?'

'It's his field and your lot are walking all over it, digging it up, finding skeletons and asking questions, isn't that enough? What's it all matter anyway? Whatever happened it all happened over fifty years ago.'

'It matters because Aunt Alice is dead, and we know someone visited her just before she died, someone who may have scared her to death.'

Peter gaped, his jaw dropped and his face was horrified. Judy leaned forward and asked firmly: 'Where did you go when you left the pub?'

'I came straight home,' the big man protested. 'Mary was here, ask her.'

Mary Jessup nodded. Her face was scared as she repeated dutifully. 'He did, about ten past ten he came in. I was watching the ten o'clock news.'

'What about Sarah?'

'She went home. I walked her there. I pass Appledown on the way.'

Judy looked at Mary. 'Did Archie go out that night?'

'No,' the answer was quick, almost tumbling out of her trembling lips. 'Dad never goes out at night, not now. That's why I stay in most nights when Peter slips out for his quick pint, to keep Dad company.'

Judy stared at them thoughtfully, weighing their body language signs and responses as much as their answers. They were alarmed. Archie was definitely hiding something, and Peter and Mary were almost certainly worried about what it might be. If she could get either of them alone she might learn something, but not while Archie was in the house listening.

Frustrated she turned again to Peter.

'Did you talk to anyone else in the Coach and Horses?'

'Not really, said hello to a couple of blokes I knew. I'd have sat at the bar on my own, but with Sarah we usually take a table.'

'Who else was there?'

Peter shrugged. 'Tommy Gallagher, behind the bar, a few young lads drinking at the bar, a young couple in the corner, Ted Blake and Wally Simms playing dominoes, about three young blokes playing darts.'

'Anybody listening to what you were saying?'

'Not as I noticed, but they could have.'

Judy frowned, and knew she was getting nowhere. She looked up at the ceiling and wondered what that bad-tempered, worried old man knew, and what he was thinking.

* * *

Archie Jessup was in fact listening. He had stopped on the landing where he could still faintly hear their voices coming up from the kitchen. He knew that when he banged the door it would never shut properly. The catch was worn with age and always slipped out again.

He strained his ears, ready to storm down again and intervene if Peter or Mary seemed about to say too much. He was silently cursing the policewoman, she was tormenting him in his own house and because she was from the police he couldn't even throw her out. He was tense and furious, his big blotched hand crushing the top of the stair rail. Mary knew nothing, and Peter knew enough to keep his mouth shut. He kept telling himself that and hoped that it was true.

Finally he heard the policewoman leave

and slowly he relaxed. He shuffled into his bedroom and watched her get into her car. The dogs were yapping at her again but keeping their distance. Good dogs, he thought fondly. She looked up once at his bedroom window before she ducked her head inside the car. She couldn't see him but she knew he was watching. She seemed to sense things even when she was being told nothing, and that disturbed him.

When the car had driven out of the yard Archie's attention wandered. He moved closer to the window and stared out toward the old airfield. He could see across to the Old Bracken field where the skeleton had been uncovered, and beyond that to a glimpse of the old runway where he had often spied Alice walking on her lonely night vigils. He had seen her stop often and gaze up at the empty eastern sky.

His anger had died and he felt a moment of grief and guilt, and a single salt tear trickled out from the corner of his painfully squinting eye. It ran down his grizzled face and into the short black stubble on his unshaven cheek. It was the first tear he had cried in fifty years, and he didn't know if it was for poor dead Alice or for himself.

13

As she drove out of the farmyard Judy was mentally reviewing all that had been said, and wondering if she could or should have handled the interviews differently. For a moment she asked herself how Ron Harding would have handled it, but she had worked with Harding for so long that she already knew. By now Harding would have jumped to the firm conclusion that the ancient skeleton in its long lost grave could only be Joe Crowfoot, and that only Archie and Charlie Jessup had a motive for his murder. They had hated Alice's 'Red Nigger', and publicly vowed to 'get him.' Harding would have attacked hard on that basis, trying to force a confession.

And now they would be arguing in the car together as they drove away, Judy reflected with a wry smile. Most of the time Harding's gut instinct was right and his direct approach achieved results, but sometimes the details needed teasing out and refining, and very occasionally he was wrong. The question was would he be wrong on this particular investigation.

Judy wasn't sure. What would be Harding's gut instinct might well be right, but she didn't think that his hard cop approach would be delivering anything more than she had already uncovered. Archie Jessup, despite his age, was still another hard-headed old bull of a man, and he would have stayed tight-lipped and resolute.

Could Archie Jessup have killed his sister Alice? He was still strong and active enough, and Judy didn't doubt that he could get angry enough to give her a good shaking, but somehow that seemed too easy an answer. He had an alibi with Mary for the night of Alice's death, but Mary was timid and obviously frightened of her formidable father-in-law. Was she frightened enough to lie for him?

If not Archie then who else would have a motive for shaking Crazy Alice to death? Peter perhaps, to protect his father. Or perhaps Sarah, to protect the memory of her father Charlie. Probably there hadn't been any intention to kill the old lady, just a moment of warning or anger that had got too violent and gone wrong.

Judy revolved the options around in her mind and couldn't decide between them. She had talked twice to Sarah, but Sarah was a strong willed woman who was giving nothing away. Peter was the weaker character, despite his physical strength and bulk, and Mary was the weakest of them all. If she could get either of those two away from that farmhouse and the immediate threat and influence of the old man, then she might learn something.

Peter would be out in the fields later, there was still beet to be lifted, and the cleared fields needed ploughing. Judy decided that she would watch and wait for her opportunity. Mary also had to leave the farm at some time. Every woman had to go shopping, even if it was only to the local supermarket. Archie and Peter both drove Land Rovers, so the small blue car she had noticed parked in one of the open sheds had to be there for Mary to use. Again, if she was patient, she might be able to catch Mary away from the farm.

Judy smiled to herself as she realized that she wanted to solve this mystery in her own way, without Ron Harding. Perhaps that was not wholly professional, but she decided she could allow herself this small indulgence.

In the meantime she needed to make a phone call to set up her next interview, so she began looking for somewhere to stop. There were no lay-bys along this winding stretch of country road, but there were field gateways. She pulled into the next one and stopped the car. Almost immediately she noticed the man leaning on the five-barred gate. He had been staring out over the field and turned his head to look at her as her car came to a halt behind him.

The man was tall, wearing a smart fawn coloured overcoat. His hair was a thick wave of dark grey, neatly combed, and the face that glanced briefly in her direction was faintly handsome, even though he was past his prime. Something about him made her curious, his passing interest in the grave site could be just that, but he had looked startled, as though he would rather not have been caught in the act. There was a tension about him now, as though he were trying to decide whether to bluff it out or walk quickly away. Judy's intuition kicked into top gear and on impulse she got out of the car.

She walked over to the gate to join him and asked innocently: 'Is that where they found the body?'

'I think so.' The stranger refused to look at her. The distant white police tent over the grave site was still just visible from the road, but now he was pretending to look elsewhere, his gaze fixed on the clouds above the Old Brackendale airfield as though he might have been bird watching.

'It's all they can talk about in the village,' Judy said. 'They have lots of theories about who he might have been.'

'They're sure it was a man?' The stranger turned now to look directly at her, his interest caught. He had sharp, searching grey eyes.

Judy shrugged. 'The police say it was a male skeleton.'

'And who do they say it might have been?'

'The police or the village gossip?'

'All of them?'

'Well, the police are not committing themselves, at least not yet. The village gossip seems to think he could have been an airman, from one of the planes that crashed here during the war.'

'Oh.' The response was vague, restrained and unsatisfied. He turned his face away again and looked down the fields.

'Who do you think it might be?' Judy asked softly but directly.

His shoulders seemed to stiffen beneath the fawn coat, as though bracing himself against the cold, or perhaps he was just uncomfortable.

'I don't know.' His voice was carefully controlled, 'Why should I know.'

'I don't know either,' Judy smiled, 'I don't even know who I'm talking to.'

He turned to look at her and seemed to fight an inner battle, he obviously wanted to escape from her, but convention and the reluctance to be impolite finally won. 'My name is Rupert Drake,' he said at last.

The name rang a tiny bell, she had heard it before but she couldn't quite remember where.

'Mine is Judy Kane,' she completed the exchange and asked, 'Are you local?'

'Sort of, I used to live around here.'

'And now?'

'Just visiting.'

'Your name seems somehow familiar.'

He smiled, responding to recognition. 'I have played the Granchester Theatre Royal a couple of times, not quite top billing, but my name was on the programme.'

'Of course, Rupert Drake the actor, you've done some TV as well, The Midnight Murders?'

'Yes, I was in that, but I prefer the live theatre. A real audience gives you a feedback, the warmth of applause and appreciation that you just can't get from cameramen and technicians.'

'I'm sure.' Judy wished that she had

actually seen him on stage but at least the ice was broken, a compliment to relax him even more and then she could quiz him gently. She tried to remember some more about Midnight Murders, but that particular crime series had finished at least a year ago. Then abruptly her mobile phone began bleeping.

Judy frowned at the interruption, tempted to ignore it. The beep tone was insistent and she dug it out of her pocket. Her thumb hesitated over the off button but then she lifted it to her ear and switched it on.

'Judy,' it was Ben's voice, angry and distressed and commanding her immediate attention. 'Sorry to call you if you're working, hope I haven't interrupted anything.'

'Well, nothing important,' she hoped. 'She moved back toward the car, giving herself some space and privacy. 'Ben what's wrong?'

He gave a short, strained laugh. 'You can read me like a book, can't you? It's this bloody letter,' she heard paper rustling as though he was screwing up the offensive correspondence in his fist.

'What's it about, Ben?'

'It's a letter from a bloody solicitor.' Two 'bloodies' in two breaths when he was speaking to her meant that Ben was savagely angry, and she could picture him lying fuming in his hospital bed. 'Mr Harvey-bloody-Pettigrew of Pettigrew, Hardcastle and Crichton, don't they sound a right trio of toffee-heads? He's representing a Mister and Mrs Michael Peachey. Young Mickey Peachey was the driver who died, the young drunk who crashed his car into me when he was driving on the wrong side of the road. Now his parents are suing me for compensation.'

'It sounds hard to believe.' Judy felt angry too, but she tried to inject a note of calm into her voice.

'Isn't it just, they are not trying to push a case for dangerous driving, they know that there isn't one, just a compensation claim. They are arguing that because I was responding to a fire call then I must have been speeding so that must make me partly to blame. They are talking about a hundred thousand pounds being the absolute minimum of what their son's life was worth.'

'Don't have a heart attack,' Judy advised. 'You're a Fire Service officer and you were on Fire Service duty. Just pass the letter over to the Fire Brigade, or your union, and let them deal with it. Harvey-bloody-Pettigrew is probably just going through the motions to satisfy a client, he can't really expect to get anything out of this. The police report has already cleared you.'

There was a long sigh from the other end. 'I know, Judy, I guess I had worked it out for myself. I just needed to blow off some steam and hear someone else say it.'

Judy smiled, 'And I was the easy target?'

'Of course, you still love me, don't you?'

'Of course I love you. One day I might even think of a reason why.'

He laughed. The tension in him was released. 'I love you too.'

'I'll come straight over and see you.'

A pause. 'It's okay. I'm okay. It's not

visiting hours. Just come and see me tonight.'

'That's a promise, if you can leave the nurses alone until I get there.'

'That's a promise.' She could picture his grin. 'See you later, sweetheart.'

She switched off the phone and put it back into her pocket. For a moment her mind stayed on Ben, and then she remembered Rupert Drake. She looked back at the five bar gate but the actor had gone. A Public Footpath sign over the stile beside the gate pointed down the edge of the field and she saw a last glimpse of the tall figure in the fawn overcoat climbing over another stile at the bottom of the field.

He was too far away to give chase, and after pondering briefly over their encounter she at last turned and climbed back into her car.

* * *

She used the mobile phone to make her planned call and with a few minutes the switchboard at the Granchester Sugar

Factory had put her through to Jim Collins. The Operations Manager was in his office, he didn't usually make immediate appointments, but in her case he was willing to make an exception. She told him she would be there in fifteen minutes. The four giant towers of the sugar beet silos were visible on the skyline, framed by the vast clouds of grey smoke and steam which showed that the factory was fully operational. She put the car in gear and headed towards them.

Ten minutes later she was at the factory gates. The guard on duty was a white-haired man with a friendly salute. He had been warned of her arrival and raised the pole barrier to let her in. From behind his glass walled cubicle he pointed her towards the visitor's car park.

Judy parked her car and walked to the reception office. Jim Collins was there to meet her, this time wearing a sober grey business suit instead of his hard hat and overalls. However, the ginger hair, beard and eyebrows made him unmistakeable. He smiled a welcome, shook hands and led her down a short, grey-panelled corridor to his own office which was only slightly smaller than reception. He waved her into a chair and took his place behind the desk.

'So how is the investigation going?' He asked cheerfully. 'What have the police discovered so far?'

'We've found the rest of the skeleton,' Judy knew that was public knowledge so she was giving nothing away. 'It was buried in a field beside the Old Brackendale airfield. Our forensic team are still peering at bits of it under their microscopes, but we know it's around fifty years old.'

'Wartime stuff, that was always most likely. We do get the odd relics from these fields, bits of shrapnel, bullet casings, that sort of thing. The skull was a new one, but almost anything can show up in a load of sugar beet. A live hand grenade turned up in one load a few years back, we had the bomb squad here. So, why are you still interested?'

'We still have to try and identify the body.'

'Nothing useful turned up with the

bones, no army boots or a flying helmet with goggles?'

'Nothing at all,' Judy wasn't yet going to mention the silver belt buckle, but she suddenly realized that Collins had raised a valid point. If the skeleton had been that of a stray airman then there probably should have been something imperishable like old boots or a flying helmet somewhere in the vicinity. The area had been thoroughly searched and nothing had turned up.

Collins took off his rimless glasses and absently gave them a polish with a large white handkerchief. 'So how can I help you?' he asked.

'We're looking at people who are known to have gone missing at around that time,' Judy told him. 'One of them worked here. He was Irish, one of the casual workers who used to arrive for the campaign season.'

Collins shrugged. 'In the old days there would be about five hundred extra workers taken on for the campaign. The job was labour intensive in those days, before the age of computers. Some of them would show up every year, others would come and go, it was a very fluid workforce.'

'This one was named Danny Farrel. According to one of the stories I've been told he disappeared after stealing some money from this factory.'

Collins looked thoughtful. He studied his glasses, was satisfied and put them back on. He tucked the handkerchief away in his desk. 'It was before my time, but there might be something, let's have a look.'

He got up from the desk and went to the shelves behind him that were stacked with document files and folders and a selection of books with a range of business and better management titles. He found the book he was looking for and brought it back to his desk, showing her the title.

'The Sweet Smell of Success, it's the history of sugar production here at Granchester. It was written by one of our retired managers about ten years ago, so it's not exactly up to date, but it covers the war years.' He thumbed through the pages, briefly scanning the chapter headings and then moving on.

'There was a robbery, during the 1944 processing season. The wages went missing. The average pay was about four pounds a week, multiply that by five hundred and you get two thousand pounds, quite a lot of money in those days. The cash was collected from the bank in Granchester every Thursday morning. We had a Chief Accountant and two clerks who were responsible for making the money up into individual pay packets. The job took them all day and then the pay packets were locked into a safe and kept overnight. Friday was pay day and the next day they would be distributed round the factory.'

Collins paused to read some of the book, and then continued. 'One Thursday night the whole lot disappeared. Someone broke into the accounts office and opened the safe. Daniel Farrel failed to turn up for work the next day and was never seen again. He became what I think you would call the prime suspect.'

Judy nodded. 'That confirms the story I've heard.'

'There's a bit more here. It seems the youngest clerk was a lad named Graham Austin. Farrel had made a pal of Austin and the two of them had got into the habit of doing some heavy drinking together. Austin admitted later to the police that there were a couple of times when he might have been drunk enough to give Farrel the combination of the safe. The boy just didn't know, but the safe had not been forced so whoever opened it had the combination numbers. Austin was sacked of course, but no charges were made.'

'With no trace of Farrel or the money that would have been difficult,' Judy said.

Collins nodded. 'They tried to find Farrel. Police enquiries were made here and in Ireland. They found his family somewhere in County Mayo, but they all went silent. The travellers are a close knit community. They don't grass each other up. So no one was talking.'

Collins closed the book and passed it over the desk. 'You can borrow this if you like. There are only a couple of pages on the robbery. Most of it is the history of the British Sugar industry in general, and this factory in particular. Granchester started up in the 1920s and managed to keep production going through two world wars. We took a couple of bomb hits during World War Two, but damage was minimal. Some of our brick buildings are original, but everything else has changed and evolved over time. It's a totally different operation now. It's quite an interesting read.'

'Thank you,' Judy accepted the book. If nothing else returning it would give her another excuse to come back and talk to him.

They exchanged a few more pleasantries before Judy got up to leave. Collins walked her back to reception and shook hands again. She got into her car, tossed The Sweet Smell of Success on to the front passenger seat and drove back to the barrier. A lorry blocked the exit road. Its driver was leaning out of the cab window with a road map in his hand, talking to the white haired gate guard who was pointing and gesturing right and left, obviously giving directions.

Judy waited patiently until the lorry drove away. The gate guard walked toward her, scratching his head, shrugging and smiling. Judy wound her window down and waited.

'Sorry to hold you up, Miss. He's one of the new lads, not sure of the quickest way to get to our factory in Norfolk.'

'It's no problem.' She returned the smile and then her hand hesitated on the gear stick. The white hair and the lined forehead suggested a man on the brink of retirement if not officially past it. There was a name tape on his company issue tunic.

'Jack Walton,' she read. 'Have you worked here long, Jack?'

'Man and boy,' Walton said cheerfully. 'I started out making tea and sweeping the factory floor.'

'Were you here during the war years?'

'Just the tail end, I left school and started work in 1945.'

Judy felt thwarted. It was just one year too late. However, she went through the motions and asked. 'Do you remember the robbery, when the wages were stolen?'

'Not really, although I did hear some talk about it. The man you should ask is probably Jim Collins.'

Judy shrugged. 'I already have.'

'Then you probably know all there is to know. Jim's old dad was the night watchman in those days.'

'Was he now,' Judy said softly. She thanked Walton and as she drove away she wondered why the helpful Jim Collins had not bothered to mention that last simple fact.

14

Judy was close enough to home to call in at the cottage and grab a late sandwich lunch. She ate at the kitchen table with a large mug of coffee and browsed through the history of the Granchester Sugar factory. The chapter covering the war years was a long one, mostly about the blackout and the problems of trying to run a twenty-four hour production operation with minimum lighting, and the wages robbery was worth only a couple of pages. The short summary that Jim Collins had given her virtually covered it all. The police investigation at the time seemed to have had very little steam and had soon died away. She guessed that manpower and resources would have been short in those days, the focus would have been elsewhere. Danny Farrel and the money had all vanished and left no clues, and that was all there was to it.

There was no mention of the night

watchman at the time. The wages office and the safe had been broken into at night and any night watchman should have been questioned. Probably he had been questioned, but nothing had come of it.

She closed the book and pushed it away, concentrating on the coffee and wondering if she was allowing herself to be side-tracked. Collins had remarked that if the skeleton had belonged to an airman who had wandered away from a plane crash then there should have been some traces of the man's flying kit. Now she reminded herself that there had been one item discovered at the grave site, the silver belt buckle with the distinctive buffalo horns. Joe Crowfoot had worn that belt in the photograph that had disappeared from Alice Jessup's dressing table. If she were working with Harding he would be telling her not to forget that.

She finished her coffee and wondered what she should do next. She wanted to talk again with Tommy Gallagher, and she had the feeling that it might be useful to talk some more with the three old church ladies who had known Alice. She really should show her face at the police station and catch up with her paperwork, and most of all she wanted to go and see Ben.

It was three o'clock and she could catch the afternoon visiting hours, but she had more or less promised Grant that she could cope with running this case, and that she would keep hospital visits to the evenings. Reluctantly she decided that she would go back to the office, it would help to bat some of her ideas around with anyone who was available, and part of her also wanted to catch up with the latest on Longship.

She went out to her car and pulled out on to the main road. A right turn was her most direct route back to the town and the police station. A left turn would take her out to the by-pass, and then a long loop back into the town again. It would take her another ten minutes but it would also take her past Blackberry Farm and she was still looking for an opportunity to catch Peter or Mary away from Archie. She might be lucky and spot Peter in the fields, or, if the little blue saloon car was not still parked in the Jessup farmyard, she could make an unscheduled stop to do some of her own shopping at the supermarket.

She made her decision and turned left. She drove slowly and when she passed the farm she gave herself plenty of time for a visual check. To her mild annoyance the blue car was still parked in the open barn, so no luck there. She drove on, still in low gear.

She passed the gateway where she had encountered Rupert Drake earlier in the morning, wondering again whether the actor might somehow be involved in her mystery. He had certainly seemed unsettled at having to explain himself to her.

Suddenly she braked the car and pulled to a stop. There had been something different about the view from the gateway, something she should have noticed. She looked over her shoulder, the road was empty of traffic and she reversed her car back into the gateway.

It was obvious now that the white SOC tent that had been set up on the second field down had been removed. The late autumn days were short and the light was failing but there was no hint of pale relief where the tent had been. Roper and his team had gleaned all that there was and packed up.

Then she became aware of something else, almost invisible in the gathering gloom she could just make out the shape of a tractor down by the far hedge. A figure moved down there, shifting away from the grave site and vanishing behind the blurred shape of the tractor.

Judy's heart skipped a beat as she realized that she probably was in luck. The tractor had to belong to Peter Jessup, and the man down there with it was most probably Peter himself. She guessed that Roper must have given him the okay to carry on and plough his field. By now he would be packing up for the day, but if she moved quickly she might catch him.

She got out of the car and locked it before climbing over the stile beside the gate, which was secured with a large padlock. Briskly she set off down the edge of the field. She was in the thick shadow of the hedgerow and for a moment she wished she had stopped to find the torch she usually kept in the glove compartment. However she didn't want to waste any time and risk losing her quarry.

The sun was already low on the western horizon as she left the car, a dull red blur below the edge of a gathering of heavy rain clouds that threatened a soaking for the end of the day. By the time she passed through the wide gap in the hedgerow into the second field it had dropped out of sight, the last flush of redness faded and the dark shadows seemed to rush very quickly over the land.

Judy left the footpath on the edge of the field and headed directly for the tractor on the far side. It was a large, modern vehicle with a high enclosed cab, painted bright green with bright yellow wheels inside the huge black rubber tyres. The colours were hard to distinguish now but she had picked them out in the seconds before the light had failed and she had left the car. She was sure that it was Peter Jessup's tractor, but now there was no sign of Peter, and she began to fear that she had already missed him. He had probably passed through the far hedge and would now be walking back to the farmhouse. She swore with frustration and began to hurry her pace. Large drops of rain began to spatter over her as the clouds decided to open up.

She was in the middle of the field, still twenty yards from the tractor, when suddenly the powerful engine started and the vehicle roared into life. Judy stopped short, startled and almost stumbling over the rough ground. She realized with a sense of shock that whoever the mystery figure might be, he or she had not simply disappeared but was inside the cab. Now that she knew where to look she could just make out the blurred human shape behind the glass of the cab walls. Then the spotlight that was fixed above the cab was switched on and the sudden beam of light blinded her. She twisted her head away and brought up a hand to protect her eyes.

She heard the engine note change as the tractor was slammed into gear and although she could no longer see she knew instinctively what was happening. The tractor had lurched forward and was charging straight at her. She turned and ran but the uneven surface tripped her, the field had not yet been ploughed but it had been torn up and left rutted and broken when the sugar beet crop had been lifted.

Judy went down on her knees, heard the thunderous roar of the tractor rushing closer and desperately scrambled up again. It was right on top of her and she remembered that these smart, modern tractors had a road speed of up to thirty miles an hour. Even if she did not break an ankle in the next few seconds it was unlikely that she could outrun it.

She blundered forward, the single bright beam of light was now throwing her own shadow ahead of her and she realized that her shadow was rapidly growing longer and stretching further ahead. The tractor was gaining and the noise behind her was deafening.

She knew the tractor was going to run her into the ground and desperately she threw herself to the left in a wheeling dive. Instinctively she had plunged her arms forward as she hit the earth heavily on her left side and she rolled herself over and over to continue her momentum. The front wheel of the tractor kicked her shoulder, helping her on her way. The back wheel was much larger, higher and wider, and the herring bone ribs of hard black rubber spun down on her. She squirmed another half roll forward and the tractor was crashing past, spewing clods of hard mud and dirt into her face.

Then she saw that the tractor was towing a plough, a battery of six massive steel blades that were just skimming the earth. They were six terrible harpoon barbs, glinting silver in the first starlight, and the outside one was going to spear her in the stomach. Judy screamed and managed a last clawing scramble to get herself out of the way. The plough blade sliced past her and missed her by less than an inch, tearing a swift rip in the corner of her jacket.

Judy lay gasping and sobbing, almost as much with anger as with terror and fear.

The stupid bastard had tried to kill her. He had deliberately tried to kill her. The rain was starting to hammer down, turning the dirt tangled in her hair and smeared across her temples into mud. She wiped it away, blinking to clear her vision. Her shoulder hurt and the pain and shock glued her to the spot.

She stared after the tractor, saw the single spotlight beam swing in a wide circle, and realized that he was coming back. He was coming after her again.

She pushed herself to her feet, ignoring the cruel stab of pain in her shoulder. She was still in danger and she looked around for somewhere to run. She was in the middle of the field with all of the surrounding hedgerows a seemingly equal distance away, all of them too far. The rain slashed down and plastered her hair to her face as she stood there trembling in the mud. The tractor completed its tight turn and the spotlight licked toward her. She heard the increased roar as the driver accelerated the engine again and raced to find her. Almost immediately she was back in that hunting beam of light, pin-pointed like a scared rabbit.

She turned and broke into another run, racing for the far edge of the field. There was a ditch there, and if she could scramble across the ditch and through the hedgerow she would be safe, but she knew that she would never make it. She was running faster this time, but not fast enough. Even the rain was working against her, driving into her face and making the earth treacherous and slippery under her feet.

She heard the maximum roar of the engine in her ears as the tractor loomed over her and felt her right foot come down and start to skid in the mud. He would be expecting her to dive and roll this time and so she had an only even chance of getting away with it. With her right foot already losing its grip she didn't even have a choice of left or right. She pushed hard off her left foot as she again twisted and dived wildly in the same direction.

The driver swerved to stay on top of her, but now the rain and the wet earth acted in her favour. As her body slapped down she skidded off to the side and again the lumbering wheels of the tractor reared high over her head and drove mud and spray into her face as they passed.

He was still pulling hard left to follow her and for the second time Judy saw the fearsome plough blades angling toward her. The tightness of the turn dipped the nearest blade so that it sliced into the earth. She felt it travel underneath her, just inches below the topsoil and acting like an almighty kick in the buttock. Again she could not control a scream, and this time the pain and fear was swamping her anger.

As quickly as she could she scrambled back to her feet, panic and the knowledge that he would try again spurring her into movement. This time she did not stop to look back for the tractor but immediately began to run again, back up the field where she had already run before. She was limping now, her hip hurt and she was almost breathless. She was soaked by the rain and she knew she was hardly capable of thinking straight. When she slipped and fell flat on her face, she could barely roll over and sit up. Helplessly she looked back for her nemesis.

The tractor was making another tight turn at the bottom of the field, the spotlight scything through the dark streaks of rain. The beam was looking for her again, but she was on the outer edge of its range. The tractor roared like a hungry beast as it plunged in her direction, and she knew that within seconds the light would find her.

She made a Herculean effort to stand up, swaying like a broken reed in the wind. The driving strength of the rain was almost enough to knock her over, and she knew that this time she was finished. Her chest was heaving but she could not get enough air into her lungs. Her whole body was oxygen starved and her legs were ready to collapse.

She stared at the oncoming tractor and bit her lip, tasting her own blood. The light found her and the tractor accelerated again. In the same moment it seemed to founder in the sea of mud. The front wheel dropped and it tilted over to the left, hanging at a crazy angle for a moment longer, and then tipping completely sideways with a crash. It lay there, cab down in the dirt, with the engine still roaring and the huge wheels still spinning, spraying up fountains of black mud.

Judy sucked in enough air to breathe again and slowly began to back away. Her head was dizzy and she had yet to work out what had happened, but she knew that it was still possible that the driver was in better shape than she was, and he or she might not easily give up the firm intention to kill her.

The spotlight on the tractor went out, causing her heart to jump again. Then the engine noise stopped and she wondered whether it had stalled or whether it had been switched off. The rain and the darkness surrounded her and she found it prudent to keep backing away.

When she reached the edge of the field she stopped. There was a ditch and now she could hide in it, or in the hedgerow that ran behind. She was already wet to the skin and filthy with plastered mud, so to crawl into the ditch would hardly make matters worse. Except to her dignity and suddenly she was damned if she was going to crawl into the ditch and hide.

She stood and waited, listening and staring into the rain and the darkness. Finally she took her police radio from her pocket and called for some back-up.

★　★　★

When Harding and two car loads of burly constables finally found her she had plucked up the courage to walk back to the over-turned tractor. She saw immediately what had happened. When her would-be-killer had made his last tight turn he had crashed into the still open grave pit where Roper and his team had excavated the skeleton. She had looked inside the cab, but one of the glass windows was broken and there was no one there. Whoever it was had survived with the ability to walk away and had vanished into the darkness.

She heard shouts and voices from the direction of the road and the gateway where she had left her car, and then she saw the fast-moving flashlights of her colleagues as they hurried towards her. She shouted back to guide them, relieved and feeling faintly sick in her stomach. She had the sick feeling under control when Harding reached her.

'What happened, Jude?'

Harding was breathless and hatless, his suit was soaked and the rain was running down his face. The bobbing flashlights converged and the constables materialized out of the pouring rain behind him. The rain dripped off the peaks of their caps and ran in rivulets down their raincoats. They were all grim faced and angry.

Judy took some comfort from the fact that they all looked like drowned rats, even though she had to be the worst mess of them all. She drew a deep breath and answered the question.

They all listened without interruption. When she had finished Harding said slowly: 'The man you saw before you left your car, are you sure it was Peter Jessup?'

Judy sighed. 'Right now I'm not even sure that it was a man. It was just a movement. The daylight was almost gone, but somebody moved across the bottom edge of this field, right where we're standing now. The tractor was parked just over there,' she pointed toward the dark blur of the bottom hedge, now visible only as a more dense line of blackness through the rain. 'I jumped to the conclusion that this must be Peter Jessup's tractor, and so it would most probably be Peter who was down here with it. Now I'm not so sure.'

'Why the doubt, if it is his tractor then he would know best how to drive it and he would have the keys.'

'It's also his field,' Judy pointed out. 'I've had time to think about it while I've been waiting for you, and it seems that there is no reason why he shouldn't be down here with his tractor. So what would be his motive for trying to kill me?'

Harding saw what she was getting at. 'You think maybe you surprised somebody who didn't want you to know that he was interested in the grave site.'

Judy nodded. 'It's beginning to add up that way. When I pulled up I saw somebody move quickly, which now does suggest that that somebody did not want to be seen. He, or she, ducked out of sight behind the tractor. I switched off my headlights before I got out of the car, so maybe whoever it was didn't see me get out of the car and climb over the style. It was already dark under the shadow of the hedgerow as I walked down the length of the first field, but I think there was just enough light for me to be seen again as I came into the middle of this field and started heading directly toward the tractor.'

'So then whoever was playing games down here realized that it was too late to get away from you,' Harding said thoughtfully. 'Maybe the bastard pan-icked, or maybe it was cold-blooded, but that's when whoever decided to run you down.'

Judy nodded again. 'That's how it is beginning to look to me.'

'A little bit back you said he or she, so what makes you think it could have been a woman?'

Judy shrugged, and winced as the

movement hurt her shoulder. 'Sarah Jessup is a woman,' she explained, 'but she's a tough and very capable woman, she runs her own farm and would certainly know how to drive a tractor.'

'So there's a wider ring of suspects,' Harding scowled. 'But none of this really lets Peter Jessup right off the hook. For my money he's got to be still in there with them.' He had noticed her flinch and remembered what she had gone through. 'That was a bad experience, are you sure you're alright?'

'I took a couple of knocks and I ache all over,' Judy said ruefully. 'But nothing hurts bad enough to be broken. I know I look all bedraggled like something the cat dragged in, so I'm not at my glamorous best.'

'You'll do for us,' Harding grinned and there were smiles all round. He put a hand on her arm. 'Come on, Jude, let's get you back to the nick, checked over, dried out and cleaned up. We can't do anything out here in this bloody weather. We'll get Roper and his team out here as soon as it's daylight, just in case there are any clues.'

They began to walk back up the fields to the gateway where the cars were parked, trudging in silence through the rain and the mud. When they arrived Harding insisted that she get into his car while one of the constables drove her car back to the police station. Judy protested, but then gave way. She had to admit that right now she didn't feel like driving. The walk though the clinging mud had aggravated her hip and left her limping.

'I'm sorry, Judy,' Harding said when they were alone. 'We're over-stretched and we've all got a full plate, but you should not have been left to go solo. Its bad practise but I just didn't expect you to run into any real problems with a fifty year old skull. I'll check with Grant, but from tomorrow we'll assign Tony Marsh to work with you. After this little episode there'll be no more of the Lone Ranger stuff.'

Judy nodded acknowledgement and didn't know whether to be glad or sorry.

15

The following morning Judy was back in the Old Brackendale field where a buzz of police activity now surrounded the over-turned tractor. The previous evening she had been whisked home for a quick shower and a change of clothes, and then a visit to the Accident and Emergency Department at Granchester General. Nothing was broken but she was now sporting some livid bruises on her left shoulder and right buttock. With Harding as chaperone she then had no choice but to return to police HQ for a more intensive debrief. She had managed to catch the last thirty minutes of visiting hours with Ben, and had finally eaten a late supper with Richard and Carol before going home to bed. At the end of it all she had felt emotionally humbled by the fierce concern and anger of all those who loved her. Even Harding, under his tough cop exterior, had been almost as furious as Ben. If either of them could have got their hands on whoever had driven the tractor, then she was pretty sure that that person would have had good cause to regret it.

The morning had started with more hard cutting questions and apologies. Grant had been absent the previous afternoon and evening, tied up in Cambridgeshire with Dave Pullen and Operation Longship, but at eight thirty he was back at his desk. Like Harding she could sense a tightly controlled anger within him. He was a man who took the care of his junior officers as seriously as the maintenance of justice and the solving of crimes, and he was equally adamant that from now on she must have a partner.

She was relieved to be out of the police station and back on the job, even though she now had Tony Marsh sticking solidly beside her. The skies had cleared after the heavy rain the previous evening, and the day was bright and sunny, although there was still plenty of slick mud underfoot.

The SOC team in their white overalls

were like a small flock of sheep as they crawled around the hedgerow which ran about twenty feet back from the bright green tractor which was tipped with two of its yellow centred, black rubber wheels in the air. The nearside wheels were down in the shallow grave and the six bladed plough was jammed up tight against the rear of the tractor on the edge of the pit. The sunlight gleamed off the slanted plough blades and Judy shuddered as she remembered how close they had come to carving her up in the mud.

Jason Roper stood on her other side and pointed out the smear of blood on the jagged spike of broken glass where the cab window had shattered as the tractor had rolled.

'Our villain must have cut himself as he was thrown against the window when the whole thing tipped over,' Roper said with satisfaction. 'So we've got a sample of his blood and his DNA. I doubt if we'll be lucky enough to have a match on our computer files, but as soon as you pin-point a suspect we'll be able to nail him.'

Marsh smiled wryly. 'So all we have to do is find him, and you already have the proof.'

'That's about the size of it.'

'Anything else,' Judy asked.

Roper pointed to where three of his team were congregated. 'We're pretty sure he smashed that gap through the hedge. It's a bit thin there and he appears to have bull-dozed his own path. The lads are looking for anything he may have left behind, a few fibres from his clothes or a drop more blood on the brambles. Just going through the motions really, because the blood sample from the tractor will be all we'll need.'

'He must have been shaken up after the tractor crashed,' Marsh observed. 'Perhaps he was stunned for a minute or two. He lost sight of you in the rain and the darkness and he probably guessed that you'd be calling for back-up. So he scarpered.'

Judy nodded, the reconstruction fitted with her own. She looked at Roper. 'Did you find the keys, or any sign that it had been hot-wired.'

Roper shrugged. 'Nothing, when we're ready to move the tractor we'll have a good look to see if anything's dropped in the pit. We're also looking for them along the hedgerow, in case he threw them away. If we can find them and get a last fingerprint we'll nail him twice.'

'Or her,' Judy said softly. She was not yet ruling anyone out.

There was a movement at the corner of the field and Peter and Archie Jessup appeared from the direction of the Blackberry farmhouse. Peter quickened his pace when he saw them, striding ahead and leaving his father trailing behind with his stick.

'What the bloody hell,' Peter roared angrily. His face was already flushed and red. 'That's my bloody tractor, what's going on?'

Judy moved towards the oncoming farmers, with Marsh promptly falling into step beside her. She reflected that it had probably been impressed upon the young DC that he would be hung, drawn and quartered if he allowed her an inch out of his sight.

'Good morning, Peter,' she greeted him calmly. 'What's going on is that someone used your tractor last night to try and kill me. Whoever it was made two attempts to run me down before it turned over.'

'What?'

Peter Jessup looked as though he had run into a brick wall. He stopped in his tracks and stared at her. Judy looked back at him and noted his wide-eyed look of astonishment, and the fact that his face was clean of any cuts or scratches, there was not even a shaving nick. His arms hung loosely at his sides and she looked at the back of his massive hands but again there was nothing. He was wearing his padded, sleeveless jerkin over a clean check shirt that was open at the neck but buttoned at the wrists.

'Peter,' she said quietly, 'would you roll your sleeves up for me, please.'

'What? Why should I?'

'Because there's blood on the broken glass of the cab window, whoever was at the wheel must have left it there.'

Peter understood, he scowled and then angrily ripped at the cuffs of his shirt, popping off the buttons. He rolled both sleeves high up on his brawny arms and brandished them at her, almost shaking them in her face. There was no sticking plaster and no bramble scratches, just sun-reddened skin and thick black hair.

'Relax,' Marsh growled. 'There's no need to overdo it.' He was tall and spindly compared to the solid bulk of the scowling farmer and Judy had to suppress a smile.

'Thank you,' Judy said, cooling it down. 'Whoever drove your tractor must have had the keys, so I had to ask.'

Peter stared at the overturned vehicle as though still trying to take it all in. Archie came up behind him and also stood staring, as always the old man's face was stony and tight-lipped.

'Where are your keys?' Marsh demanded.

Peter turned to look at him. The flare of anger seemed to be replaced by bewilderment.

'Under the seat,' he said simply. 'I always leave them under the seat.'

There was a moment of disbelieving silence.

'I might lock it if it's near the road,' Peter offered defensively. 'But out here on the fields or on the farm I don't usually bother. I might not be the next one to use it. Dad likes to keep his hand in and plough a few furrows, so we always leave the keys under the seat. Dad walked three fields to a tractor once, and then found that he'd forgot the keys and left them hanging on the hook behind the kitchen door. Swore a bit about that, didn't you, Dad. Since then we usually just leave the keys with the vehicles. There's usually nobody interferes with anything away from the road.'

Archie was making solemn nods each time Peter mentioned his name. Marsh looked incredulous. Judy didn't know whether to believe them or not. If they had been lucky enough never to have anything vandalized or stolen then it might all be true. She looked around the field and noted that none of it had yet been ploughed.

'Which one of you brought the tractor up to the field last night?' She asked.

'I did,' Archie said shortly.

He offered nothing more so Peter filled in. 'Traffic gets heavy on the road first thing in the morning, all those people rushing to work, especially now with the sugar beet campaign under way. Mid afternoon road traffic is light so Dad brought the tractor here ready for me to make an early start this morning. We were going to come up together with the old tractor and a scoop bucket to fill in your hole. She's not so wide, easier to drive between the fields. Then I could get straight on with ploughing while Dad took the other tractor back.'

Marsh looked at his wristwatch. 'You call this an early start?'

'He was up all night,' Archie spoke up to defend his son. 'He was over at Appledown. Sarah called about midnight to say that one of her cows was having trouble dropping a calf. Our usual vet was out on another call. Peter went over to help.'

Peter nodded. 'The old cow took her time. One of the calf's legs had got twisted and stuck. By the time it was all done the cocks were crowing, so Sarah made us a mug of tea and fried up eggs and bacon. When I got back to Blackberry I noticed that you lot were all out here on Old Brackendale again, so me and Dad came over.'

There was another uncomfortable pause. Peter knew they were doubtful about the keys. Judy finally looked directly at Archie.

'What time did you leave the tractor here?'

'Just before dark, drove it along the road and then down into the fields. It was dark when I got back to the farmhouse.'

'Was that before or after the rain started?'

'The rain came down just as I got back to the farm. It was dark then.'

Judy frowned. If he was telling the truth then he had left the scene just before she had arrived. His face gave nothing away but there were no cuts or scratches on his grizzled old cheeks and none on his hands. The old grey canvas coat he wore covered his arms, but it seemed that he always wore the same coat and it would have protected him. One pocket was partly torn away, but it was a very old coat.

'Did you see anyone near here before you left?'

Archie shook his head.

Judy frowned. She could almost believe that this stubborn old man might have been bloody-minded enough to want to run her down with his tractor, just for disrupting his life, prying into his secrets and trespassing on his fields. Only one thing did not fit. Archie was sour and capable but he was slow, and the movement that had attracted her attention the previous evening had been quick. She didn't think that Archie could have been that nimble.

'So what were you doing out here on your own anyway?'

The belligerent question caught Judy by surprise. She wasn't prepared to be put on the defensive. Archie glowered at her and the look demanded a reply.

'I was passing,' she said slowly. 'I saw someone down here. I thought it might be Peter, and there were some more questions that I wanted to ask him.'

'What about?'

Peter's tone was not so aggressive. It registered his annoyance but was mostly curious.

'It hardly matters now.' Judy saw no gain in admitting that she had wanted to talk to him away from his father. She went on quickly, 'Where were you while Archie was bringing the tractor out here?'

Peter shrugged. 'Loading beet with the other tractor, I had to load up Sam Arnold's truck ready for first delivery this morning.'

Judy glanced in the direction of the hard pad where the sugar beet was piled ready for loading. It was two fields away, screened by a couple of hedgerows. She hadn't been aware of any activity there last night, but from here it was not visible. However, if Peter had been there and Sam Arnold had been there with his lorry then Peter had an alibi. It would be easy to check and she didn't think that Peter was stupid enough to lie, unless somehow Peter and Sam were in this together. Suddenly Judy felt the beginning of a headache.

On the Appledown side of the field a large black mastiff dog suddenly bounded into view. It stopped short and squatted, front paws down, head high up and staring, and Judy recognized Sarah Jessup's dog. A moment later Sarah appeared from the corner of the hedge, calling the dog sharply to heel. She strode toward them with the dog padding obediently behind her. She wore a long raincoat and canvas hat and carried her stick. She was looking at the over-turned tractor and her greeting echoed Peter.

'So what's all this about?'

'Someone tried to kill me last night.' Judy looked her directly in the eyes. 'Just as it got dark and the rain started. So where were you at that time?'

Sarah looked startled, and then affronted. She planted herself squarely in front of Judy, leaning slightly forward with both hands folded on top of her stick. 'I was bringing home the cows,' she said flatly. 'I let them graze through daylight, bring them home for milking as soon as the light goes. Soon it won't be worth taking them out at all. I feed them in the sheds through winter.'

Judy nodded. A thought struck her. 'You look pretty fresh for a lady who was up all night.'

Sarah grinned. 'I'm used to all that. Farming folk don't keep town hours.' She looked over to Peter. 'I spoke to the vet just now. He's going to come over later to check the new calf.' She returned her gaze to Judy. 'Then I saw that something was happening over here again, so I wandered over, just being nosey.'

Judy wondered if it was all too neat and convenient. Sarah had just confirmed Peter's story of being up all night with a cow in labour without being asked. Then she reminded herself that as far as she knew they did not need any kind of alibi for last night. The time in question was the late afternoon when she had been attacked. Her headache throbbed a little harder.

'Is that all?' Sarah asked bluntly.

Judy nodded. Sarah had taken offence, so now it had to be hit hard or back off. Judy couldn't think of another hard direct question so she backed off. Sarah walked past her to join her cousin and uncle and the three Jessups began discussing the problem of getting the over-turned tractor upright again. Roper moved closer to Judy, a look of enquiry on his face.

'Get fingerprints and blood samples from all three of them,' Judy said. She had already antagonized the whole family so she might as well get the job done. 'Tell them it's just for the process of elimination.'

Roper nodded. Judy turned away.

'Where to now,' Marsh asked, as he fell dutifully into step beside her.

'The nearest pub,' Judy answered. 'They should just be opening, and you can have the pleasure of buying me a large white wine.'

⋆   ⋆   ⋆

The pub Judy had in mind was The Coach and Horses, which was the next port of call on her list. By the time they arrived she was all professional again and settled for an orange juice. Marsh bought himself a half of bitter. Tommy Gallagher served them. For the moment he had no other customers so he had no escape.

'Stay and talk to us, Tommy,' Judy invited.

Gallagher leaned his elbows on the bar and propped his white-whiskered chin in his hand, his favourite gossiping stance. 'So what can I tell you, my darling — have you heard the tale about the bishop, the choir boy and the actress?'

'None of your naughty stories, Tommy, it's too early in the day. The last time I was in here you told me a story about the evacuee boys and the missing vicar.'

'Aye, I remember all of that.'

'So why didn't you tell me that Grace Wilkes still lives here in Brackendale, and that she still attends the church less than a hundred yards from here.'

The white eyebrows lifted and Gallagher rubbed a finger thoughtfully along the length of his nose. 'I suppose it must be because I didn't know that.'

'Tommy, you know everything.'

'I know almost everything about most of my customers,' Gallagher corrected her. 'And most of what happens here in the village. But as far as I know Grace Wilkes has never been inside the Coach and Horses, if I saw her in the village I probably wouldn't recognize her, and being the old sinner that I am I don't attend the church.'

They stared at each other. Gallagher's blue eyes were wide and innocent. After a minute he lifted his shoulders and then let them drop again in an expressive shrug.

'Alright,' Judy let it go. 'Think back to that night when Crazy Alice died. Peter and Sarah Jessup have claimed that they were in here earlier that evening. Can you confirm that?'

Gallagher stroked his beard between his fingers and thumb. He was concentrating and trying to cooperate. 'Yes, I believe they were. They only stayed for an hour or so, just the one drink. They didn't stand at the bar. They sat at that table just there.'

'Could you hear what they were talking about?'

'As far as I can remember they were talking mostly about Crazy Alice, and about the old skull. I wasn't taking much notice, but they were not keeping their voices down.'

'So anyone who was in here could have overheard them?'

Gallagher nodded.

'So tell me again, who was in here?'

'Just some of the local lads,' Gallagher recalled, 'Wally and Fred playing dominoes as usual, a few of the sugar factory workers at the end of their shift. Three of the gypsy lads from the traveller's camp were playing darts.'

Judy and Marsh exchanged glances.

'Name them,' Judy said.

'Robbie Farrel, his mate Sean, another one, didn't get his name.'

Robbie Farrel, and Alice had been in love with a Danny Farrel all those years ago. Judy felt her intuition kicking in, and with it frustration. Grant and Harding had the travellers in the frame for the ram raids and so she couldn't go there yet. Was it a coincidence or a connection? Either way, for now she would just have to put that question on hold.

Marsh was savouring his bitter. Gallagher was still thinking. Neither of them had noticed her interest.

Gallagher continued. 'Then there was Jim Collins, the manager up at the Sugar Beet Factory. He drops in most nights for a pint and a whisky chaser on his way home.'

Judy's invisible antennae picked up again, but Gallagher had not finished.

'And the stranger,' he said pensively. 'Now what did he say his name was? Duck? Drake? Rupert Drake — said he was an actor. Funny thing, his face seemed somehow familiar, although I'm not a theatre man and I don't think I've ever seen him on the telly. It was like somehow, I should have known him. Now he was interested in your old skull. He stood here with a gin and tonic in his hand but hardly touched it. I could swear his ears were wagging, like he was soaking up every word.'

16

Judy had waited all day to talk to Ben, eager to turn over the possibilities that her talk with Tommy Gallagher had generated. She had discussed them with Marsh, but her late arrival partner still had a lot of catching up to do and was still absorbing information. Ben was more familiar with the case and she was beginning to realize how much she was depending on his input. However, Ben had other things on his mind.

'Dave West came in to see me this afternoon,' he said as soon as she had kissed him and settled herself in the chair at his bedside. She knew Dave as one of his colleagues from the Fire Station and was vaguely aware that he was also the officers' representative for the Fire Brigade Trade Union. 'The Union has taken up my case and appointed a solicitor to see off Pettigrew Hardcastle and Chrichton, and the bloody Peacheys.'

'Well that's good news,' Judy was pleased to see him buoyant.

'It's a bit of a relief, Jude. I've had nothing else to do but to lie here and worry about it. Dave reckons that our side is confident that there isn't even a case to answer. The police investigation has already cleared me and we know that Mickey Peachey was drunk and driving on the wrong side of the road. Our man hasn't been in to see me yet, but he's got the police report and all the facts. He's sure that Harvey-bloody-Pettigrew will back down when he sees that we've got some real weight behind us and that he has a real fight on his hands. It's almost a foregone conclusion that he'll advise the Peacheys to drop the charge. It means that they can't rob us of my pension and our cottage and savings.'

'That is marvellous.' Judy leaned forward to give him another hug and a kiss and his arms were strong and reassuring around her. She suddenly realized that she too had been secretly worrying about the possible horrendous cost of this overhanging court case. She had pushed the nagging fear into the back of her mind and tried to ignore it, but now, inside herself, she was weak with relief.

When she came up for air she had to push his arms away, smiling as she disentangled herself.

'Easy now,' she said breathlessly. 'There is a limit to how far we can go on a hospital ward.'

Ben grinned and restricted himself to squeezing her hand. He relaxed and closed his eyes for a moment, then looked up at her seriously.

'I've been doing a lot of thinking, Judy, there's not much else to do while I'm lying here waiting for you.'

Judy looked back at him warily, she knew him well enough to guess that this casual preamble had some heavy content.

'What have you been thinking about?'

'About us, the future, things in general.' He paused, watching her.

'Go on,' she prompted.

'Well, I suppose it soured me off, this compensation claim, and the whole sick compensation culture that goes with it. It seems that everybody is trying to screw everybody else, and the big law firms encourage it because they are making pots of money. I suppose some people do deserve their compensation money — I do feel sorry for the Peacheys and those three kids in the other car — but there is always someone else who has to pay, people like us who are just unlucky enough to have someone trip up on their path, or have a drunk driver crash into them out of nowhere.'

'But it's all on the way to being sorted now,' Judy reminded him patiently. 'We've got the union and a big law firm on our side now.'

'I know, but like I said, it soured me off. It's just one symptom of all that's wrong with this lousy country. We have the highest cost of living in the world, the highest taxes, everyone and his brother are always moaning, and for nine months of the year the weather's grey and miserable. Winter is almost on us again and we hardly seem to have had any summer. I think I've had enough.'

Judy nodded slowly. She was beginning

to see where this might be going.

Ben got to the point. 'You remember we were talking about retiring to Spain. Well, what I was thinking was why wait until retirement age. I'm finished with the Fire Service anyway.'

'We still don't know that for certain.'

'Yes, I know I'll walk again, it's only a matter of time, but I don't think I'll ever be quite the man I was, not A1 fit for an active career. I'll have my pension, if our lawyers can keep it safe from the Peacheys' lawyers, and we've paid off a fair bit of our cottage. We could invest in that little bar in Spain right now, and have the rest of our lives to enjoy it.'

His words were something of a bombshell and Judy was momentarily at a loss to respond. Ben gripped her hand tighter and gave full beam to his infectious grin.

'How about it, Judy, goodbye grey skies, hello blue, sand, sea and sangria for the rest of our lives.'

'It sounds good,' she said at last. 'But even if your career is over, and we can't be sure about that, mine definitely isn't.'

'I know,' Ben sobered. 'You're a good cop, Judy, a Detective Sergeant already and you could go a lot higher, Inspector at least, Superintendent maybe. You know how to read people, and you're good at wrinkling the truth out of situations. But is that really how you want to spend the rest of your life, investigating sordid little crimes and digging into other peoples' grubby little lives and secrets?'

'You're trying to make it sound worse than it is,' Judy accused him. 'I get a lot of job satisfaction from what I do. It's not all about catching the guilty ones. It's also about clearing the innocent, and giving the victims a chance to move on and rebuild their lives.'

'I'm sorry,' Ben squeezed her hand again, gently this time. 'I know you're not one of the hard and cynical kind.' His grin flashed. 'I guess I couldn't have married a female version of Ron Harding.'

'The mind boggles,' Judy said.

'God forbid it,' Ben added.

They both laughed.

'But seriously,' Ben pressed again while

her mood was lightened. 'We have talked about retiring to Spain when we've both earned our pensions. Well, now it looks as though I could be getting mine early. We may not have to wait. We could leave England, the Fire Service and the Police Force, sooner rather than later, give it all up for the good life on the Costa Brava.'

Judy thought about it. 'The sun, sea and sangria sound fine. But we'll still have to work, and I'm not so sure that I'm ready to exchange police work for a job behind a bar. Later in life, yes, when I have to give up my career anyway, but now is too soon.'

'It's not too soon for me,' Ben was disappointed. 'It's beginning to look like my best option, a healthy swim in the sea every morning, chatting to bikini-clad girls over our bar for the rest of the day.'

'The healthy swim in the sea I might allow,' Judy said severely.

Ben laughed. 'Alright, I won't be able to keep my eyes off the bikini-clad girls, but I promise to keep my hands only for you.'

'You'd better,' Judy leaned down and

kissed him. The idea of a lifestyle with plenty of sun bathing and warm sea swimming was suddenly tempting.

'Someone tried to kill you yesterday,' Ben reminded her. 'I don't want that to happen again.'

Judy had a quick mental flashback of herself standing in the mud of Archie Jessup's field in the appalling darkness and the pouring rain. The single light of the tractor blazing out at her as it tried to run her down, the deadly steel plough blades slicing towards her. Compared to that image the idea of sun, sea and sangria was definitely more enticing.

'I'll think about it,' she promised.

And Ben smiled.

★   ★   ★

That night her sleep was broken several times as she woke up with the nightmare of the tractor trying to run her down and Ben's dream of living in Spain all mixed up together in her head. The last time she awoke her alarm was ringing, and although she now felt ready for some deep sleep it was time to get up. As she showered her head cleared and she knew the bad experience of having someone trying to murder her would fade. However, Ben was right, something like it could happen again, and Spain would be a nice climate, and an easier lifestyle.

Easy, but boring, there was a buzz in police work that she knew she wouldn't get from pulling pints of Stella and mixing up jugs of red wine and orange juice. For her it wasn't the right move yet, but for Ben perhaps it was. She knew Ben wouldn't push it if she said a firm no, but she didn't want an unhappy Ben. This could put a strain on their relationship and she wasn't sure if it was worth it. So far their marriage had mostly been one of harmony and she liked it that way.

She dressed and grabbed a quick breakfast, coffee, fruit and cereal, and then drove into the police station to collect Marsh. From there on she tried to forget Ben and Spain and concentrate on the case in hand. She still wanted to know who had killed Alice, and now who had tried to kill her. She guessed that it was probably the same person.

'Roper took the fingerprints and blood samples you ordered,' Marsh greeted her. 'They clear all three of the Jessups. The blood sample on the broken window glass came from somebody else.'

'So we'll relay that to the Jessup family,' Judy decided. 'It gives us an excuse to re-visit one of them, and perhaps calm some ruffled feathers.'

'Which one?'

'Sarah Jessup.' Judy had no hesitation. 'She's the only one who is even remotely likely to be reasonable.'

Marsh didn't argue and they drove out to Appledown Farm in Judy's car. It was a grey morning, threatening rain. The leaves were thinning on the trees and soon there would be just the stark bare branches of winter. Not like sunny Spain. Judy pushed the intruding thought away.

As they approached the farmyard they passed a small herd of black and white Friesians in a field of pasture. Sarah's cows, Judy guessed. Sarah would probably be back at the farmhouse by now so the timing was probably right.

As they drove into the farmhouse Jess barked from inside the house. By the time they had got out of the car and walked up to the door Sarah had opened it and stood waiting for them.

'You've got a cheek,' she said sourly.

'It goes with the job,' Judy said. She tried a smile. 'Sarah, I know we've upset you and all your family, but we do still need your help.'

Sarah grimaced. 'They took all our blood and fingerprints.'

'It has helped,' Judy assured her. 'The blood on the broken window was not yours, or Peter's or Archie's. So now we can rule you all out. We had to be sure. I'm sorry.'

'You've upset them all you know. You'll never get a civil word out of Archie now.'

'I never did get a civil word out of Archie,' Judy admitted ruefully.

Sarah laughed. 'Well he is a grim old bugger, so I suppose nothing's changed.'

'Yet you like him,' Judy guessed.

'Two of a kind,' Sarah said. 'All of us Jessups are grim old buggers at times.'

Judy waited. Sarah seemed undecided.

She was blocking half the doorway, the dog squatted solidly beside her, completing the barrier.

'We still have to find out who killed your Aunt Alice,' Judy reminded her. 'You must want to help.'

Sarah relented, her round, work-lined face seemed to soften. She sighed and moved back into the house, pulling the dog away from the doorway.

'I suppose you had to do your job,' she conceded. 'And yes, I do want to know who frightened Aunt Alice.' She led the way into the kitchen and sat down at the table. Judy and Marsh sat facing her. The dog watched them dubiously and then decided to wander outside.

'Fire away then,' Sarah said. 'What else can I tell you that we haven't gone over before?'

'Think back to the night Aunt Alice died,' Judy said. 'She was alive when you left her cottage. You went to the Coach and Horses and had a drink with Peter. Try and remember every detail of what you and Peter talked about that night. I think that someone may have overheard something that may have led them to visit Alice.'

'We talked about Aunt Alice. We talked about you going up into her bedroom and making her cross. We talked about that old skull turning up at the sugar beet factory. We talked about your lot digging up Archie's field.' She sounded bored. 'We've done all this.'

'You talked about Joe Crowfoot,' Judy prompted.

'Yes we talked about Joe Crowfoot. We went over all of that old story.'

'What about the other one, the Wild One, the gypsy boy?'

Sarah nodded, for the first time she showed a flicker of interest, as though she was thinking back. 'We did talk about Gypsy Danny. Danny resented Joe, everybody knew that. So I guess Joe must have resented Danny. They were rivals for Aunt Alice's attention. And Archie and Charlie hated them both.'

She was looking straight at Judy now, her eyes thoughtful. 'Aunt Alice talked about that before I left her that night, and I passed it on to Peter. I think Aunt Alice thought that it might not be Joe in that field, that it might be Danny. After all, he disappeared too. Joe might have flown out on that last mission with the Kentucky Lady, but nobody ever had any idea of what might have happened to Danny, unless he ran off with the stolen money from the sugar factory.' She spread her hands helplessly. 'It's all a muddle, isn't it?'

'What do you think,' Judy pressed her. 'Do you think Archie and Charlie might have killed Joe or Danny?'

'My dad wouldn't,' Sarah was defensive. 'Uncle Archie did have a black temper though.' She pursed her lips in that disturbed Jessup expression. 'I think Aunt Alice thought they may have done.'

'And you discussed all of this with Peter that night in the Coach and Horses?

Sarah nodded.

'So think back to who else was there, was anyone taking any notice of what you were both saying?'

'Not that I noticed.'

'So tell me again who was there.'

Sarah shrugged. 'Ted Bates and Wally

Simms, but they were only interested in their dominoes.'

'Forget them. What about the three lads from the traveller's site?'

Sarah looked blank.

'The three who were playing darts, were you sitting near the dart board?'

'Near enough, I suppose. They could have overheard, but I didn't notice.'

'Jim Collins was at the bar, do you know him?'

'The manager from the factory. He said good evening as we came in, good night as we went out. That was all. He was up at the bar talking to Tommy.'

'Was he listening to you and Peter?'

Again she shrugged her shoulders. 'Not that I noticed, but he could have heard. I suppose anyone could have overheard. We had no reason to whisper.'

'There was a stranger at the bar, probably wearing a fawn overcoat. He said his name was Rupert Drake.'

'I remember the man in the overcoat, good looking sort of man, dark hair with just a bit of grey in it. He was up at the bar, beside Jim Collins. He had his back to us most of the time.'

They were both silent for a few moments. Judy had no more prompts to make and just waited. Finally Sarah said, 'If anyone was listening to me and Peter talking then it was probably old Tommy Gallagher himself. He talks a lot, but he doesn't miss much.'

★   ★   ★

'Did we learn anything from all that?' Marsh asked as they drove away, and Judy had to admit reluctantly that they hadn't.

★   ★   ★

The rest of the day was no more fruitful. Judy still had the idea in mind that there could be more to be learned from the three old ladies at the church, the twittering birds in the bright flowered dresses. However, on this occasion when she called at the church she found the door into the porch solidly locked with a large padlock.

'Vandals,' Marsh guessed. 'These days

the bad boys don't stop at nicking the lead on the church roof, they'll take anything that's not nailed down inside. The days when you could leave an unattended church wide open are long gone.'

Judy nodded and fished out her notebook. She had taken down the three names and addresses but after a tour of the village each one in turn drew a blank. At the third house they visited, the home of Muriel Abbot, a curious neighbour raised her head over the adjoining fence.

'Muriel's out,' she informed them. 'There's bingo twice a week in the old cinema in Granchester. Her friends called for her in a car about an hour ago. That's where they'll be.'

'Thank you, we'll call back another time,' Judy said.

She led the way back to the car. Marsh dutifully followed. Behind them the neighbour looked disappointed, she had obviously hoped for some gossip in return.

They returned to the police station, and took time for a sandwich and a cup of tea in the canteen. There was a report from Roper waiting on Judy's desk, but no new revelations from the SOC team. Peter Jessup had brought up another tractor with tow chains and a lifting bucket to haul his over-turned tractor and the plough out of the grave. Roper's team had then gone over the ground again, inch by inch, but with no results, and finally Peter had been given the okay to fill in the grave and get on with his ploughing.

Judy threw the report to Marsh who read it with the same weary resignation. There was nothing left for them to do except fill in the afternoon with the waiting piles of deskwork. Harding and Grant were again both out, tied up somewhere with their major concerns. Judy found herself troubled and restless. She was no nearer to doing anything other than guess at who might have killed Alice, and she kept thinking about Spain and Ben. Her paperwork was an unwanted chore. She was glad when it was time to pack it in and call it a day.

She said goodnight to Marsh and the

few officers who were left and went out to her car. She drove home with Ben on her mind, wondering if he would raise the question of Spain again, and how she would answer him. She didn't want to say an outright no, and she didn't want to say yes. She knew she would stall for more time and it made her uncomfortable.

Damn it, she loved Ben and she wanted him to be happy. She wanted both of them to be happy. Everything had been fine the way things were, with both of them forging ahead with their careers. Now it had all changed.

She reached the cottage and parked the car. It was a couple of hours after sunset and everything was in pitch darkness. It was one of those cloud covered nights with no moon and no stars. She had a torch in the dashboard but she was familiar with her own garden path and she didn't need it. She got out and locked the car, swapping the keys for her door key as she walked up to the small porch and her front door. The air smelled damp, the beginning of fog, or perhaps it was going to rain again.

She stopped at the door, inserted her key and pushed the door open. It was dark, silent and empty inside. No Ben. Ben was still lying in hospital. The thought tugged at her heart and saddened her. She reached for the light switch but her fingers never found it.

There was the sudden rush of movement behind her, two figures looming fast out of the night. She managed to half turn before a rock hard fist punched into the side of her head. Her brain was shaken, lights exploded inside her suddenly spinning head. She felt rough, powerful hands grab her arms from behind, wrenching them back into more pain as her shoulder blades touched.

Something dark dropped in front of her eyes and all vision was gone. She felt something coarse and scratchy against her face, a sack or a hood of some kind had been slipped over her head. She couldn't breathe.

She panicked, fought, tried to scream.

Then the blackness shut down completely.

17

There was pain in her head, a dull blinding ache that refused to let her open her eyes. There was pain in her arms which were somehow twisted up behind her back, and the sore fire of pain around her wrists. Her shoulder throbbed, in fact all the bruises and hurts she had suffered in her encounter with the tractor were throbbing again.

Judy groaned, fought the pain and forced open her eyes.

She was in a small room lying on her side on some sort of a couch. The light from an overhead bulb made her squint and she felt tears beginning to prickle. She blinked and told herself firmly that she must not cry.

The furniture was small with more cushioned seating around a central table, and fixed glass-fronted wall cupboards full of bric-a-brac, pictures of horses and dogs and people, some crystal glasses, small brass ornaments and a collection of horse brasses on black leather straps. There was a glimpse of a miniature kitchen beyond a dividing work top that was littered with beer cans and the remains of takeaway meals. Everything was fitted to make the maximum use of the available space and she realized that she was inside a large caravan, or a small mobile home.

'She's awake, Robbie.'

The hard voice pulled her attention to the two men who sat on the other side of the central table. The speaker was a thickset man who wore faded blue jeans and a black tee shirt. He had straw coloured hair and a day's growth of stubble on his chin. He was staring at her with cold, speculative blue eyes.

His companion had dark black hair, slicked back with some kind of hair oil. His lean face might have been handsome if he had smiled, but now his mouth was tight-lipped and humourless. He wore a black shirt with the collar open at the neck, and a fancy gold trimmed black waistcoat. The fan of cards in his hand, the beer cans, the remaining card deck and the piles of loose change on the table between them completed the image. He looked like a cheap gambler from some old black and white B movie.

'So she is, Sean,' he said softly. 'So she is.'

Judy searched her memory and put the names together with the names she knew. Sean and Robbie, Sean Ross and Robbie Farrel, the connection was easy. She groaned inwardly as she realized that despite all her care and caution she had definitely cocked up and compromised Operation Longship. Grant and Harding would not be pleased.

Robbie Farrel carefully placed his cards face down on the table. 'We'll finish this game later.' His tone made it more of an order than a request. 'There's still money in the kitty.'

Ross shrugged. He had a poor hand and had lost interest in the game now that the woman was awake. He leaned back in his seat to watch.

Farrel stood up and moved round the table to stand over Judy, staring down at her. He was tall, having to stoop a little to get his head under the light and its lace fringed lampshade. Judy judged them to be both in their early twenties. Farrel looked hard and muscular. Ross looked equally tough, more squat and solid but not running yet to fat.

'You know me,' Farrel said.

'I do now,' Judy answered. She was surprised to find that her mouth wasn't gagged.

'You knew me anyway,' Farrel said harshly. 'You saw my face through the windscreen of the tractor. I saw you staring at me.'

'So it was you.' Judy felt a tingle of horror that made it difficult to keep her voice calm. 'If it makes any difference I didn't know. You may have seen me clearly, but that damned spotlight was in my eyes. I was dazzled. All I could see was the outline of a face behind the glass and the blur of the windscreen wipers. Until now I didn't know who it was.'

'Damn it,' Ross roared. He slammed his fist down on the table and sent coins and cards scattering on to the floor. 'We didn't need to do this, Robbie. I said we didn't need to do it.'

'Shut it, Sean.' Farrel turned on him with a snarl. 'It doesn't matter now, it's done. She's been asking too many questions and it was only a matter of time before she came round here looking for me. I wasn't going to just sit here and wait to see if she could recognize me. This way I get to ask her questions, and she's going to bloody well answer me.'

'It's still a bloody mess,' Ross grumbled. 'You went along with it,' Farrel reminded him. 'We still do what we were going to do. Nothing's changed.' He grinned suddenly, an appeasing leer. 'You can still have your fun.'

The belligerence went out of Ross. He relaxed and grinned in turn. Both of them looked back at Judy.

Judy's skin felt as though it was crawling with lice. She suppressed a shudder and had to struggle even more to keep her voice level. She ignored Ross and looked at Farrel.

'What I don't understand,' she said

slowly, 'Is why you tried to kill me in the first place.'

'It was your own damn fault,' Farrel scowled at her. 'You were coming straight at me. I saw your car stop, so I ducked behind the tractor out of sight. Then I saw you coming down the field path, before the rain started there was just enough light. I thought you were going to stay on the path and pass along the edge of the field. The door of the tractor was unlocked so I got inside to hide. Then you cut across the field and came straight toward me. I knew you had spotted me then, and I realized who you were, the pony tail gave you away. You were the bloody policewoman asking all the questions.'

'Why should that worry you?'

'That's none of your business, not now.'

'So how did you know me?'

'Saw you in the Coach and Horses, talking to that daft old Irish sod. We came in for a pint. Sean ducked into the gents. The tight-arse plays any trick to let me get to the bar first to get the beer in.'

'I do not,' Ross said indignantly. 'I needed a piss. I always buy my round.'

'You always buy the last round. Most often you get away with buying one round less than everybody else.'

Ross grinned. 'It's not my fault if I have an over active bladder.'

'So you hung back in the corridor and waited.' Judy guessed. She wasn't interested in their amiable squabble. 'You must have overheard some of my conversation with Gallagher, enough to know what we were talking about.'

Farrel turned back to her, scowled but nodded. 'I knew Gallagher would finger me if I showed my face. So I collared Sean and we went out again.'

'That tells me how you knew my face and recognized my hair style, but it still doesn't tell me why you wanted to avoid me.'

'Because you're the bloody police, isn't that enough.'

'I suppose it is.' She looked at him warily. 'Did you know the keys were under the tractor seat, or were you just lucky enough to find them?'

'I found them. That old farmer was stupid enough to leave them poking out from under the cushion.' He lost patience suddenly and grabbed her by the shoulders, hauling her into an upright sitting position and pushing his face close to hers. 'But you're not here to ask questions, Madam Smarty-knickers. You're here to answer questions.'

Judy felt fear flash through her. His fingers and thumbs were digging hard into her shoulders, and she had a vivid mental flashback of poor Crazy Alice lying dead on the mortuary slab. Rawlings had showed her the blue fingerprint bruises where someone had gripped and shaken Alice violently enough to bring on a heart attack. Now she could feel the same pattern of bruising forming on her own shoulders.

She swallowed hard and then said, 'What do you want to know?'

She already knew, but she wanted confirmation, and she was aware that somehow she would have to buy herself some time. Eventually she would be missed, but probably not until she failed to turn up for work tomorrow morning. She wondered how long she had been unconscious, whether it was already tomorrow. Then she thought that that was a crazy thought, it was never tomorrow, but Robbie Farrel was giving her an answer.

'Who was it?' He demanded. 'The old skull that was found at the beet factory and the skeleton you dug up in the beet field? Who was it?'

'We don't know,' Judy said honestly.

The slap across the face stung her cheek, rattled her teeth and slammed her head back, but the mental shock was worse. It felt as though her mind had blown, or her brain had seized up.

Farrel had let go of her left shoulder to make the slap, but now he grabbed her again and gave her another furious shake. Judy knew that this was how Alice had died.

'You know,' he shouted. 'By now you must know. You've got all those guys in white suits. You do all this forensic stuff, all this DNA stuff. So you just tell me who it was. I want to know.'

'We don't know.' Judy had to gather her wits. 'DNA testing can only confirm something when we have two samples to match together.' She saw for the first time the grubby bandage on his right wrist, probably where he had cut himself on the broken glass of the tractor window, but she decided not to use that example. She thought of another. 'If we want to match a child to a parent we can do it if they share the same DNA, but we have to have a sample from both parties.'

'You're lying.' He slapped her again. 'It's been over a week now since you dug up the skeleton. You know who he was.'

'We don't know,' Judy repeated. She could taste her own blood and it felt as though one of her teeth was loose. She was afraid, but she knew she could work this to her advantage. It was an interrogation in reverse, she was on the receiving end, but if she played it right she could still get some answers. 'The bones were fifty years old. But you are right. DNA testing could help to identify him, if we had some idea of where to start looking for a match. Who do you think he might have been?'

'You don't get it do you?' He gave her another shake. 'I ask the questions.'

Judy closed her eyes and tried to focus her mind. All along she had felt that if the death of Crazy Alice hadn't been the result of an in-family quarrel, then it had to be someone who had listened in to the talk between Peter and Sarah. Now her present situation confirmed that Robbie Farrel had indeed been paying attention to that conversation as he played darts nearby. The way that Alice had died was due to the same sort of violent shaking that Farrel was now doing to her. The picture was all fitting together.

She opened her eyes and looked back into his glaring face.

'There are only three possibilities. The prime candidate has always been Joe Crowfoot, who was Alice Jessup's Red Indian lover, but you wouldn't be interested in him. Then there was George Wilkes, the vicar who went missing, but he's hardly likely to have any meaning to you either. That only leaves the Gypsy boy, Danny Farrel, the same name as yours, the same family. He must have been a relative.'

'My dad's father, my grandfather,' the admission blurted out.

'So Danny Farrel went back to Ireland, and fathered a son?' Judy was uncertain, this didn't fit the picture.

'No, you silly bitch, Danny made my grandmother pregnant before he left Ireland, before he came over to England, before he met that Alice bitch. He never came back to Ireland. Nobody ever saw him again.'

'We thought the family protected him.'

'The family never knew anything. It's always been the big family mystery.'

'And you were trying to solve it.'

The puzzle was fitting together but he was losing patience again. He gave her another savage shaking that rattled her teeth and made her dizzy.

'Shut it, just shut your mouth. You keep forgetting that I'm the one who is asking the questions.'

Judy's eyes were screwed tight shut, trying to hold back her tears. From her right hand side she heard a door open, the movement as someone stepped up into the caravan, and then a new voice, startled and angry.

'Robbie, what the hell are you doing? I heard you shouting and — oh, my God, what have you done?'

There were a few seconds of silence, and then Sean Ross answered in a voice heavy with menace.

'Billy, sod off and leave it. It's none of your business.'

'You be quiet, you young fool.' The voice was shrill with alarm. 'Robbie?'

'Sean's right, dad, it's none of your business. Just go back out, back to your own van and your own bed, and forget what you've seen.'

Judy opened her eyes and twisted her head. The new arrival was an older, more shrunken and weathered image of Robbie Farrel, Robbie's father, obviously. His face was appalled. He came further into the van, craning his head to look behind Judy's back.

'Who is this girl? Are you both insane? Why have you got her hands tied up behind her back?'

Robbie pulled back, letting go of Judy's shoulders, his hands ready to push his father away.

'We're telling you, it's none of your business.'

'This is my camp. You're my son. You're doing this in the middle of my people. Of course it's my business.'

Judy had fallen back as she was released. She tasted more blood from a split lip and made the effort to speak.

'I'm a police officer.'

Billy Farrel looked down at her, his eyes wide. He had the expression of a rabbit caught in a torch light, knowing that the boom of a shotgun would come next.

'Oh, my God,' he said again. He pulled her forward and twisted her away from him, his movements spurred by panic but suddenly deft and quick. He began pulling at the rope that bound her wrists, his fingers plucking at the knots.

'Let's get this off you,' he glared at his son. 'Do you know what you're bloody well doing?'

'More than you do. Stop that.'

Billy Farrel's nut brown face had drained to white and he was trembling, but he continued to pull at the knots. Judy leaned her body forward to give him room.

Robbie Farrel released her, transferring his grip to his father as he grabbed the older man again by both shoulders. 'I said stop it, Dad,' he bellowed the words into Billy's face as he gave him a fierce shake. Ross had lurched up from his chair and moved quickly round the table to grab Billy from behind. Together they hauled him away from Judy.

'It's too late to interfere, Billy,' Ross snarled into Billy Farrel's ear.

'Sean's right,' Robbie said. 'This time you listen to us. You do what we say. It's too late now to just let her go.'

'For God's sake,' Billy was petrified. 'If the others hear all this, if the women find out — '

Judy had straightened up again, watching, listening and learning. Suddenly she realized that this was not an isolated caravan, she was in the middle of the traveller's site. There were other caravans and homes near, within screaming distance. The travellers would normally stick tightly together, but there would be limits. Billy Farrel was already showing that these two young villains had gone beyond those limits. She opened her mouth to scream.

Some instinct warned Robbie to look down at her. He saw her lips parting and saw the sudden flash of hope in her eyes. He pushed his father hard into Ross as he swung away and grabbed for her head, one hand slapped hard across her mouth and the other clamped on the back of her neck. She writhed and choked.

'You stupid old bugger,' Robbie hissed savagely. 'You almost invited her to scream her bloody head off.' He snatched at the black and red chequered neckerchief that Billy wore at his throat and used it as a gag, quickly knotting it around Judy's mouth. Judy tried to bite him but failed and received another angry slap.

They were all silent for a minute, all mentally reviewing the situation, and then Billy said feebly, as though it were a weak defence, 'I can't see why you didn't gag her to begin with?'

'Because I wanted to talk to her,' Robbie said.

'What about?'

'About our Granddad, about your dad, I suppose in a way I did it for you, you silly old sod. You've always wanted to know what happened to him. It's always been the big family mystery. I thought I could find out.'

'How?' Billy was quiet now, still stunned, but curious as much as scared.

Robbie shrugged and opened one of the fitted wall cupboards. He fished out a framed photograph from behind all the other bits and pieces of brass and china dogs and horses.

'Here,' he shoved it under his father's nose. 'Is this your man, is this Granddad Danny?'

Judy recognized the photograph which she was sure was of Joe Crowfoot, the picture which had vanished from Crazy Alice's dressing table.

Billy took the framed photograph and held it in both hands, staring at it. Ross had released him now and stood back. Billy looked up at his son and shook his head.

'No, this isn't Danny Farrel. Who is it? Where did you get it?'

'I took it from the old crazy woman's bedroom,' Robbie said. 'She's supposed to have had a fling with Granddad Danny, before he disappeared.'

Billy dropped the framed picture as though it had become red hot. It smacked down on the table but the glass didn't break. Billy's face had a new look of horror as he stared at his son.

'The old crazy woman died. What the hell were you doing in her bedroom?'

Robbie shrugged again, as though it had all become unimportant now. 'I went to see her. It was after the skull was found, while the police were still digging for the skeleton, the stuff everybody's been talking about in the village. I heard these two farmers talking in the Coach and Horses, about Crazy Alice and how the old woman thought that the skeleton just might be Danny Farrel.'

He was confirming what Judy had

already deduced, but the chilling thing was that it no longer seemed to matter to him how much she knew. He went on in the same bored tone, 'So I went to talk to her, just to talk. But the stupid old cow had a heart attack. I only gave her a little shake, just to rattle the truth out of her, and she dropped dead on me. I carried her up the stairs and put her into her bed, to make it look like she died in her sleep. She was already in her nightdress and a dressing gown, so I just had to get the dressing gown off and get her into the bed. I hung the dressing gown behind the bedroom door. Then I saw the picture. I took it away to show you, but then I wasn't sure, so I just stuck it in the cupboard.'

Billy's face was still white, and now there was a sheen of sweat glistening on his wrinkled forehead. He looked down at Judy.

'What about this one?'

'She knows too much,' Robbie said grimly. 'I knew that before long she'd be round here asking questions. Then she nearly caught me at the grave.'

'What grave?' Billy looked punch drunk, as though he was taking a mental beating.

'The grave where they found the skeleton, in the old beet field on the other side of the airfield, I just wanted a look, to see where old Danny died. She turned up, coming straight toward me. I tried to run her down with the tractor, but she got away. I thought she must have seen my face, and I figured she must know if it was Granddad Danny. So me and Sean grabbed her, to find out and then get rid of her.'

Billy groaned and hung his head in his hands.

'You daft, young bugger, I can't believe all this. It's all madness.' He looked up at Sean Ross. 'And you, why did you go along with it?'

Ross grinned inanely.

Robbie said simply. 'Sean's a mate, and before we killed her we were going to have some fun. She's not a bad looking bird, quite tasty.'

'Dear God,' Billy said, and from somewhere he plucked some courage. He glared at them. 'There'll be no killing here, and no fun. There are women and children on this site, other families. Decent people, not like you black-hearted spawn. This is their home too. They won't accept it. Neither will I. The women would tear you apart themselves.'

'They won't know,' Robbie grated. 'You won't tell them.'

'No fun,' Billy croaked. 'If the women ever found out — '

He didn't finish. Robbie and Sean looked at each other, frowning. Then, for his father's benefit at least, Robbie compromised.

'All right, no fun. Not here. But we still have to get rid of her,'

'How?' Billy almost shrieked. 'How are you going to kill her?'

'With these,' Robbie flexed his large bare hands. 'I've strangled rabbits before.'

'God help us, boy, a policewoman aint no rabbit.'

Robbie shrugged. 'Maybe not, but her neck will still break. It'll just take a bit more throttling and squeezing, that's all.'

'No,' Billy said. 'No.'

'No other way,' Sean Ross agreed with Robbie.

Billy looked from one to the other. 'What are you going — where — ' With Judy listening he couldn't get himself to ask how they intended to dispose of the body.

Robbie understood anyway. 'There are plenty of fresh ploughed fields around here, so no one is going to notice a bit of turned earth. Old Danny stayed buried for fifty years. We'll just put her a little deeper.'

Billy swallowed hard, looking for a last line of resistance. 'We have to tell Tinker,' he said desperately. 'We can't do this without telling Tinker.'

'Tinker Jim doesn't have to know anything.'

'He's my brother, he's your uncle, and he's The Gaffer. He'll decide what to do. He'll know what's best for us, for all of us.'

Sean and Robbie exchanged glances, the business was getting out of their hands and they were not happy.

Billy dug into his pocket and pulled

out a mobile phone.

'You do nothing,' he insisted. 'You do nothing until I've talked to Tinker. You hear me.'

He didn't wait for an answer but backed up a step and then barged out of the door and fled from the caravan. Sean started after him but then stopped and looked at Robbie. Robbie shook his head briefly. They both knew they couldn't afford to make too much noise or fuss. They didn't want to alert the rest of the camp. They knew they wouldn't be able to control the women.

$\star$ $\star$ $\star$

After five minutes Billy Farrel came back into the caravan. His face was still pale, but at least the responsibility had been taken out of his hands.

'The Gaffer's coming over,' he told them simply. 'He's not too pleased with you bloody pair, but he's bringing a closed van and a couple of his own lads from River Farm. This is the first place the police will look so it's too dangerous for all of us to leave her anywhere in this area. He'll take her back to Norfolk.'

They all looked at Judy.

'And then what?' Robbie asked.

'They've got an old car engine block and some old chain at River Farm, and a boat on Dalton Broad. Dalton Broad leads into the whole lake network, so they'll take her down to one of the deeper broads, chain her to the engine block and dump her over the side. It's the safest way for all of us now.'

Judy's eyes were open wide and inside her heart felt as though it was frozen into a block of ice.

18

It was late evening when the police patrol car turned off the Granchester by-pass and cruised slowly along the Old Brackendale road. It passed Appledown Farm, and then Blackberry Farm. Both farmhouses showed lights, warm squares of yellow marking the ground floor windows, but only attracted passing interest. Police Constable Frank Wallis was at the wheel, and he eased his foot a little more off the accelerator as they approached Hawthorn Cottage.

They had orders to include this small detour as part of their regular patrol route. The order had originated from Detective Inspector Ron Harding after the attack on Judy Kane, and had been reinforced by their uniform sergeant Tom Ford. They were to be discreet, but just keep an eye on the place and make sure everything looked okay.

The cottage was in darkness. Wallis

slowed the car to a crawl.

Ray Finch peered through the front passenger window, and then looked at his wristwatch. 'It's too late for hospital visiting,' he said dubiously, 'and a bit early for bed.'

'She had a hard day yesterday,' Wallis said. 'She could be taking an early night, or she could be with her sister. I think she's been having her evening meal round there while Ben's in hospital.'

His partner twisted his neck as they rolled past, looking back over his shoulder. 'Stop, Frank,' he said suddenly. 'It doesn't look right.'

Wallis stopped the car. Finch opened his door and got out. 'I think the front door is open,' he said as he went to investigate.

He carried a flashlight in his hand and switched it on as he walked up the short path. The door was partly open and he saw the keys hanging in the yale lock. He moved the torch beam around the small porch and saw that some of the trellis work of the archway was freshly broken. A sweep of the torch beam at ground level

336

showed trampled flower beds on either side of the porch, and another set of keys, Judy's dropped car keys, glinting back the light.

Finch didn't need to see any more. Initially he didn't even need to check the house. He turned and hurried back to the police car and its radio.

*   *   *

There was a clock on the wall of the small but compact kitchen, which Judy could just see by moving her head forward to look past an intervening wall cupboard that blocked part of her view. When she first noticed it the hands showed two thirty in the morning. She calculated that she had been awake for at least a couple of hours, which meant that she had probably been unconscious from the time of the attack until around midnight. She remembered the punch to the side of the head, her temple still ached where the blow had struck, and guessed that it was that punch that had knocked her out.

Sean Ross and Robbie Farrel again sat

facing each other over the small central table, half heartedly dealing and flicking the cards. They had no real interest in the game and their faces were sullen. They played without speaking, showing their hands, shrugging and sulking by turn. The scratch of the loose change as it was moved back and forth was the only sound. Several times Ross looked at Judy, his eyes hot and brooding, then he would glare at Billy and reluctantly resume the unwanted game.

Billy Farrel sat stiff and uncomfortable on the couch against the opposite wall of the caravan. His arms were folded tight across his chest, his body language shouting that he wanted no real part of any of this. His jaw was clenched tight, his lips a thin pale line across his lined face. He refused to look at Judy, but she was thankful for his presence.

Twice Robbie had told Billy to go back to his own bed, but Billy was adamant that he was staying until Tinker arrived.

'Just sod off and leave it.' Ross had backed Robbie the second time, balling a big fist.

Billy had flinched, his eyes blinked and his mouth trembled, but he stood his ground.

'And leave you alone with her.' He managed to spit out in disgust. 'You still want to have your fun you randy sods. But I tell you the women wouldn't stand for it. If they found out they'd have my balls for breakfast as well as yours. They'll turn the blind eye to a bit of thieving, but not to this.'

Ross started to rise from his chair. Robbie looked at him hard and briefly shook his head. Billy was Robbie's father and although they both wanted the old man out of the way there was a limit to what they could do, and to how far Robbie was prepared to go. Even if they threw the old man out the row would wake the rest of the camp, and they knew that Billy was making no idle threat. They would definitely have the women to contend with, and probably most of the older men as well.

Judy was almost afraid to move, not wanting to draw any attention to herself, but she was stiff and cramped and finally had to try and ease herself into a more comfortable position. Sean and Robbie both glanced at her briefly and then back at their cards. Judy stretched her legs and shifted her weight from one shoulder to the other. Suddenly she was aware that there was a little more movement in her hands. Her wrists were not lashed quite so tight together. She could move one numb wrist against the other. The discovery brought a sudden sharp pain of blood flow as the circulation there increased.

Sean Ross looked at her again and she froze. She couldn't avoid his eyes, but he was not interested in her face. His gaze dropped to the level of her breasts and stayed there a moment. Robbie turned a card and flicked another coin into the kitty, raising his bid. Ross grunted, a frustrated sound, and looked morosely to his cards.

Judy closed her eyes and lay still. She could still feel the pulsing tingle in her wrists. After a few moments she partially opened her eyes. Sean and Robbie were both focussed on their game. She tried moving her wrists again and this time she was sure. The rope was loose. Billy had plucked quickly at the knot, and although he had not been given enough time to free her he had slackened it off a little.

She watched the two card players through half lidded eyes and began gently moving her hands behind her back, trying to fully restore her circulation and perhaps loosen the rope a little more.

Time dragged. She could no longer see the clock and she was concentrating now on trying to appear motionless while her hands were busy behind her. She twisted each wrist in turn, feeling for the knot with her fingers, trying to get a finger and thumb grip on one of the loose ends of the rope. She tried with the fingers of her right hand and then the left, then the right again, failing every time. Frustration welled up inside her and she felt a damnable wetness behind her eyes. She wanted to weep.

Billy got up suddenly and walked through the small kitchen to the back of the caravan. He disappeared from sight and Judy felt a cold chill seep through her bones. She shivered and lay still. The card game had stopped. Sean and Robbie had lowered their cards and were looking at each other, then as if by some unanimous telepathic agreement their heads swung together and they both looked directly at their helpless captive.

Judy opened her eyes fully and glared at them, putting all the defiance she could muster into the look. She couldn't speak with the rough gag still in her mouth. They didn't. The silence hung heavy with menace in the small caravan. Then the toilet flushed and Billy came hurrying back, still zipping his fly. He didn't trust the two younger men either. He sat back in his place and folded his arms again over his thin chest, watching but saying nothing.

Judy felt relief. The card game resumed, as sullen and brooding as before.

Judy felt weak and wretched. She didn't want to anger them or provoke them in any way, and it was a long time before she risked working her hands again. There was no gain in the small amount of movement in the rope, and all her efforts began to seem hopeless. She could now twist her hands around without pain, except for the harsh abrasion of the rope, but that was all. She could not shake them free.

After what seemed an eternity the waiting ended. Suddenly there was the sound of a vehicle arriving, a flash of headlights passing across the caravan window, tyres skidding in the dirt and the brief sound of an engine before it was switched off. Relief flooded across Billy Farrel's tense face and he jumped up quickly and almost ran to open the door. Robbie threw down his cards and with a final sigh of disgust swept his hand across the table to scatter the pack and the loose money on to the floor.

There was a low murmur of voices outside the caravan, but the greetings there were brief. None of the speakers wanted to rouse the rest of the camp. One sleepy voice, a woman's voice, enquired as to what was going on, but was told softly but curtly to go back to sleep. Then Billy quickly reappeared. He was followed by a tall man wearing a long black leather coat, and a black felt hat with an incongruous feather tucked into the hatband. The door was firmly but quietly closed behind them.

For a few moments the silence continued. The new arrival surveyed the scene inside the caravan and his lip curled in a slight grimace as he met the eyes of the two young men at the card table. They glowered back, but had enough sense to wait until they were spoken to. Then his gaze settled on Judy and became sorrowful.

Judy stared back at him. Tinker Jim Farrel had an imposing presence. He was the head of his clan, The Gaffer, and he knew that he had their respect. His height helped, but his weathered, gaunt cheeked face had the browned age lines of long experience. He was in his seventies but his eyes were sharp with deep creased corners. The feather in his cap was the brown tail feather of a pheasant, Judy noted, her trained mind even now recording every minute detail.

Tinker Jim pursed his narrow lips in a

way that reminded her suddenly of Archie Jessup, and for a moment she wondered what might happen if these two dominant old patriarchs ever came up against each other. She knew instinctively that on some levels they were two pig-headed old bastards out of the same antique mould, although Tinker Jim looked much smarter and ruled a larger empire.

He didn't speak to her, but finally looked back to Billy, who now stood patiently and nervously waiting.

'Alright, Billy Boy, so tell me again why it is that you have to drag me all the way down here in the middle of the night.'

Sean Ross started to speak, but the tall man fixed him with a vicious glare, a sharply out-stretched hand and an admonishing finger.

'You shut up. I'm talking now to Billy.'

Ross closed his mouth, biting his lip.

Tinker waited, and after swallowing hard a couple of times Billy told his story. In places it was a stuttering tale, with a few false starts and frequent anguished glances at the stony face of his son. Tinker listened without expression or emotion, standing tall with his hands folded in front of him. In the black coat his graveside stance and his face would have been suitable for a funeral, and Judy realized with awful anguish that this was precisely what was to come, her funeral.

When Billy finished there was another pause. Billy was still pale, all the colour had been drained out of him hours before and he had recovered none of it. Tinker Jim stared down at his own boots, deep in thought.

Robbie drew a breath but before he could say anything the commanding hand was raised again. Finally Tinker Jim looked at him, his face and eyes were cold.

'I hear you were trying to find out what happened to my poor brother Danny. That's commendable, but the way you went about it is just plain daft. You've as near as damn it screwed up every bloody thing. You haven't got half a bloody brain cell between the two of you. I'll have to decide later how I'm to deal with you, but right now we have this young woman to consider.'

He moved to look down at Judy, towering over her as she lay helpless and afraid. He sighed, as though there were a great and terrible weight on his shoulders.

'Do you have children?' he asked sadly.

It was a surprise question, and one she could not answer with the gag in her mouth. However, it was a rhetorical question and not one that she was expected to answer. He went on in the same sad, detached tone.

'I hope you don't have children. It would be too awful if you did. But you understand that foolish as these boys are, they are part of my family. God help me, but for my sins, and theirs, they are still my responsibility. I'll have to punish them some way, but I can't let them go to prison. I have to fix this mess, and unfortunately there is only one way.'

He stood with his hands folded in front of him again, that awful graveyard posture, and sighed heavily.

'It's not something that I would want to happen. But then, life doesn't always work out the way we want it. Call it fate, I suppose. Did you know that I never wanted to be a horse thief, but to your sort that's what I am. The first horse I ever stole was a chestnut stallion, a lovely animal, beautiful to look at, sleek to touch, and fast enough to be a racing champion. I didn't want to be a thief, but I did want that horse. So I stole him away one dark night, with never a thought to the consequences.'

'My father wouldn't let me keep him though, that's the pity of it. He was stolen property and as soon as my father saw him he made me take the horse to a fair in the next town and sell him on. I cried, so I did, at having to let him go. But the money was nice, and it came so easy. My father let me keep the half of it. So that's how I began.'

He shook his head with regret and looked almost fondly at Robbie. 'And this damned nephew of mine, I don't suppose for a moment that he wanted to kill that poor old crazy woman, or to harm you. He just wanted to solve the family mystery, and find out what did happen to my long lost brother. And like me he was too young and too wild to think about the consequences.'

He was looking at Judy again, almost pleading now. 'Fate leads us down its own pathways, girlie, that's the way it is. I have to help them now. It's nothing personal to you. I'm sorry.'

Judy stared up at him as he finished his apology. She would have been practically speechless even without the gag. The bloody old hypocrite actually expected her to understand and forgive him. The fear in her suddenly fumed into anger, but there was still nothing she could do.

Tinker Jim turned away from her and his tone became more business-like. He leaned forward, palms down on the table, his eyes fixed on Robbie Farrel.

'So tell me now, and tell the truth or by God I'll have the skin flayed off your arses, did anyone see you bring her here?'

Robbie looked affronted. He said a short and emphatic, 'No.'

'We're not stupid,' Sean added, but he was ignored.

'So where did you grab her?'

'She's got a cottage, not far from here. Her old man's in hospital, crashed his car and broke his leg, so we knew she'd be coming back alone to an empty house. That's where we waited for her.'

'You're sure no one saw you, or heard you, no nosey neighbours.'

'The next house is a hundred yards away. No one saw or heard us. I'll swear it.'

'Alright, I'll believe you.' The old man frowned fiercely, narrowing his eyes. He thought hard for a moment. 'Billy says you've talked to her. You grabbed her because you thought she saw your face when you were daft enough to drive at her with a tractor. She says she didn't, but she sure as hell knows it now?'

Robbie nodded gloomily.

'So the fact is she didn't know it was you before you grabbed her, so there is no way she could have told anybody.'

Again Robbie nodded his head.

Tinker Jim shook his own head in disgust. 'My God, what a pair of bloody fools you both are. It's the two of you that I ought to be chaining up to an old engine block and dumping in the middle of the broads. Drowning is almost too damned good for you, but it would probably save me a lot more future trouble.'

Robbie looked down at the table and kept his silence. Sean's fists were clenched and white across the back of the tight knuckles, but he too kept his lips closed tight.

Tinker Jim straightened up and studied Judy for another moment. 'I'm tempted to take that gag out of your mouth and let you talk for yourself, but if you let out a yell I don't think that even I could control the women in the camp over this. So, I'll have to take young Robbie's word that you couldn't have blabbed before they picked you up. My best guess is that if I did ask you anything you'd probably lie to me anyway. I'll say it again. I'm sorry, girlie, but these young idiots have left me no choice.'

He turned back to Robbie Farrel and Sean Ross.

'I've got a closed van outside with two of my lads sitting inside and waiting. You two can take her out and get her inside the van, and be bloody quiet about it. You will both stay here and act innocent if the police do come sniffing around. And both of you can be bloody grateful that I'm clearing up your mess and taking her off your hands.'

19

The dilapidated wartime control tower at the end of the old airfield was shrouded in darkness, the squat hulk of a ruined square that was barely discernible in the gloom. Inside the bare concrete room on the upper floor that had once been the radar room, Detective Sergeant John Kershaw stood behind a pair of powerful night glasses that were mounted on a full height tripod. The glasses were aimed through the broken fragments of glass that still clung to the ancient, bare metal frames of the only window. Beyond the window and the outside sagging balcony, a hundred yards away down the short grassed slope with its tangles of intervening bracken and blackberry bushes, was the Old Brackendale travellers' site.

Kershaw was a tall, tough young man with dark hair. He was another hard cop, Ron Harding had been his role model and Judy had once described him to Ben as a Harding clone. That was back in the early days after her transfer from the uniformed branch, before they had all settled down and she had become an accepted part of the Crime Team.

Kershaw had the night watch again and he didn't know whether to be glad or sorry. The knees of his trousers were still wet from crawling along the old drainage ditch he had first discovered as a boy. It had been fun at first when the ditch was dry, but not after rain, and after a week of it he was getting a bit tired of sneaking about in the dark. It made him a key player for tonight's business but it also meant that he was probably going to miss the action, and that was a big minus.

He had to crouch down a little to keep his eyes glued to the eye pieces of the big binoculars which were focussed on the only caravan among the dozen or more mobile homes which still showed lights. His eyes were tired and sore and he rubbed them frequently. He had a Detective Constable beside him to share the watch, but only occasionally did he relinquish his position, and then only briefly.

He and his partner had both brought flasks of hot coffee and plastic boxes of canteen cheese and pickle sandwiches to see them through the night, but so far neither of them had given a thought to drink or food.

They both knew that Judy Kane was missing.

There was a five foot high wooden fence around the perimeter of the camp, screening most of what went on inside. Their observation point was only high enough to give a full view of the far side of the camp, and unfortunately the caravan which currently occupied their undivided interest was on the near side, close against the fence. Their prime job was to note who came and went, and when, and Kershaw had watched when the small white van arrived earlier in the evening. He knew from earlier observations that it was the vehicle which was normally used by Robbie Farrel and Sean Ross.

The van had pulled up close in front of

what had now become the target caravan, so he had been unable to see clearly who had emerged. However, he had got the impression that below the level of the fence they were carrying something heavy between them.

He had also observed the large grey minivan that had arrived much later. As far as he could tell only one person had emerged from the van, a tall man in a black coat with a ridiculous feather in his hat. The lights in two other mobile homes had flicked on briefly but then went out again. Kershaw was certain that the new arrival had entered the target caravan. Since then there had been nothing more to observe.

Kershaw had reported both incidents over his radio link to the radio control room at Granchester Police Station. He had also been able to report the licence plate number of the grey minivan.

Now he watched and waited. He had already carefully scanned the perimeter fence, and noted a loosely boarded section which looked as though it would cave in quickly under a few determined kicks. He wasn't going to miss out on any action if he was given half a chance.

* * *

Judy made no attempt at resistance as Sean Ross and Robbie Farrel moved in on either side of her and hauled her upright. She thought that if she was lucky she might get one chance and the time was not yet. Anything that happened inside the caravan would be muffled and would not help her. She needed to be outside, and able to make a noise. Any sort of noise, to kick over a dustbin or a milk bottle, to kick in a headlight or anything glass that would break, to kick one of them in the balls if she got the opportunity. Her only hope was to alert the sleeping camp to what was happening.

Her legs were stiff and weak and threatened to collapse beneath her. She sagged as they got her out from behind the table and into the small open space in the middle of the cramped lounge. Billy and Tinker Jim stood back to give them all room. Judy lifted her knees up and down to get the blood flowing, stretching her legs to ease her muscles. Sean and Robbie understood what she was doing and allowed her a minute to let her legs come alive. They didn't want to carry her, but their patience was limited. All too quickly they were hustling her out of the caravan.

Billy opened the door for them. Sean went out first and turned to help her down the two steps. Judy looked over Sean's blonde head to take in the loose circle of darkened caravans. There was not a light anywhere and no sign of life. There was a motley collection of mostly old and battered vehicles parked between the vans. A mongrel dog roped to the wheel lay under one of the homes, its head up, looking at her. She willed the stupid animal to bark but it refused. The smell of the men was familiar and its bored face slumped down again on its paws.

Sean pulled at her left shoulder, Robbie pushed her from behind. She went down the steps, staggered and Sean caught her.

She felt revulsion at being so close, but concentrated on looking round. The darkness was not total. There was a hairline crack of red in the eastern sky. It was nearly dawn. She looked for a dustbin or milk bottles, but there was nothing within reach, nothing to kick.

She thought of turning quickly, lashing out with her feet at the metal side of the caravan, but the thought came too late. Robbie was already coming down the steps behind her, pushing her away from the van. It was all happening too fast, her brain, like her legs, was too stiff and too slow.

Robbie had her right shoulder again, Sean was on her left. They were also aware of the dangers of being heard or seen and quickly hurried her towards the grey minivan. The back doors were pushed open from the inside. Two more hard and greasy-looking young thugs were waiting for her. One of them jumped out and held the doors wide. Kick the door she thought wildly, last chance.

The noise, when it came, was abrupt, screaming and dramatic, and it was not of her making. Judy stood as stunned as the rest of them as the shrieking wail of an emergency vehicle siren started up quite close, gaining in volume with every frozen second. She looked toward the sound and saw a spinning blue light flashing and approaching fast above the line of black hedgerows along the road that led up to the camp. Behind the light she could see the silver steel glint of ladders clamped to the top of the large red fire engine.

'Bloody hell,' she heard Tinker Jim curse from the open doorway of the caravan behind her, 'the bloody police.'

'No.' Billy Farrel's eyes were sharper and he was further forward. 'It's the Fire Brigade.'

'What do they want?' The old man sounded as though he had survived the first shock of hearing the siren, but his voice was still strained and wary.

'They come here sometimes,' Billy said, the familiarity of the fact slightly easing his mind. 'The younger lads collect scrap and burn off a lot of rubbish. They make a lot of smoke sometimes. Then some idiot phones the Fire Brigade.'

'There's no smoke now,' The Gaffer was still edgy. 'Not at this time of night.'

'Going past then,' Billy said hopefully, 'A fire somewhere else, or a road accident.'

They waited. The fire engine was hurtling up fast, and for a moment Judy feared and the others hoped that it would flash on past the camp entrance. Then its driver stamped on the brakes at the last possible moment, spun the wheel and the big red engine turned on skidding wheels and plunged into the heart of the camp. It stopped dead in a screech of sprayed dirt and stones in the dead centre of the circle of homes, only yards short of the waiting minivan. Judy and the two men who held her were spot-lit in the bright blaze of its headlights.

There were two police cars tucked in close behind the fire truck, using it as cover, and suddenly their blue lights and headlights flashed on as they skidded to a stop on either side of the fire engine, adding to the brilliant blinding display of circling blue and white light.

Each car was packed with the maximum number of brawny young constables who now came spilling out in force.

Sean and Robbie had instinctively drawn back towards the caravan they had just left, still dragging Judy with them. Then Sean broke and ran.

Judy recognized the white helmet with the single black rank band of a Station Officer in the officer's seat in the front cab of the Fire engine. With the lights dazzling her she couldn't see his face, but her heart leaped joyfully as she thought Ben. Then she realized it couldn't be Ben, he was lying crippled in hospital and this Station Officer was swinging open the cab door and jumping down cat-like with the full use of both legs.

He was a tall man, as tall as Ben, but the fire tunic hung loose on him, he was leaner. The chin straps were loose on his fire helmet and he reached up quickly to take it off. She saw black hair, wild and tousled, not Ben's blonde hair. Now she recognized Ron Harding.

Harding swung his right arm back, passing the helmet over his left shoulder, holding it by the protective brim. Then his arm flung out straight, hurling the heavy white helmet like a discus thrower. It was a trick she had only seen once before, in an old James Bond film. A character named Oddjob had worn a bowler with a steel brim which he could throw with the precision of an assassin's blade. Harding threw the fire helmet in the same way, and with the same effect. It spun through the air and hit Sean Ross square in the back of the neck. Sean's run finished in a headlong dive that brought him smashing down flat on his face.

From somewhere behind the caravan Judy heard the sound of splintering timber, as though someone had just kicked their way bodily through the fence. Then John Kershaw appeared, flying round the end of the caravan and throwing himself on top of the sprawling Sean.

For a moment it seemed as though the whole tableau was frozen. There were lights on now in all the caravans and shocked and startled faces were beginning to appear in the doorways and at the windows, the faces of men, women and wide-eyed children. Some of the men had started to come forward, aggressive and angry, but those who had stepped down from their caravans were quickly flanked by policemen working in pairs. A minivan had arrived, unloading another influx of constables, all of them in black flak jackets and some of them armed. If there had been any gaps in the police ranks there were five burly firemen climbing purposefully out of the fire engine. Ben's colleagues, and her colleagues, all faces she recognized, and Judy felt a huge swell of gratitude and relief. A large grey Rover car appeared. Operation Longship was Go, and Detective Superintendent Charles Grant had arrived to take personal command.

For a moment Judy almost forgot that she was still bound and gagged, with Robbie Farrel's arm still hooked around her chest, almost crushing the life out of her. It was so good to see all those familiar, supportive faces pouring out of the invading vehicles. She had been rescued and the relief drained her. Then she heard the loud click as a blade sprang open, a glint of steel flashed in front of her eyes, and she realized that it was not yet over.

Robbie Farrel had pulled out a knife. Until now she hadn't realized that he had a weapon of any sort, but the clasp knife had been closed and concealed in one of his pockets. He held it now with the blade across her throat, the cold razor edge touching her cheek.

'Stay back,' he screamed at the oncoming wave of policemen. 'Stay back or God help me I'll kill her.'

The wave stopped, each man becoming still but holding his place, mouths tightened, knuckles tightened around truncheons. At one end of the line a constable in a flak jacket slowly knelt, a machine pistol levelled in both hands. Harding had pulled open the Velcro fastener of his borrowed fire tunic and his right hand had eased inside. His eyes were hard. Judy knew that Harding was firearms trained. There would be an automatic holstered inside that tunic.

'Give it up,' Tinker Jim said wearily

from the top of the caravan steps behind them. 'It's all over now, son.'

Robbie wasn't listening. 'I'm getting out of here,' he shouted at the ring of frozen faces. 'She's coming with me. If anyone moves I'll cut her bloody throat.'

He started to move sideways, hauling Judy with him. He had heard the crash of breaking timber just before the copper on his left had appeared to pounce on Sean, and he guessed that the man had come through the weak spot in the fence. There must be a hole there now, and if he could get through it there were bushes and tree cover not too far away. He wasn't thinking any further than just getting out of the camp, out of this bloody glare of lights and hostile faces, and just making a run for it.

Judy allowed herself to be moved almost to the end of the caravan. Robbie's grip on her was tight and hurting but it was only a one armed grip. She gathered her courage and then ducked her chin tight to her chest to protect her throat. Her hands were still tied behind her back but she had enough room to move them.

She blessed Billy Farrel for just slightly slackening off the rope around her wrists as with both hands she reached back and grabbed for the crotch of Robbie's trousers and its contents. She squeezed and twisted with all her strength. It was a double twist, clawing and hurting his most vulnerable parts, and at the same time twisting her upper body out of his grasp.

Robbie howled, the knife blade gashed hotly into her cheek, and then she was falling away from him.

Her shoulder hit the wall of the caravan, stopping her from falling all the way. Robbie was stumbling away from her, the troops were moving forward, but she wasn't finished yet. As Robbie started to run she went down on her left knee and swung her right leg out in a far reaching sweep to hook one of his ankles from under him.

Like that of Sean Ross before him Robbie Farrel's face smashed down in the dirt as he was flung full length to the ground. He struggled to get up, pushing himself from the earth, and for a moment he was crouched on his hands and knees, facing away from her.

Judy used her shoulder and the side of the caravan to get herself back on to her feet, stepped unsteadily forward, and took great satisfaction in kicking him as hard as she possibly could between his unprotected legs. Robbie screeched in agony and sprawled forward again. Seconds later Tom Ford, Tony Marsh and two of the nearest constables had all thrown themselves on top of him.

Judy leaned back against the caravan wall, using it to prop herself up. Without it she would have collapsed. Her cheek stung like fire and she could feel blood dripping down her chin. She saw Harding coming towards her and heard him wince. Then he was gazing up at the widening crack of dawn in the eastern sky. His hand rested comfortably on her shoulder, a steady, reassuring squeeze.

'I didn't see that,' he said loftily, and grinned. Then he reached down into the melee of bodies on the ground before them and found Robbie Farrel's left ear. He twisted it viciously. 'And you didn't feel it, you young bastard — not if you know what's good for you.'

★   ★   ★

While Harding gently removed the gag from Judy's mouth and the rope from her bound wrists, Charles Grant emerged from behind the wheel of his Rover and walked calmly forward. The circle of police and fire service personnel parted to let him through. He strolled up to what had been designated the target caravan, where Tinker Jim and Billy Farrel stood waiting in the doorway.

Grant nodded politely to the older man. 'I take it that you must be Tinker Jim Farrel, sometimes known as the Gaffer.'

Tinker Jim nodded slowly, and stepped down to ground level to face him.

Grant offered his card. 'I'm Detective Superintendent Charles Grant of the Breckland CID. You might say that I'm The Gaffer for these gentlemen.' He waved a hand expansively around him.

Tinker Jim nodded again, without

looking at the card. He took off his black felt hat with the jaunty pheasant tail feather and clasped it with one hand to his breast. His head was almost bald, except for a few wisps of grey hair. Without the hat he was a very old man. He sighed and inclined his head briefly. He still had nothing to say.

Grant had noticed the mobile phone that was still gripped in the old gypsy's free hand, and shook his head wryly.

'If you were trying to phone home to River Farm, or to the cousins at Bleak Fen, I can tell you what's been happening there. The police forces from Norfolk and Cambridgeshire have raided both camps. It was a simultaneous, co-ordinated three county operation, in force and I believe a clean sweep at every site. At River Farm they found a stolen Range Rover hidden under some sheets of tarpaulin, your favourite ram-raiding vehicle, and no doubt ready for the next job. At Bleak Fen the Cambridgeshire Police already had enough evidence to make convictions. You will be helping us with our enquiries as we sort out all the charges over the next few days, but I don't think we'll be releasing many of you without a charge.'

He paused and then smiled. 'It's actually good to see you here. When my opposite number in Norfolk alerted us to the fact that you and two of his prime suspects had driven out of River Farm we feared you might slip the net. But all's well that ends well, as Shakespeare would have said.'

20

Grant and Harding filled in the rest of the explanations, and Judy told her story, as they drove her back along the now familiar route to Granchester General Hospital. Harding had stopped the bleeding and applied a dressing to the shallow cut across her cheek, where fortunately the knotted gag had helped to check the slice of the blade, but the wound still needed stitching and medical attention.

Grant drove the car, his own Rover, while Harding sat beside her on the back seat. Colin Bradshaw had arrived to take command of his own personnel, bringing with him a genuine Station Officer to take charge of the fire engine and return it to the Fire Station. Tom Ford and John Kershaw had been left in charge of mopping up the police operation, weeding out all those suspected of being part of the ram-raiding crimes and ferrying them down into the holding cells at the police station.

Judy told her story briefly, her face hurt abominably and they were sympathetic enough to leave the details for another time. However, she had to ask them how they had managed to make their cavalry charge so quickly.

'We had your house watched,' Harding admitted. 'Just a passing check that the patrol cars made on their normal rounds. One patrol spotted that your door was open. That's how we knew something had happened. I hauled in Tony Marsh and quizzed him about your movements, and then found reasons to make snap visits to both the Jessup farmhouses. There were no guilty reactions anywhere, so then I went to see Ben. I know you share most things with him and I guessed you would have had plenty of time to talk at his bedside. He was able to tell me about most of what you had been working on and what you were thinking.'

'We should have known,' Grant apologized from the front of the car. 'We had a lot on our minds but we should have known.'

Harding nodded agreement, and then continued. 'John Kershaw reported some unusual late night activity at the travellers' camp, and that information reached me while I was with Ben. Ben's gut instinct was the same as mine, and he came up with the idea of using a fire engine to cover the raid. He told us there were regular calls to rubbish burning fires on the camp, so they might not be too alarmed to see a fire engine coming. The police cars could tuck in out of sight, close behind the fire engine.'

'That idea took a bit of persuasion to put across,' Grant said wryly. 'I spent an hour talking to Colin Bradshaw. His boundary rules are not to get too closely involved with police operations, except in a back up capacity. But this was for Judy Kane, the wife of one of his fire officers, so we found ways to bend the rules. I put in an official request for the Fire Service to stand by because I believed that the travellers would attempt to burn large amounts of evidence.' Judy could see his smile in the rear view mirror. 'Ron borrowing Ben's uniform and actually riding in the fire engine was something we are both supposed to not know about.'

'Operation Longship,' Judy asked, 'was that scheduled for tonight?'

'No,' Grant answered. 'We were almost ready to go, but the date had yet to be finalized. When we realized that you were most probably being held at the Old Brackendale camp we made the decision and brought everything forward. Once I had Bradshaw's co-operation I spent the rest of the night switching phone calls between Geoff Geeste and Dave Pullen to get everything synchronized, but they've pulled out all the stops too so that we could still hit all three sites at the same time.'

Judy felt a warm glow inside as she thought of all that rushed effort on her behalf, and the glow spread as the thought sunk in that most of it had been initiated by Ben.

'It was Ben's idea,' she wanted to hear it again, 'to use the fire engine to lead the charge.'

Harding nodded. 'And a good one, it gave us an edge of surprise. We needed to be in the middle of them before they had a chance to hurt you. Of course, I had to order a couple of nurses to hold the big fellow down or he would have been there himself, with or without his broken leg.'

Judy couldn't smile, her face hurt too much, but her eyes were grateful. 'Thanks for coming in his place.'

Harding did smile, and he squeezed her hand. 'It wasn't just me. You're a popular girl, Judy Kane. I could have filled that fire truck and the police vehicles three times over. Every single man on both stations jumped up to volunteer.'

$\star \quad \star \quad \star$

It was two days later when Judy parked her car beside the handkerchief green in the heart of the tiny village of Brackendale. It was a gloriously sunny autumn morning with a slight breeze that gently swirled falling leaves from the old chestnut tree as they settled on the car's bonnet. She was parked opposite the

Coach and Horses, and from here she could see the grey flint church tower rising above the thatch of the surrounding cottages. Everything was quiet and peaceful. The old picture postcard cliché came to mind, and she thought that like old jokes the old clichés were sometimes the best.

She sat for a moment. There were seven stitches under the clean dressing taped to her cheek and she still had to be careful when she tried to talk or smile. Operation Longship had been a resounding success, with all three police forces enjoying a chorus of media praise, but she was trying to put all of that out of her mind. Officially she was on sick leave, but there was something she still needed to know. She now knew who had killed Crazy Alice, but she had yet to discover the true identity of the skeleton that had been dug up in Archie Jessup's beet field.

She got out of the car and locked it. She spared another passing glance to the perfect setting for the rambling old Tudor pub and the ancient church, but they were not what had brought her here this morning. She walked over to one of the cottages, Number Three, The Green, the address she had down in her notebook for Grace Wilkes. A blackbird began to sing somewhere in the chestnut tree as she knocked on the cream painted door.

After a moment the door opened, and she received a total surprise.

The man who answered the door was Rupert Drake.

For a moment Judy was at a loss for words, but Drake was not. He wore a knitted cardigan in brown and yellow check. At the V throat there was a neat white shirt collar and a yellow bow tie. His silver streaked hair was perfectly combed back and his handsome face wore an amiable smile of welcome. He was, as ever, the polished actor.

'Well now,' he said mildly. 'It's the lady police officer. I told mother you would be coming to see us eventually.' He stepped back from the door, holding it open. 'Do please come in.'

Judy stepped warily inside, into a comfortable and surprisingly large sitting room where corn coloured curtains matched the three piece suite of arm-chairs and settee. The pile carpet was a deeper shade of gold with a pale green rug to break up the overall colours of the furnishings. The walls were painted soft green, and broken up by framed pictures and shelving units full of tiny porcelain figures. The ornaments were mostly shepherd boys and shepherdesses, or ladies in swirling gowns with hats and baskets.

Grace Wilkes sat on the settee, behind a small coffee table that was set for morning tea. She wore another flowered dress, this one a pattern of white daisies. With her grey hair and another welcoming smile she looked like someone's cheerful old grandmother, but suddenly Judy was not so sure.

'Yes, do come in, dear,' Grace said. 'Will you have some tea? Clarence, be a dear and fetch another cup.'

She moved into the corner of the settee to give Judy room to sit beside her. Judy accepted the invitation but watched as Drake disappeared into the kitchen. He returned almost immediately with an empty cup and saucer and he knelt on the carpet to fill the cup from the china teapot on the coffee table.

'Milk and sugar?' he asked mildly.

Judy nodded. 'One sugar, please.' She looked from one to the other and said slowly, 'Mother? Clarence?'

'Oh yes, Clarence is my son,' Grace said proudly. 'My only son, he's a good boy.'

Judy was still perplexed. The man she knew as Rupert Drake handed her the cup of tea and then straightened up. He was smiling.

'I was christened Clarence Wilkes,' he explained. 'But when I took to the stage it didn't seem to have quite the right ring for a future star, so my agent decided that I had to be re-born. I wanted to be Richard Drake, but there were too many excellent Richards around in those days, Richard Burton, Richard Todd, and Richard Green — he was the old black and white TV Robin Hood, of course.' He shrugged his shoulders. 'And so I became a Rupert. My agent thought that Rupert Drake had the right touch of class.'

Judy managed a half smile and sipped her tea. It was hot and she started to put the cup and saucer down on the table, and then changed her mind. Rupert Drake, who had been Clarence Wilkes, was a tall man, lean and fit, and he remained standing, blocking the door and her exit. She remembered that acting was his profession, and all acting was a form of deception. He appeared to be mild and harmless but again she was not sure.

She felt almost trapped again. Perhaps the experience of being held captive at the travellers' camp was too fresh and recent in her mind, but she felt a renewed chill. She was probably being paranoid, but she kept the teacup and saucer in her hands, deciding that she could always throw the hot tea in his eyes if it became necessary.

'You've hurt your face, dear,' Grace Wilkes said and her tone was full of concern.

'Just a small accident,' Judy brushed it aside. She paused. 'You were expecting me?'

Grace nodded. 'Clarence said you would come here eventually. You're a clever girl, and a determined one. You want to know the truth.'

'What truth?' Judy said softly.

'Why, the truth about Joe and Danny.'

'And you know the truth?

'Oh yes, dear. I've always known.'

Rupert Drake cleared his throat, an apologetic sound. 'I didn't know, not until a couple of days ago. That's why I came home, when I read about the skull and the skeleton being unearthed. I thought that it might be my father, but it wasn't. Mother finally told me everything.'

'So who was the body in the beet field?' Judy asked. 'Was it Joe Crowfoot?'

'No, dear,' Grace sighed, and used a small lace handkerchief to dab away a tear. 'Poor Joe flew out on that last mission with the Kentucky Lady. He died with the rest of his crew. It was Danny who was buried in the beet field, Gypsy Danny, Alice's Wild One.'

Grace looked down at her handkerchief and twisted it in her hands. Rupert Drake stood silent, head slightly bowed. Judy waited.

A silent minute passed before Judy

asked, 'What happened?'

'Joe came to me that night,' Grace said quietly. 'The night before his plane flew out for that last mission over Germany. He came to see George, actually, but George had gone up to London, looking for those two poor evacuee boys who had run away.' She looked into Judy's eyes. 'Joe was a red man, but he was a good Christian boy, did you know that? He learned his Bible at a Christian Mission Hall on the Navajo Reservation.'

'I didn't know that,' Judy said softly, but she remembered the Bible on Alice's dressing table.

'Well he was. That was one of the things he and Alice had in common, she was brought up in the church. She loved her Bible too. When they started courting they came to church together, our church, here in Brackendale, every Sunday if Joe could get away from his camp. So when Joe was in trouble it was only natural that he should come to the vicarage to find George. He wanted to confess. He knew that every mission he flew could prove to be his last. He was looking for George to make his confession, to make his peace with God. The Navajo Mission Hall he attended at home was a Catholic church, so he needed that. But George had gone up to London. There was only me. And Clarence, of course, but Clarence was only a baby.'

She stopped, and again Judy waited while she dabbed at her wet eyes.

'Poor Joe,' she continued at last. 'He came to me with blood on his hands, Danny's blood. They had fought a terrible fight. Joe had been out with Alice and he had taken her back to Blackberry Farm. They always said goodbye at the gate, just out of sight of the farmhouse, because Archie and Charlie were so mad about it all. Joe would then just watch to see that Alice got safely to the door, and then he would take the short cut along the field path to get back to the airfield. Archie and Charlie knew all of this. They told Danny where he could hide in ambush and attack Joe from behind in the dark. And they paid him to do it, two hundred pounds, all in those old white five pound notes.'

'Joe told you all of this?'

Grace nodded, her grey starling's head bobbing briefly. 'Danny was waiting behind the hedgerow, and he had a spade which he was planning to use to kill Joe and then bury his body. But Danny had been drinking, he was a bit slow and clumsy, and Joe was sharp and alert. Danny took a big swipe at Joe with the spade. Joe reckoned it would have sliced his head off if it had hit. But he heard it coming and ducked. The spade missed and Danny almost fell over with the force of his swing. Then Joe got close and they fought.'

Grace sniffed, and now there were tears trickling down her cheeks. In her mind's eye she could again see Joe Crowfoot standing distressed and dishevelled in the old vicarage kitchen, spilling out his story with the red blood on his hands, his clothes torn, his face filled with anguish.

'Danny had taunted Joe,' she remembered all that Joe had told her. 'Danny wanted Joe to know that Archie and Charlie had paid him to do this, but that he would have done it anyway, without the money. Danny was so jealous of Joe, he wanted Alice for himself. Then Danny charged at Joe again with the spade, but he tripped in the tangles of grass and bushes. Joe hit him, punched him on the jaw with an almighty right hook. It snapped Danny's head back and broke his neck. Joe hadn't wanted to kill Danny, only to defend himself, but he broke Danny's neck.'

Grace subsided into more sniffles and Judy waited until at last she composed herself to finish her story.

'After it was done Joe used Danny's spade to dig a grave. The night was pitch dark and no one had seen or heard anything. Joe put Danny in the grave and covered him up. He took the spade away and threw it into a deep-water ditch beside the next field. After that he came to me. I didn't know what to do, but he was distraught. He knew he had to fly on that last raid over Germany. Finally I said that I would hear his confession, I was the vicar's wife, and that I would repeat it word for word to George when he came home. I told him that when he returned from the flight over Germany he could still tell George himself, and that even if he didn't I would tell George for him, and that God would understand. I didn't know then that I would never see either of them again, not Joe, nor George.'

There was an even longer silence while Judy digested all that she had heard. Then she said doubtfully.

'We found Joe's silver belt buckle in the grave.'

'Joe's shirt was torn open, his face was all scratched. I think his belt was hanging open too. The buckle must have been torn off in the fight.'

Grace stood up suddenly and went over to an oak writing bureau that stood in one corner of the room. She came back with a handful of white paper which she handed to Judy. There were forty large white five pound notes, still crisp and new, the sort that had been obsolete for forty years or more.

'Archie Jessup's blood money,' Grace said bitterly. 'It's what he gave to Gypsy Danny to make sure that The Red Nigger stayed away from his sister.'

She put the money on the coffee table in front of Judy and sat down again, her tale finished. She looked tired and even older than before.

'She finally told me last night,' Drake offered. 'I always knew there was something, and even after the skull and the skeleton were found it still took a few more days to get it out of her.'

'It was a confession,' Grace said slowly. 'I was the vicar's wife, and it was the same as if Joe had confessed to George. I had to keep it secret.' She paused and more tears trickled from her eyes. 'And there was Alice to consider. Alice was my friend. I couldn't ever let Alice know what had happened. It would have hurt her too much. It was bad enough that she didn't know what had happened, but it would have been worse for her to know the truth. I couldn't say anything to anybody while poor Alice was still alive.'

'So it was Danny Farrel in the grave. Joe Crowfoot was shot down in his Flying Fortress over Germany. And my father died in the London Blitz.' Rupert Drake recited the facts to clarify them for himself as much as for Judy, and it was the third statement that affected him the most. He drew a deep, noisy breath that might have covered his own sorrow.

Grace Wilkes looked up at her son.

'I did go and look for him. The very next morning. I took the train up to London and found my way to Burton Street. It was awful, every house in the street had been bombed to rubble. There were fires everywhere, it was all still burning, smoke and fire and people running, and shouting, and screaming, bodies and bits of bodies, people with blood on them — ' The images were still alive in her mind, even after all these years, and now she broke down fully and wept.

Rupert Drake knelt at the end of the settee and put his arms around her shoulders. Grace pressed her tired old face to her son's chest for a while, and then finally composed herself and drew away. She dabbed with the handkerchief some more, while Judy patiently waited.

'I found a woman who said that George, or someone who might have been

George, had been asking his way to Freddy and Herbert's house just before the air raid started.' Grace was remembering aloud, not really talking to either of her listeners. Her eyes were vacant as she stared at the opposite wall. All that she saw was memories. Her voice was low.

'I found the house, what was left of it. It was just like all the others, a pile of hot bricks, broken doors and window frames sticking up, all black and eaten by fire, broken furniture and crockery. There were people digging and crying all along the street, looking for survivors, pulling out bodies. I dug with them, and cried with them, for three days, with my bare hands, I just dug and dug in the rubble of Burton Street.'

She looked down at her hands holding them in front of her. They were wrinkled and shaking, the backs brown mottled with age, but these were not the hands she saw. 'I dug until most of my nails had come away, until my hands were all raw and bleeding. We found a leg, I think it was a woman's leg, it was white and smooth with no trouser leg — just a leg that ended in a red stump, all messy with black ashes. We found a man dead and pulled his broken body out, but no one alive. We found poor little Herbert. I think it was Herbert. His poor little face was crushed. Anyway, it was his jersey, I'm sure I saw the darn I did myself to repair the sleeve. At least the boys got home. I couldn't find George. There was nothing of George.'

She made an effort to come back partially to the present and looked at her son. 'I stayed for three days, looking for your father. There was a school where one of the classrooms was still standing. The Salvation Army had set up a soup kitchen there, and provided some blankets. There were survivors gathered there, women and children, old people, all those left who couldn't dig. I had some food there, not much. I couldn't bring myself to eat much. When I was exhausted I slept in a corner under a blanket they gave me. When I woke up I went back to the digging.'

She shuddered with all the memories, closed her eyes for a moment and then opened them again.

'There was a man who helped me. His name was Derek. He worked beside me, showed me what to do and where to go. He was an Auxiliary Fireman, but he lived on Burton Street and he had lost all of his family there, so like me, for three days, he was just digging. We pulled broken beams out together, cried together. But he was strong, for three days he was my rock. I leaned on Derek. He gave me his helmet to wear when the air raids started again, but they bombed other streets. Burton Street was already flat. Derek found me a first aid post and made me get my hands bandaged. Then he found me some gloves from somewhere when I insisted on going back to the digging.'

It was confession time for Grace and she was begging her son to understand. 'I think I fell in love with Derek. Things change so quickly in wartime. Bonds form almost immediately. I knew in my heart that George was dead, even though I had to keep digging. All through those three days I knew that he was never going to come back, that I was never going to find him. At the end I just wanted to stay with Derek. But there was you Clarence, you were my baby. I had left you with a neighbour but for you I had to come back. I never really looked at another man again, not after George and Derek, it was all too much.'

There was a long silence, while Rupert Drake continued to hold his mother tight, gently stroking her grey hair. Finally Grace stirred herself, remembering Judy and turning her head so that they were face to face.

'Well, dear, now you know all my secrets. I went up to the Blitz because I loved George. I think that by the third day I was staying because I loved Derek. In the end I came home again because I loved Clarence. It's what we're born for, isn't it, the things we women do for love.'

Judy didn't know how to answer. She inclined her head in silent agreement.

Another quiet minute passed, and then Rupert noticed that Judy still held her full cup and saucer in her hands.

'Your tea has gone cold,' he said mildly. 'Would you like me to get you another?'

* * *

When Judy returned to her car she sat for a long time with her hands resting on the wheel, staring across the green at the church tower without really seeing it. She was reflecting on all that she had just heard, and especially on those parting thoughts on what a woman would do for love.

She thought of Alice Jessup, poor Crazy Alice, forlorn and lonely, never married and forever searching the night sky for the sound of an aircraft engine and the return of the man she had loved.

She thought of Grace Wilkes, exhausted but still digging in the burning rubble of the Blitz, until her hands were raw meat bleeding into the ashes.

Both women had been torn between two men. Alice had been courted by Joe Crowfoot and Gypsy Danny. Grace had lost her husband, and the chance to make a new love with Derek. Both of them had lived alone with their memories for the next fifty years.

That was what they had done for love.

And what would she do for love.

For her it was easier. She only had one man, and he was alive. Ben was at home, at the cottage, waiting for her. He had been discharged from hospital the previous day, making a brave display of mastering his new crutches.

And suddenly she knew what she was going to do.

She started the car and drove home, to tell Ben that if this was what he really wanted, then they were going to Spain, together, to run that little bar they had dreamed about for the future.

THE END

THREE DAYS TO LIVE
SEA VENGEANCE
THE BIG FISH
FALCON SAS — BLOOD RIVER
FALCON SAS — FIRESTRIKE
PERSONS REPORTED

We do hope that you have enjoyed reading this large print book.

Did you know that all of our titles are available for purchase?

We publish a wide range of high quality large print books including:

Romances, Mysteries, Classics
General Fiction
Non Fiction and Westerns

Special interest titles available in large print are:

The Little Oxford Dictionary
Music Book, Song Book
Hymn Book, Service Book

Also available from us courtesy of Oxford University Press:

Young Readers' Dictionary
(large print edition)
Young Readers' Thesaurus
(large print edition)

For further information or a free brochure, please contact us at:
Ulverscroft Large Print Books Ltd.,
The Green, Bradgate Road, Anstey,
Leicester, LE7 7FU, England.
Tel: (00 44) **0116 236 4325**
Fax: (00 44) **0116 234 0205**

A TIME FOR MURDER

John Glasby

Carlos Galecci, a top man in organized crime, has been murdered — and the manner of his death is extraordinary . . . He'd last been seen the previous night, entering his private vault, to which only he knew the combination. When he fails to emerge by the next morning, his staff have the metal door cut open — to discover Galecci dead with a knife in his back. Private detective Johnny Merak is hired to find the murderer and discover how the impossible crime was committed — but is soon under threat of death himself . . .

THE MASTER MUST DIE

John Russell Fearn

Gyron de London, a powerful industrialist of the year 2190, receives a letter warning him of his doom on the 30th March, three weeks hence. Despite his precautions — being sealed in a guarded, radiation-proof cube — he dies on the specified day, as forecast! When scientific investigator Adam Quirke is called to investigate, he discovers that de London had been the victim of a highly scientific murder — but who was the murderer, and how was this apparently impossible crime committed?

DR. MORELLE AND THE DRUMMER GIRL

Ernest Dudley

'Dear Mr. Drummer. Your daughter is safe . . . If you want her back alive it is going to cost you money . . . Don't call the police . . . You are under observation, so don't try any tricks.' A note is left in the girl's flat by her kidnapper. Her father, Harvey Drummer, turns to Dr. Morelle and Miss Frayle to help him secure his daughter's release. The case proves to be one of the most baffling and hazardous of the Doctor's career!

MONTENEGRIN GOLD

Brian Ball

Discovering his late father's war diaries, Charles Copley learns that he had been involved in counter-intelligence. When Charles is approached by an organisation trying to buy the diaries, he refuses. But he is viciously attacked — and then his son is murdered . . . Seeking revenge, he is joined by Maria Wright, daughter of his father's wartime friend. They are led on a journey to the mountains of Montenegro — and thirty years back in time in search of a lost treasure.